Groping for Luna

Pam Summa

To Hilda –
Hope you enjoy the artists from another view. XOXOXO
Pam

Groping for Luna

Pam Summa

Mystic River Ink
Somerville, Massachusetts

Cover design by Emily Arkin and Pam Summa
Book design by Abe Foreau

Back cover image:
View of the Moon, by John Adams Whipple, February 26, 1852
Daguerreotype, made by the use of the fifteen-inch telescope.
Courtesy of Harvard College Observatory, Harvard University.

Ten percent of the profits from the sale of this book will be donated to the Mystic River Watershed Association, a group of organizations and individuals who work to protect and restore the Mystic River.

ISBN: 0-9724752-7-3
Printed in Canada

Mystic River Ink trade paperback edition/October 2002

Mystic River Ink
P.O. Box 441357
Somerville, MA 02144
http://www.mysticriverink.com

This is a work of fiction. The characters exist in a parallel universe.

To Jessie Summa-Kusiak
—my daughter, my deejay—
who convinced me to
take it to the street.

And to Emily Arkin
and Hsuan Tsen,
my first street.

Whachacallit? When you look at the sky in a poetic sort of way? You know, when you grope for luna…

Los Pixies

I.

Angel was in love again. He'd met this woman at a gig. She'd been tending bar. Joe didn't remember any woman bartender from a gig.

"She's smart," Angel said. "She likes me."

That was nothing new. Angel attracted women like honey attracted flies. Stringer, singing lead in a voice that ranged from full moon mellow to alley cat screech, should have gotten more action but it was Angel with his high cheekbones, long black hair, and zigzag lightning tattoos on either bicep who had more women than he knew what to do with. But Angel's luck with women ended with the body count.

"A smart bartender," Joe said.

"Alice is an artist," Angel said. "A printmaker. She's only a bartender at night."

She could be trouble. Angel did that, he got into trouble. She was probably ready to try anything. Or she was already into everything and wanted Angel to keep her company doing it.

But Angel seemed okay. He still fooled around with other women, at least this Alice person didn't have a leash on him. But he was at her place more than he was home.

One night Joe came early to the club where they were playing and saw Angel with a woman Joe didn't know, dancing to the band that was on before them. She was on the skinny side, with a big mouth and shoulder-length dark brown hair in one of those what-the-hell hairstyles. She was wearing black jeans and a t-shirt Joe recognized. He'd lent it to Angel. Angel wasn't as tall as Joe, but the t-shirt had fit him okay. On her it was too big.

Angel spotted him and grabbed the woman's arm, yelled in her ear, and pointed towards Joe. Angel moved through the crowd, the woman in tow. Joe didn't try to arrange his face; he knew it wouldn't give anything away.

Angel introduced them, this is Joe, this is Alice. Angel was wanting them to like each other. Alice said hi, how are you, heard a lot about you.

"Hi," Joe said. He smiled with just his mouth, trying to figure her. He watched her face turn wary. That was okay, he wasn't afraid of that. Angel didn't notice.

Joe reminded him how much time they had before they went on.

"Nice meeting you," he said to Alice.

"You too," she said.

But Angel had noticed. "Hey man," he said to Joe before they went on, "you could have been more polite."

Joe tuned his guitar. "I was polite. I said 'nice to meet you'."

Angel lit a cigarette, blew smoke at Joe's guitar. He had a don't-bullshit-me look on his face.

"I was thinking about something else," Joe lied.

"Well try to focus."

Joe focused. During a break, when Angel had gotten hung up with some friends, Joe made a point of speaking to Alice.

"Nice shirt," he said. It was dull purple, faded from many washings.

"Thanks," she said. "It's Angel's." She had a margarita in one hand, a piece of lime in the other. She rubbed the lime along the rim of the glass and then sucked salt off the lime.

"Actually, it's mine," he said, sipping beer. "Angel borrowed it."

She licked salt off her upper lip. "You want it back?" she asked. She wasn't flirting.

"No," he said. Then he scanned the crowd like he was looking for something interesting enough to hold his attention. "He'll give it back when he's through with it."

Joe meant, when he's through with you. He glanced at her; she was rolling her eyes. When he caught her doing it she gave him a blank fuck-you look.

Angel showed up then, saving them the trouble of further conversation.

Joe was a surprise to Alice. Angel had said Joe was like a brother. Joe and Angel lived together, had started the band together, although Stringer, as the front man, wanted to think it was his band. When Angel went into rehab their old band fell apart; when Angel came out, Joe was already putting together another band, talking to agents, lining up gigs. He didn't treat Angel like an ex-junkie, he treated him like a musician.

Alice had expected someone more like Angel. Quieter, maybe, but not someone who looked like a smile would crack his face. Not someone who took one look and wrote her off forever.

Alice had met Angel one night when she was tending bar and he was playing. He came over to the bar and he and Alice started talking. People talked to bartenders. She told him she liked the music. He seemed as pleased as if he'd never heard this before. The bar emptied, she closed down. He helped her collect ashtrays, he put the chairs on the tables while she and the other bartender closed out.

Alice's car wasn't running, as usual, and Angel didn't have a car. After a night of playing, Angel was as wired as Alice was after a night of bartending. "Do you feel like walking?" Alice asked him. He said he did.

It was a good night for walking. The air was cool and silky, with the little sharp teeth of autumn in it. Angel asked how she liked bartending and she said she did it to support her habit. He got a funny look on his face.

"What habit," he said.

"Printmaking. You know, woodcuts, etchings, like that." She laughed. "What, did you think I was a junkie?"

"You could have been," he said. "I was." He didn't look at her. He didn't hang his head, either. "A couple years ago," he said. They kept walking while he waited for her to decide about him. He hadn't told her enough for her to decide anything yet.

"Why would you do something like that?" she asked. She sounded annoyed.

"I was an asshole." Now he sounded annoyed.

"So why'd you quit?" She knew he didn't want to talk about it, but he'd brought it up.

He raised his eyebrows and then his shoulders. "I didn't want to sell my bass," he said.

"You were gonna sell your *guitar*?" She was shocked. "Are you kidding?"

Angel looked at her and laughed. She knew why it was funny and she was still shocked.

"I didn't, though," he said. "I've still got my bass and I'm as clean as clean." He grinned at her. It was an invitation written in flashing neon letters a foot high, but Alice had never been good at deciphering that kind of message. What she read most clearly was the dare between the lines. She wondered what she'd see if the plug was pulled on all that.

"Is that so," she said, flat.

His grin lost some wattage, but it didn't fade entirely. "Yeah," he said. "It's definitely so."

Their footsteps sounded loud on the pavement. It was late; this block was deserted except for them. "Listen," Angel said, and then nothing else. She looked at him so he would know she was listening.

He stopped to light a cigarette. He cupped his hands around the match as it spurted and caught fire. He leaned his head down to the flame and his face turned gold with ragged blue shadows. He would be good to draw, Alice thought. He would be great to draw if it turned out there was something to him.

He blew smoke. "You want to talk?" he asked.

"Yeah," she said.

"Okay," he said, looking around at the empty street. Then he looked at her. "What do you want to talk about?" It was a very small smile, this time. Alice liked it much better than the other one.

"I don't know," she said. "You could tell me the story of your life."

"Well," he said. "I will if you do. Where do you want to start?"

"The beginning."

Once they had decided what to talk about, they couldn't shut up. Angel was from Tucson, a big family, two older kids, three younger, and no reason to be as crazy as he had been. They talked about people who had helped them. Angel talked most about his friend Joe; Alice talked about Christine, her second foster mother.

Alice's mother had run off with a neighbor when Alice was a kid; her dad had started drinking, lost his job, and finally lost Alice to the court system. Her first foster family needed the money the court paid them for her; they gave her all the housework to do. All the cooking and the laundry. At first Alice tried to please them. She worked hard. They were pleased. They gave her more work. After six months she realized it wasn't going to get any better. She scorched the shirts, starched the lingerie, burned the dinner.

Angel laughed himself sick. Alice had told the story to be funny, but Angel's reaction made it funnier. It made her feel like it hadn't been so bad because here she was, years later, making him laugh.

Angel's own story of heroin addiction was not funny. He kept it short and to-the-point.

Near morning Angel gave all his money to a street person. Alice held onto her tips, which would just about cover her outstanding electric bill. She had eggs and bread and coffee at home. They got to her house as the sun was coming up. They took off their shoes and tiptoed up the creaky stairs, trying not to wake the downstairs neighbor, an old man who lived to complain about the noise. They were giggling hysterically. The downstairs door opened just as they got inside of her apartment; imagining his ire they collapsed with laughter, trying to stifle the sounds against each other. One thing led to another, right there on the floor. The man downstairs thumped the ceiling. Good thing, too, it gave Alice the breathing space to look for condoms.

She hoped the expiration date wasn't up. They finished in bed. It was a botched job, that first time. They kept laughing. When they woke up in the afternoon they did it again. They didn't laugh this time.

They barely had time to shower and eat before Angel had to go. Angel's band had another gig that night; at the door he asked if he could come back afterwards. It would be late, because he'd have to help break down and load the equipment, and borrow a car or get a ride.

"Get some condoms while you're at it," she said. "I'm out."

She didn't feel that casual. She called her friend Lynn as soon as Angel had left and told her the whole story.

"A junkie musician?" Lynn said. "Oh god, Alice. Just what you need. Verbal abuse wasn't enough?"

She was talking about Alice's last boyfriend, a year ago now.

"Ex-junkie," Alice said. "And he's not like that. He's not at all—he doesn't feel sorry for himself. He's sweet. He's the sweetest man I've ever met."

There was a long silence on the other end of the line. "Well," Lynn said. "When's his birthday?" Lynn was an astrologer; she always wanted to know birthdays.

"I didn't ask," Alice said. "What if he doesn't come back tonight? I almost don't want to be here in case he doesn't come back."

"If he's as great as you say he'll be back."

Alice bored Lynn telling her how wonderful Angel was, how he had given twenty bucks to a street person because he didn't have anything smaller, how he had this big, beautiful mouth and was the best kisser Alice had ever met, probably the best in the world. Then she felt superstitious. What if she had to tell Lynn what a shit he was tomorrow, what if he didn't come back? She was out of food. She bought a frozen dinner for one. If he didn't come back she didn't want that extra food staring at her. But she could clean the apartment. She had to do that anyway. She could do the laundry. She didn't want to smell him in the sheets if he wasn't going to come back.

By eleven o'clock her apartment was as clean as it would ever be and the laundry was clean, folded, and put away. Her bed was a little too pristine. It looked like an altar. She sat on the pillows to mash them and rolled around on the bed to wrinkle the sheets. She looked through some books, but she didn't feel like reading. She flipped through the four channels her little black and white TV set got. An old movie was on; she watched it and didn't know what it was about. Another one came on; one o'clock. Well, that didn't mean anything. She watched the second one in bed, half-asleep. She woke up at the end, when the station went off the air. Three a.m. How late was late?

She poured herself a shot of tequila, turned off the lights, and sat in bed to have her drink, looking out the window. She heard someone come in downstairs; it was the neighbor across the hall. Sounded like a heavy date. The man downstairs came out and told them to be quiet, some people slept at night, not like rabbits.

It should have been funny. Nocturnal rabbits? Alice thought about how it would have been funny if Angel were here. She knew he wasn't coming. "Shit," she said out loud. Then she turned on her side and lay still, pretending she was going to sleep. It was probably just as well to be a little miserable now as a lot miserable later. Angel was so sweet, so easy, he probably picked up women all the time. She turned on the radio, low, so she could stop listening to the cars going by. Then she put the radio in bed with her and pulled the covers over her head.

She finally slept. It was the kind of sleep that feels like you're still trying to go to sleep. She came wide awake to the sound of the buzzer. Someone was leaning on it. The clock said 5:13 and she stumbled to the door, hauling on her bathrobe, buzzing back. The door to the apartment across the landing was opening, and the door downstairs. Was it a fire?

"What the hell?" said her neighbor across the hall. He had a towel around him. The man downstairs was yelling, someone was standing on the other side of the door, rattling the knob. Alice ran down and opened the door.

Angel reeked of alcohol. She wanted to run back upstairs.

"What are you letting him in for?" the man downstairs demanded. Her upstairs neighbor had gone back to bed, slamming his door to let them know what he thought. Angel looked dazed.

"He's a friend of mine," Alice said. She took Angel by the arm and led him upstairs.

She sat him down at the table. He put his elbows on the table, his face in his hands. When she asked him if he wanted a cup of coffee he nodded.

She made coffee, nothing to say. How was she going to get rid of him? She wanted to get rid of him, now.

"I couldn't find you," he said to her back. "I don't know your last name. I couldn't remember which house it was. I must have tried all the houses on the street."

"What'd you do, ring every bell?"

"Only three. Besides yours."

Great, she thought. My neighbors must love me.

"There was a party. Joe wanted to go, he said he'd give me a ride if we just went for awhile. Then he met this chick—"

"Woman," Alice said.

Angel looked at her. He waited for her to say whatever it was. "It might seem weird for a bartender," she said, "but I don't like being around really drunk people."

"Because of your dad, right?"

"I just don't."

He got up and went into the bathroom, closing the door. She could hear him retching, then water running. He came out with his face wet, drying himself with his shirt. Even his hair was wet, like he'd stuck his head under the faucet. He smelled like toothpaste. His eyes were bloodshot and he looked like hell.

"I was nervous," he said. "I was afraid you'd change your mind. Have you?"

"I don't know," she said. Why didn't she just say yes I've changed my mind goodbye? "Sort of drunk is one thing, really trashed is another. I don't even want to start."

"Well, I'm not going to promise never to get trashed," he said. "But how about if I keep away from you when I do it?"

She liked him for not saying he was never going to do it again. She liked him for not being abject or trying to charm her. It made her feel that he was taking her seriously. She fought against liking him for that.

"I'd worry," she said.

"No, I mean, not so you'd worry. Not when we were going to see each other."

"Can you do that?"

"Sure," Angel said. He smiled, faint. "It's something I learned in rehab."

She looked into her coffee cup. He bent his head down to see her face.

"Alice?"

"No second chances on this," she said.

Angel hadn't needed any second chances. He only got trashed with the band, usually when they'd finished a long job or there was a big party. He warned Alice in advance.

She had a key made for him. Lynn met Angel, and in spite of her reservations, she liked him. Alice was free to be as in love as she wanted.

Angel kept a cheap guitar at her house for writing songs. Most of his clothes were at her apartment. She wore them more than her own. She could smell Angel in them. He smelled like cat's fur, like a cat sleeping in the sun.

Angel still lived with Joe, but neither Alice nor Angel suggested she spend time with him there. Alice didn't even like calling Angel at home. When Joe answered he pretended not to recognize her voice, as if she was only one of the many women who called Angel. At gigs Joe nodded to her. Once he even said hi. Compared to the rest of the band he was effusive.

The drummer, a baby-faced guy named Dan who would have been built like a football player if he gained thirty pounds, had never yet addressed a word to her. When Alice started showing up at gigs, sitting with Angel afterwards, Alice figured Dan might begin to notice that she was an actual living being. Once when Dan was talking to Angel and Alice, who after all was sitting right there, made a comment, Dan stared at her in genuine surprise. Did he think she was a mute?

Stringer, the lead singer, was friendly when they first met. He told Alice he was a feminist, and that he was married, like he thought she was interviewing him. He was one of those good-looking guys who had no sex appeal whatsoever. How did he manage it? Angel told Alice his wife Julie looked just like him. Angel called them Ken and Barbie. Stringer reminded Alice of a used car salesman, up in your face one minute, no time for you the next.

Alice tried talking about the band thing to Angel. Angel was smart about people, but he didn't quite get it. Her gossip outlets were Lynn and their friend Matt. Lynn had gone out with a musician for a while, and Matt had been in a band himself, so they both knew what she was talking about.

"I remember that 'it spoke' attitude," Lynn said. "Sometimes the guy's a jerk, but sometimes it's just the band. If you run into him by himself, he acts like a normal person. You have a conversation, he remembers your name...it's weird."

"Bands are like hydras," Matt said. "Even when they're infighting they're still one thing all together, and everybody else is an outsider."

"Did you ever act like that?" Alice asked.

"Probably. It's nice, if you've always been the outsider, to be at the center of things. But it's hard to keep doing it when you figure it out."

"I guess I should feel complimented that Joe doesn't like me," Alice said. "At least he noticed I'm alive."

"I wonder why he doesn't like you," Lynn said. "You don't even know him."

Alice said she thought it was a combination of possessiveness and plain old sexism. Now that he'd helped Angel through a bad time, Joe thought he owned Angel; he didn't want any competition, especially from a mere female.

"Is Angel on to any of this?" Matt asked.

Alice made a face and waggled her hand.

Lynn and Matt came along the next time Alice went to see the band. When Lynn saw Joe performing she said it could be a god's-gift-to-women thing, nothing personal. Alice didn't get that.

"What, just because he can play guitar?" Alice asked.

"Well, look at him," Lynn said.

Alice looked. Joe was medium tall and slender. He had two eyes, a nose, and a mouth. His hair was about a yard long, light brown and healthy. It was always clean. When he was onstage he flung it around tastefully. He never acted goofy, like Angel did. He acted like he couldn't be bothered. Just now he was naked from the waist up.

"You've got to admit," Lynn said, "he's a pretty hot tamale."

Alice didn't have to admit anything. "He doesn't even look like he's alive. He's probably an android."

"I think he does. And he writes those gut-wrenching songs. Doesn't it make you wonder what's going on inside?" Lynn was teasing Alice, who didn't feel like being teased.

"No," Alice said, grumpy. "What do you think?" she asked Matt, who was unusually quiet.

"I hope he's gay," Matt said. "Introduce me."

"That's an idea," said Alice. "You can keep his mind off Angel."

"Don't joke," said Matt. "I think I'm in love."

Alice introduced Matt and Lynn to Joe after the set, hoping for Matt's sake that Joe was neither homophobic nor racist. Alice dragged her attention away from Angel long enough to notice Matt saying something that made Joe laugh. Lynn was laughing, too. When the band started packing up Matt thanked Alice for introducing them.

"You're still in love and you talked to him?" Alice said.

"He wasn't that bad," Lynn put in. "I wouldn't call him a raging extrovert, but he was okay. Reserved, but pretty nice."

"A real human being."

"Well he probably is, Alice," Lynn said. "Most people are."

Alice thought Lynn had treated him like one of her kids having a bad day. Lynn was a daycare teacher, and a good one. Especially good with kids having a bad day. She and Angel had hit it off right away. But Lynn and Angel were both like that, they thought the best of people. Alice didn't. She waited to see.

"He invited us to a party tonight," Matt said.

"Oh no," Alice said. She had heard about the party. She guessed what was coming next.

"You have to go. We can't go without you."

Alice groaned. A party of drunken musicians was not her idea of a good time. "The things I do for your love life."

"What have you done? You've never done anything," Matt said.

The party was at Angel and Joe's house. Alice had avoided the parties; she felt like this was a test.

Angel didn't act like it was a test, he acted like it was a party. The place was mobbed with people Alice didn't know; the music was loud, people were dancing. Lynn had gone home from the club; she had to work in the morning. Alice saw Matt talking to Joe and some other people but after awhile he cornered Alice and said he was leaving.

"Leaving? You can't leave. What about your quest for love?"

"He's wonderful," Matt said, "but he's not gay."

"Maybe he just needs to be talked into it," Alice said.

Matt shook his head. "I don't do that anymore. I'm going home to soothe my wounded heart."

"What can you do at home? They have tequila here."

"That's what you do. I'm going to take a bath and sing sad songs." Matt gave her a hug and was gone.

While Alice had been talking to Matt, Dan's date had started dancing with Angel. She'd been making eyes at Angel all night and was finally drunk enough to act on it. Dan was in the kitchen talking loudly to two other guys; he didn't even notice. Why the hell didn't Dan's date make eyes at Joe?

Joe leaned against a wall, taking notes on the natives. Alice couldn't tell if he was as wrecked as everybody else seemed to be; he looked the same as usual. He glanced in her direction so she looked away. But she could feel him watching her. She caught him at it and stared back.

Joe acted as if Alice had been trying to catch his eye. He strolled over to her.

"You don't come here much," he said. Alice had never been to Joe and Angel's apartment. "Come on," he said. "I'll give you the guided tour."

Now it felt like a test. With Matt gone, she was alone in enemy territory.

"Okay," Alice said. She wasn't afraid of Joe. She followed him into the kitchen, where Dan and the other two guys sitting at the table were having a heated discussion about who was the best drummer in the world. None of them looked up.

"The way he fucking plays against the fucking beat," Dan was saying. "He's a fucking genius." He was so excited he was spitting as he spoke.

"This is the kitchen," Joe said. He looked around at the kitchen. He stared briefly at the guys arguing. They were getting louder. Joe didn't crack a smile. Alice guessed his kitchen always looked like this, beer cans and overflowing ashtrays and musicians turning up the volume. But Angel would have seen the humor.

"Bathroom's back there," Joe said, lifting his thumb at a doorway.

"I know," she said. Back hall, bathroom, back door. She'd already checked the exits.

The only other room was the bedroom, right off the kitchen. The door was open; Alice stuck her head in.

Angel and Joe shared this room like two kids in their parents' house. There were two beds, one on either side of the room. One bed was made. That side of the room was neat, if not clean. The other side was a mess. The bed was a nest of blankets and clothes. Alice moved towards it as if Angel's bed were a refuge. Then she saw the photograph tacked to the wall over the bed. It was black and white, torn out of a magazine, curling at the edges.

The woman in the photo had lips dark with lipstick, big naked breasts, legs wide apart. She was wearing a garter belt, black stockings, and high heels. She was using her fingers to spread herself open, showing off what was only normal equipment, minus the hair. She looked like a plucked chicken, ready for the pot.

Her long blonde hair fell over her face and her tongue poked out between her lips. She stared at Alice. Alice felt like she'd been punched in the stomach. She turned her back on the picture and went and sat down on the bed that was made. She looked at the photograph, at the woman sticking her tongue out.

"Can you tell which side of the room is Angel's?" Joe asked. He was smiling slightly, like he knew exactly how the photograph had affected her and was pleased about it.

"This side," she said, meaning the side she was on. She wasn't going to ask if she was right. He sat down on the unmade bed.

"How can you tell?" he asked.

"If you bleached your hair and turned into a woman, you'd look just like that," she said, lifting her chin at the woman nailed to the wall. "It's got to be yours."

"Yeah?" he said, turning his head to look at the picture. "Is that a compliment?"

So she'd been right. She was so relieved she didn't bother answering. Angel wasn't so neat at her house. Neither was she. They lived in a mess of clothes and books and tapes.

She didn't want to sit here with Joe anymore, playing cat and mouse. She wanted to dance. She got up and walked out of the room without saying another word to Joe. She cut in on Dan's date slow-dancing with Angel. The woman pretended not to notice Alice's first tap on her shoulder, so Alice "tapped" her harder the second time.

They left around four. Joe tried to convince them to stay. "It's just getting good," he said. Alice kept her mouth shut. She felt like he was trying to turn her into Angel's cop.

"You can tell me what I missed," Angel said, putting his arm around Alice's shoulder. Joe looked at them, shrugged, and went back inside.

Walking home, Angel asked Alice what she and Joe had talked about.

"He wanted to show me the house, since I'd never seen it. We didn't talk about anything. I couldn't believe your side of the bedroom was so tidy."

Angel laughed. "I am tidy," he said. "Don't I always do the dishes?" That was true. He did the dishes and swept the kitchen floor. Her concession to cleanliness was to scrub the bathroom every few weeks.

"You don't like him," Angel said. "Do you."

"Nope," she said.

"When I was in rehab," Angel said, "he called my sister Deanna, the one person in my family who could deal with it, and told her what was going on."

"I know he's a good friend to you," Alice said. "I just don't like him."

"Why not?"

"Because he's a manipulative shit," she said, really angry.

"He's my best friend."

"I know. I hear what you're telling me. But he's not my friend." She wanted to say, and he wants to make sure he keeps you to himself. "Does he have any girlfriends?" She thought a girlfriend might keep Joe occupied enough so he'd loosen his hold on Angel.

"Off and on," Angel said. "No one steady. You want him to have a girlfriend?"

"Yes," said Alice, fierce. "I do."

At the studio she told Lynn about the scene in the bedroom. Carla, another member of the printmakers' co-op, was there too. Carla was a pirate where men were concerned. She had Japanese chrysanthemums and dragons tattooed on her breasts, so no one could say they hadn't been warned. She wasn't a romantic. Her advice was always more practical than Lynn's or Alice's.

"I went out with a guy once who had these photographs of women with golf balls stuffed into their crotch," Carla said. "Close-ups of the ball and the crotch, that was it."

"Golf balls?" Lynn said.

"Is that a metaphor?" Alice said.

Carla laughed. "For what?"

"I don't know. What's the turn-on?"

"I asked him," Carla said. "He couldn't explain it."

"Was he a golfer?" Lynn asked.

"No," Carla said. "He was an environmentalist. He hiked a lot. He wanted to save the spotted owl." That cracked them up.

"I think," Carla said, when they had calmed down, "it's the different species thing."

"What different species thing?" Alice asked, thinking Carla meant the spotted owl.

"Men being a different species from women," Carla said. "I mean, think about it. Can you imagine a woman getting turned on by something like that?" None of them could.

"I always thought Angel was the same species as me," Alice said. "But he lives with Joe, and I can't imagine any woman doing that. Maybe he's the same species, a different tribe."

"Maybe he's the missing link," Carla said.

"I wouldn't worry about Joe," Lynn said. "Angel doesn't seem to care."

"I'm not worried about Joe," Alice said. Angel was loyal. He would be loyal to Joe and Alice while they hated each other. "I just want to punch him. Or I want to hook him up with some dragon lady and see him go down in flames."

"Introduce me," Carla said, and they laughed.

Alice expected to reach a point when she got used to Angel, when she felt a little bored and dull, a lag time when she could catch her breath. Five months going on six, and it hadn't happened yet.

He wrote songs at her house. She showed him her prints. He helped her get through an opening when she was berserk with terror by sticking close to her and making dumb jokes. He had a good eye, which was a great relief to Alice. He said she had a good ear.

He liked to walk. He would meet her at the bar, or she would meet him at a gig, and they would roam all over the city, looking at everything, talking about music and art and band gossip, turning the small events of the day into stories to tell each other.

They watched late movies in bed sometimes, like an old married couple. Alice even tried reading her favorite books to him. Angel fell asleep, so they stuck to the late movies.

They went to hear music together. Angel crowd-surfed while Alice watched him being passed around by other people's hands, proving that his faith in humanity was justified. He seemed purely himself then, out of control and laughing about it. One night he got her to do it.

"You know you want to," he said.

She did want to, but she was too chicken. "What if they drop me?"

"They're not going to drop you," he said. "You're a woman, and you're light. They'll be fighting to hold you up." He put his hands on her waist and lifted her up, and three guys next to them held out their hands.

"Angel!" she yelled.

"Try to stay on your back," he yelled back, as she was lifted onto the top of the crowd.

If she stayed on her back, no one could grab her breasts and crotch. They could grab her ass; they did. But she moved so fast over the waving field of hands it hardly mattered. A guy crowd-surfing in front of her, with a shaved head and a face like a ferret, called out as he went, "Hold her up! Hold her up!" They grinned at each other like long-lost kin. She wasn't just held up, she was tossed high into the air, and wherever she landed there were more people, passing her on. What a rush! Totally out of control, with no faith whatsoever in humanity, Alice was passed along anyway. By the time she came back to Angel she was laughing, she was as high as she'd ever been.

"See?" he said.

He still didn't come home all the time. Different tribes, Alice told herself, or Angel wanting to get trashed with his friends. But she didn't like it.

Once the band went out of town for a week and Angel was back for two days without calling her. Alice, imagining Joe answering the phone, didn't call. She dreamed that Angel was fucking the woman over Joe's bed.

The next night she went to an art opening with Lynn that she had hoped to go to with Angel. Alice and Lynn got dressed at Lynn's house, like they were getting ready for the prom. They wore eye makeup and jeans. Alice wore a thrift store blouse of Lynn's; it was slithery and funky and sexier than Alice's clothes. She hit on a guy she knew vaguely from art school. He was ready for a one-night stand. She wasn't. She backed off. He got interested in somebody else within five minutes.

Alice stood at the fringes of various conversations. She was thinking she would go wait in the car when Matt showed up with Chuck, another printmaker from the co-op. They saw each other all the time, but they greeted each other with glad cries, as if they'd been stranded on separate desert islands for years.

Matt and Alice danced. Matt was a good dancer. Alice had met Matt in art school, in the cafeteria line. She had been having a bad day until then. She had just realized that the new guy she'd met was not for her and, to top it off, nothing she had drawn for the past six weeks had worked. Her figure drawings were awkward and out of proportion, the heads and bodies had no relationship to each other. They had a mind/body split. She was staring morosely at the little dishes of strange foods sitting on beds of ice, wondering if this was to be her lot in life, when this gorgeous guy with dreadlocks who was standing behind her said, "The bread pudding is safe," and she realized she was holding up the line. She took the bread pudding, embarrassed, and moved on. He looked like he was from Jamaica but he had no accent. At the hot food line he peered at the stew. "What do you think?" he said, noticing her watching him.

"Dog food," she said.

They ate together, and Alice told him about being unable to draw, because he asked her why so dismal. He had thought it was love, himself. He was the one who began the love sucks conversation, so she found out right away that he was gay. She fell madly in love with him anyway. Then they had a huge fight about Picasso, she fell out of love, and they stayed friends.

Matt was not in love with anybody right now. He asked about Angel and she told him, as usual, more than she meant to. They went out and sat in the car, Matt giving her serious advice that she immediately forgot.

They all ended up at Lynn's house, eating popcorn and smoking pot, gossiping about the show. Alice felt depressed and disoriented the next day, like she had landed on this planet through some cosmic error and whoever was responsible hadn't noticed it yet. It was her usual pot hangover. She had smoked because she wanted to forget about Angel and laugh. She had to work that night; she went straight from Lynn's house to the bar.

She got off at one in the a.m. and walked home. It was a long walk; it gave her time to think. Was she supposed to be getting over Angel now? Is that what it was time to do?

Angel was asleep in her bed when she got home. Now he was here, she wanted to kill him. He woke up when she came in, saving her the trouble of waking him. He was glad to see her.

"Where were you?" he asked.

"Where were you?" she answered.

"At a very long party," he said.

"You didn't call me. You didn't tell me where you were."

"I called you," he said. "You weren't home. You wouldn't have liked the party, Alice."

So don't go, she thought.

Angel took hold of her fingers and moved her hand back and forth like it was the rudder of a boat. "Parties aren't as much fun as they used to be," he said.

She hoped that meant he wouldn't go anymore, and she wouldn't have to say anything about it.

"Where were you?" he asked again.

"At an art opening." She thought about the guy she'd almost

picked up, imagining that she had picked him up and hoping that Angel would read her fantasy, take it for reality, and be jealous.

"Was it fun?" he asked.

She shrugged. "It was okay." She tried to say it like she was hiding something. He smiled and pulled her into bed next to him, not jealous at all, as if he knew exactly what she was doing.

"I talked to Deanna on the phone last night," he said. "The wedding's next week. They want me to come." Alice wondered who "they" were; Deanna was the only person in his family he kept in touch with. She'd been planning her wedding for months now.

"Are you going?"

"I asked Joe to fix it with the gigs so I could take off for a week or so."

A week or so! He'd just gotten *back*.

"Can you afford it?"

"They're sending me a plane ticket," he said. She settled herself next to him so she could be miserable in comfort.

"I haven't seen them in a long time," he said. "But I didn't want to. All at once I do."

Alice hadn't seen her mother in fifteen years. Her father had gone into AA, met a woman there, and remarried. They had two kids from her former marriage. A couple of years ago Alice had gone to their house for Thanksgiving. Lynn had thought she should find out about her mother. But there was never any time to ask. Her father, almost as if he knew she wanted to ask, kept himself busy with the rest of his family, with his real family.

She'd come back to her real home, here, her real family, which was Lynn and Matt if it was anybody. Matt thought she was lucky, having no one's expectations to live up to. His parents kept waiting for him to get married, or at least get a girlfriend, as if being gay was a rebellious phase he was going through. Alice didn't feel lucky.

“I wish I could take you,” Angel said.

Alice’s self-pity, which had become a hard knot in her chest, began to dissolve. Angel was here now. That was what counted, wasn’t it?

“Next time,” Alice said. “We could go in the clunker.”

“Naw, I’ll buy a real car, something that runs. We can camp out in the desert.” This was an ongoing fantasy of theirs, driving and camping in the desert. “We can drive all night and listen to the radio,” Angel said. “Or we’ll get a decent tape deck.”

“We can steer by the stars,” Alice said, getting carried away. “I’ll learn all their names. I’ll get a sky map.”

“But the roads will take us there,” Angel said. “Unless you want to go cross-country and ignore the roads. Maybe I should get us a jeep.”

“We can go on horseback,” Alice said. “We’ll ignore the roads and have a vision quest.” Except weren’t you supposed to do that alone?

“Are you supposed to do a vision quest alone?” she asked. “And how are we going to listen to plugged-in music on horseback?”

“Solar batteries and a boom box?” Angel said. “I don’t know. We’ll wing it. We’ll make it up as we go.”

II.

The printmakers were having a show in the co-op gallery. Angel scheduled his return to coincide with the opening. He would still be gone for a week, but those would be heavy working days for Alice. She only had one drawing for the show; she needed two more pieces for it. She could work hard with no distractions, go flat out to the deadline, and have Angel's return to look forward to at the end of it.

Alice was going to take Angel to the airport but her car broke down again, so Joe drove Angel to the airport and Alice came along. There was one passenger seat; Alice sat on Angel's lap and he wrapped his arms around her waist. The back of the van was empty except for a mattress, some amp cords, and used paper coffee cups.

"It's safer if Alice rides in the back," Joe said. Alice was surprised he had used her name. He usually referred to her as "she". He was wearing sunglasses in spite of the overcast.

"It *feeeels* better if she rides right here," Angel said. "Don't worry, if we get in an accident I'll hold onto her." Alice didn't think that was what Joe was worried about. He wanted Alice in back with the other trash.

Joe didn't argue. He didn't even sulk. He started talking about how it had been when he went to his brother's wedding, seeing all these people who either remembered you from when you were a kid or didn't know you at all. "They kept asking me when I was getting married," Joe said, "or looking at me like they thought I was there to take hostages. One of my aunts got loaded on champagne and said, 'Your hair looks good. It must be a lot of work.' We talked about conditioners."

Angel laughed. From the safety of Angel's lap, Alice looked at Joe with interest. She had never thought of him having a family, being connected to anyone outside the band or having anyone to deal with besides his own irascible self.

"I should probably get shit-faced," Angel said. "That would reassure Deanna, anyway."

"What do they say to you at your family things?" Joe asked Alice. Was he trying to be polite?

"I don't have family things," Alice said.

"Alice is a solo act," Angel said.

Joe didn't say anything. "I keep in touch with some of the other foster kids," Alice half-explained. "But none of us expect anything from each other like that."

There was a silence. Alice wished she hadn't said anything. Under her jacket, Angel rubbed his thumb over her hipbone.

"What time's the plane leave?" Joe said, and the talk turned mundane.

Joe got the boarding pass so Angel and Alice could have some time together. They only had a few minutes. Alice hugged Angel tight. Angel gave her a long involved kiss, not minding the people passing by.

"I wish you could come with me," he said.

"I wish I could too."

"They'd probably put you in the downstairs bedroom where they could keep an eye on you, and me as far away as possible."

"Maybe I'll have enough money to get the car fixed by the time you get back. I could pick you up."

Angel kissed her again.

Then Joe was back with Angel's ticket. His sunglasses reflected the overhead lights in twin stars. Alice felt embarrassed, kissing Angel in front of Joe. Angel wasn't embarrassed. He took the ticket, gave Alice a last hug. He hugged Joe. Then he was on his way.

"Call when you get in," Joe yelled to his back. Angel raised his arm to show he'd heard, but he didn't turn around.

Alice would have watched until Angel was out of sight, but Joe was ready to go. "I'm parked illegally," he said.

Alice hadn't noticed. She'd been too busy hoping something would happen at the last minute to keep Angel in town. There was a ticket on the windshield. "Fuck," Joe said, and flipped it into the back of the van. He lit a cigarette and got in. Alice stood waiting on the other side of the van. "It's unlocked," he yelled.

Feeling stupid, she got in. With any luck he would just ignore her for the rest of the ride. He started up the van, but he didn't go anywhere. He turned his head and stared at her. The cigarette was stuck in the corner of his mouth. Smoke curled up around the opaque black lenses over his eyes.

Did he think he was in a gangster movie?

"What," she said.

"Seat belt."

She put on her seat belt. He put the van in gear and pulled out of the lot.

"Where to?" he asked. "You're on the way to work, aren't you?"

"You can drop me at the bus stop."

"I'll take you to work. The Neptune bar, right?"

"You don't have to."

"I told Angel I would."

She rolled down the window a couple inches.

"Smoke bother you?" he asked.

"No. I just want some air to mix it with."

They drove the rest of the way in silence. It was not comfortable, but Alice figured it was better than talking. The discomfort kept her from missing Angel so much. Seven days!

She wanted to think about last night but there was no way she was going to think about anything that personal in front of Joe. Who knew what he could sense from behind those sunglasses? She watched the scenery out the window. It was grey and brown.

"Thanks for the ride," she said when he had pulled over near the bar.

"How late do you work tonight?"

"One," she said.

"Have a good night."

She thought he was being sarcastic; she didn't answer.

Actually, she was glad to work. Thursday night was busy without being totally insane and she got along with Freddie, the other bartender. He was fast without being harried, he didn't have moods, and he was good at handling drunks, not one of Alice's strong points. The band was decent, and the owner wasn't coming in. It was a good night.

Around midnight Freddie "broke" a bottle of tequila, and he and Alice made margaritas. The band finished and the bar emptied fast. This gave Alice and Freddie time to play air guitar and jazz up their margaritas. They played the Hendrix version of "All Along the Watchtower" on the jukebox and sang along. Alice got into it; she imitated Stringer's nasal vibrato snarl, Angel's war dance. She played air guitar while tossing her hair around in a don't-hate-me-because-I'm-beautiful sort of way, being Joe. She shrugged one shoulder back and bumped her air guitar suggestively with her hip, as if working the hetero female element of the crowd. She was snickering wildly.

Freddie flopped around like a loose-jointed doll, imitating somebody, she had no idea who. He made Alice laugh so hard she drooled. He couldn't carry a tune and he sang louder on the notes he couldn't hit. Alice sang louder too. She thought she sounded great.

One of the regulars still left at the bar applauded them. They turned around and took a bow, laughing and out of breath. When she straightened up Alice noticed someone else watching them, over by the door. He was wearing a leather jacket Alice had last seen on Angel. But it wasn't Angel.

Alice's laugh died a short, painful death. Her neck buzzed with heat, and then her face. How long had he been standing there?

Joe watched her turn red, looking interested. He came over and pulled up a barstool. "Can I still get a drink?" he asked.

"Sure. What do you want? A margarita? It's on the house." She was talking too much, trying to act normal, to pretend she wasn't blushing.

"Just a shot," he said.

She poured him a hefty slug. "How'd you like the band?" she asked. "I thought they were pretty good."

"I just got here. I thought you might need a ride home."

"Oh." Alice guessed Angel had asked him to. She wished he hadn't.

Joe swallowed tequila. "You sounded just like Stringer," he said. "But Angel plays his bass lower and he doesn't do that other shit." He twitched his shoulder and flung his hair back, showing her the other shit.

She could feel her blush returning tenfold. She searched her mind for a snappy comeback but all that came out of her mouth was "Mmm." Oh fuck it. So he'd caught her imitating him, so what.

Joe drank tequila and smoked while she and Freddie cleaned up. Joe didn't say anything, which should have made it easier to ignore him.

Then Alice was done; she split tips with Freddie, put on her jacket, and stashed the rest of the tequila in her shoulderbag.

Joe and Alice came out of the bar into a drizzling rain.

"Angel got in okay," Joe said.

"That's good," Alice said. The streetlights had haloes, the neon made ghost snakes in the mist. She thought about Angel in Tucson, surrounded by cactus, endless desert, and family. She wished Joe were Angel.

Joe wasn't wearing his sunglasses. He was treating her like she was someone he knew and took for granted, like a friend.

"How'd he sound?"

"Fine," Joe said, which told her nothing. If he really had been a friend she would have pumped him for details, or he would have heard what she wanted to know and answered without being pumped.

Angel had run into some of his old friends. He was already partying with them. Alice, on the other hand, seemed to be taking a week-long separation like a sojourn in hell. In the van leaving the airport, she'd been like a dog who's just seen the last of her litter carried off by strangers.

Joe didn't want to feel sorry for Alice. He wanted to find out what she was about. Angel had never been with anyone for this long and now his sister was getting married. Weddings affected people weird.

Coming into the bar tonight, watching Alice before she'd seen him, he was almost glad that she didn't look so wilted. Then he heard her doing Stringer's voice, saw her doing Angel's war dance. It took a while longer to recognize himself. She had been imitating what Angel called Joe's "come fuck me" moves, only with no finesse. She looked like a kid pretending to be a rock star in front of a mirror. He thought it was funny.

"Don't you hate drunks or something?" he asked her.

"What?" Her mind was a million miles away, probably in Tucson.

"Why do you work in a bar?"

"I like the hours," she said. "I'm counterphobic."

"What's that supposed to mean?"

"If you're phobic and you're afraid of something, you keep away from it. If you're counterphobic, you rub your nose in it."

"Until it goes away?"

"The drunks don't go away."

"I meant the fear."

Alice thought about it. "That hasn't happened yet."

"So who drank?"

"What?"

"Someone you grew up with?"

"My dad," she said.

He'd surprised her. She must think he was a moron. That was okay. It'd be easier to keep her off balance. "My mom ran off with some guy," she said, like she was talking about the weather. "Then my dad started drinking." They got in the van.

"Don't you ever lock it?" she asked him.

"Nothing to steal. It's a piece of crap anyway."

"It runs," she said. She remembered to put on her seat belt. She put her bag in her lap and folded her arms over it, protecting her solar plexus. Or the tequila.

He started up the van. "You wanna go someplace and drink that?" he asked. She glanced at him. He could feel her trying to figure out what was going on. He eased out into traffic, watching the rearview mirror and the road, giving her space.

"What kind of place?" she asked.

"An outside place," he said. "It's pretty."

He could almost hear the wheels turning. He thought she was the kind of person who would take a dare. He had been careful not to make it sound like a dare. He figured she would take the dare to prove something to herself, but not if she thought she had to prove anything to him. Especially not then.

"Okay," she said.

He took her to the cemetery. They sat on the gravestones, passing the tequila bottle back and forth. Joe drank more than Alice. He had a hard head that way. To get her talking he talked about personal stuff. He told her his older brother Frank was doing well with a small business, a small house, a small family. Joe didn't mean to sound snide about his family. They accepted him, even though he was a broke musician living with Angel and working as a security guard to keep the money coming in.

"You're a security guard?" Alice said. "Don't you get the creeps, being alone in an empty building at night?"

"I get bored. Sometimes I take the guitar and write songs. An alarm got set off once, and it turned out to be a rat or something chewing on the wires. A break-in would have been okay with me. I would have gotten to see how good I was at aikido for real."

"What's that like? Aikido. How'd you get into that?"

"I started with karate, when I was a kid. I used to get picked on a lot. I was a skinny little kid and I stuttered." He hadn't meant to tell her that, but it wouldn't hurt. Women always liked hearing how you had been picked on and survived.

"You stuttered?" Alice asked. "When did you stop stuttering?"

"Around puberty," he said, to shut her up and finish his story.

She cracked up. "That would be a problem," she said. "Hey, b-b-b-b-b-baby, w-w-w-what's happenin?" She thought she was hilarious. But he was laughing too.

"So what about the aikido," she said.

"I kept getting beat up. My dad took me to a karate class. The first year I hated it; I wanted to quit. He wouldn't let me quit until I learned something. By the time I learned something I was hooked."

"But aikido's a whole different thing from karate, right? Aikido's self-defense, karate's attack."

"Yeah. In aikido you use your enemy's aggression against them. You let them defeat themselves."

"You psych them out? I'll bet you're good at that," she said. He was good at that, but since it was how he planned to defeat her he didn't want her thinking about it too much.

"That's not exactly aikido—psyching people out. You just try to stay in harmony yourself. So what did you do? For self-defense." Everybody had something. He passed her the tequila. Truth serum. She took a long swig.

"I got real *bad* at what I was doing," she said, and told him a story about scorching the ironing and burning the dinner at the first foster family she'd stayed with. "I even starched their underwear. They knew I was doing it on purpose. I'd been so good and careful before. I'd been so fucking scared," she said, sounding angry. "I lucked out with the social worker, though. She didn't listen when they said I was a 'big problem.' She listened to me. She crossed those people off her list and sent me to Christine. Christine just kept taking kids because she knew they needed her, not for the money. She's the one who pushed me to go to art school."

Joe took the bottle back. Alice wasn't drinking out of it anyway.

"How old were you when all that happened?"

"I was thirteen when I got sent to Christine."

Jesus H. Christ, Joe thought. Thirteen years old and you've got nobody. That's what Angel had meant, when he said Alice was a solo act. Would that make her tougher, or easier?

Joe held up the bottle. Alice shook her head. The overcast was getting lighter, not much.

"You know," he said, "I couldn't figure out why you and Angel were together until now."

"I didn't have the tits for the job?"

He shrugged. "Who can tell?" He meant her clothes. She wore baggy t-shirts and sweaters that hid everything. Tonight she'd worn a bartender's apron around her waist and it was the first he knew she had a waist. She started laughing and couldn't stop. He figured she was getting smashed.

"Well," she said, "I didn't know why Angel was friends with you *at all.*" Then they both laughed. Joe decided he was not entirely sober himself.

He drove her home, running the red lights carefully.

"You know where I live," she said.

"I've driven Angel here enough times." He realized he hadn't found out anything much about Alice. He'd talked about himself, relaxed too much. "You work tomorrow?"

"No."

"Want to go see something?"

"What kind of something?"

"Nature," he said. He wanted to see the trees anyway. He hadn't been there in too long. Two birds with one stone.

"Yeah," she said, sounding surprised about it. "I would."

"I'll pick you up at noon."

"Noon? It's almost noon now."

"You can sleep in the back. It's a long drive."

"You're so flexible," she said. "It must be the aikido."

"It's a long way," he said. "Eleven would be better."

"I'll see you at noon."

Alice was ready at noon, barely. She brushed her teeth, washed her face, took a five minute bath, put on clean underwear and t-shirt, a big sweater, and black jeans. She brewed a cup of coffee in her commuter mug. She made a couple of bread and butter sandwiches, washed some grapes and threw them in a paper bag. Then she was ready to spend a day in the country, checking out her rival. When Joe rang she slipped on her jacket, stepped into her unlaced boots, and came down the stairs.

She drank her coffee while they waited in line for the ferry. They went and stood on deck for the crossing, staring at the water and the mountains half-visible in fog. Joe had his own coffee. He ate a couple of Alice's grapes. He had as little to say this early as she did. They communicated in grunts. When it was time to get in the van again Alice crawled in back and lay down on the mattress and went to sleep.

She woke up a couple hours later when they stopped for gas. Alice went to the bathroom, and then got more coffee. She gave Joe a bread and butter sandwich. He'd bought some homemade split pea soup across the street and they dunked the bread in it. Alice hated split pea soup. It was slimy and who would want to eat anything that color? But this was good. She ate so much of Joe's soup he had to go back and get another cup. She felt better, more awake, and curious about where they were going.

"Want me to drive?" she asked.

He didn't. The road turned a corner and there was a lake. The water was silvery. Clouds rolled in over the hills across the water, changing the light. It was like one of those old photographs, when they didn't know what they were doing yet and everything was as accidental and meaningful as it is in a dream. The road twisted around steep-sided mountains, thickly forested. The water looked cold and deep.

In late afternoon they reached the place Joe was taking them. He parked the van and they walked among trees. Trees always had some kind of presence, but these were old, with roots reaching down to the center of the earth. Alice felt small and obtrusive, like a gnat. She stepped softly. Moss and centuries of tree leavings made the ground springy. She wandered away from Joe, following something.

One tree in particular spoke to her. She put her hands on its bark, its rough skin. After awhile, she put her cheek against it. It didn't mind. What was it Dylan Thomas said? Something about a green fuse. She felt the green fuse; she felt the tree life pulsing under the bark, a slow drawing-up of water to air. All her own worries floated to the surface. Then the tree pulled them away from her. Gnat worries, they were gone in a moment.

She looked around, feeling watched. No one was there. It was the trees watching her. She lifted her shirt, unzipped her jeans, and pressed her belly against the tree. She was asking for a blessing.

Later, Alice found Joe. He was sitting on the ground, his back against a tree. His hands rested on its roots, his eyes were shut. He had taken his sunglasses off. It was only then that she realized he'd had them on all day.

She felt like a voyeur. She was going to go away, but his eyes opened. He looked straight at her. His eyes were light, blue or green or both.

He didn't say anything. He stood up slowly, dusting leaves off his butt. Alice followed him back through the forest. On the path he stopped and picked up something—a feather?—and put it in the pocket of his biker jacket.

Alice had a stone in her pocket. She had found it at the foot of the tree and waited until she knew it was all right to take it. They came out of the trees and saw the sun dropping below the cloud cover before it fell into the ocean.

They watched from the van as the sun changed. The top of it flattened, the yellow giving way to dark pink streaked with black, like someone had painted an ink wash across it. It moved down the sky and was gone.

For one moment Alice forgave everybody, even her parents. She stared at the place where the sun had been, her eyes burning.

Joe lit a cigarette. He rolled down the window to let the smoke out. He drew deep, making the ash glow red, and exhaled smoke on a long sigh.

“I’ve been trying to work out how to get Angel to cut loose from you,” he said.

“I noticed,” Alice said. Well she had. He hadn’t bothered to hide it from her, although he’d probably hidden it from Angel.

“I mean today.”

“Today?”

“Since he’s been gone.”

The road was empty. No one was around except Alice and her enemy. She put her hands in her pockets. Her hand closed around the stone.

“So what are you going to do?”

He started up the van. “I just did what I’m going to do,” he said. “I told you.”

When he finished the cigarette he lit another one off the butt before mashing the first one in the ashtray. The sky was dark, the sun gone. Alice watched in the rearview mirror; only reddish-tinged clouds were left. Joe chain-smoked.

“Why’d you tell me?” Alice asked, miles later.

“So you’d know,” he answered.

“If you’re gonna keep smoking, give me one.” He gave her one. She lit it, breathed in shallowly, and blew smoke in a thin stream.

“Do you smoke?” he asked, like he didn’t think she did.

“It keeps my eyes from watering when everyone else is smoking,” she said. It made her dizzy. It reminded her of the first year of art school, before she’d quit smoking. It gave her something to hold onto that was also a weapon—fire.

“You could be trying to throw me off by being honest about what you’re doing,” she said. “That would be an aikido move.”

In the light from the dashboard she saw his surprise. “I could be,” he said.

“You’re not going to scare me away from Angel,” she said, suddenly furious.

"I know that," he said, being angry back. "I'm not an idiot."

"No," she agreed, blowing smoke. You're a manipulative shit.

The road curved back and forth along the water. Fog and mist hid parts of it. Joe concentrated on driving. Alice put her feet up on the dashboard and leaned back against the seat. "When were you born," she said. "November?"

"Halloween," he said. Alice started laughing. "What's that got to do with anything? That supposed to make me a zombie? Night of the living dead?"

"It makes you a Scorpio," she said.

"So fucking what?" He hated astrology. If he was what he was, then he wanted to be it on his own.

"Lynn's an astrologer," she said. "Not me. She thought you were a Scorpio."

"Really," he said, mashing out his cigarette. He'd heard all this Scorpio shit before. One of his old girlfriends had used it to explain everything she didn't like about him. He didn't ask why Lynn had thought he was a Scorpio. "When were you born? You're one of those signs that's supposed to be real nice, right?"

Alice snorted. "November," she said. "The seventeenth."

"No shit?"

"I usually don't tell people." She put out her cigarette in the ashtray. She had an evil smile on her face. "I make them guess. Then I watch them cringe."

"Angel's born in the spring," he said.

"But he's a Pisces. If anybody can slip through the net, it's him." She filched another cigarette from his pack on the dashboard. Now that they were both Scorpios, he figured she thought she didn't have to ask. "Scorpios have to work at it. Angel just goes his own way. I kept thinking, if he was out there in those trees, he wouldn't feel small and unworthy. He'd take off his clothes and run around."

Joe glanced at her. Her eyes were shiny. She held one of his cigarettes in her hand and forgot to light it. He hated astrology and he hated nonsmokers who bummed cigarettes and he hated crying women. Did she know how much Angel went his own way? Did she know about the other women? But she was right about one thing. "I brought Angel out here once," he said.

"You did?"

"He took off his clothes and ran around."

Joe stopped at the next town, which consisted of a filling station, a gift shop, and a restaurant. They pooled their money and bought as much food as they could get: a fish dinner, a bowl of stew, two cups of coffee. They split everything. Alice stuffed the extra rolls into her pocket.

As if making up for being quiet all day, they talked all through dinner. Joe talked about aikido, about how important it was to know how to defend yourself. He thought Alice should learn some self-defense. He thought, although he didn't say it, that she believed in people too easily.

Alice said that making prints was her self-defense. As long as she was working she was okay, no matter what else happened. She said she tried to follow whatever hooked her, figuring she'd learn the technique along the way. "I get lazy and scared. But if I keep at it I forget all that other shit, how I'm not as good as I want to be, what other people are going to think, and go for something simple."

"Like what?"

"Like the shadows that bring things forward," she said.

That didn't mean anything to him. "What do you mean hooked?" he said, going back to what she'd said earlier.

"'We never know what is of overmastering importance,'" she quoted, "'until it has overmastered us.' So you stick with whatever hooks you, no matter how silly or wrong it seems. Because it might turn out to be the really important thing."

"Sometimes what hooks you is exactly what you don't need," Joe argued.

"You mean drugs."

"Not just drugs. There's lots of stuff."

"Well, that's not the stuff I mean. Or maybe it is. Leave drugs out of the argument."

"Okay," Joe said. "Make it a bad relationship. You're with someone who makes you feel like shit. There's nothing to do but leave, and you can't leave."

Alice looked at him like she thought he was talking about himself. He was talking about everybody. "But then you do leave," she said, "and you don't make that mistake again. Because you found out something that you didn't know before and couldn't have learned any other way."

"Unless you keep doing it because that's what's hooked you. People get hooked on bad relationships."

"Then you didn't do it to the end the first time. You stopped before you were finished with whatever you needed to find out. So the trick would be to make sure you're finding out something...or maybe I've got the emphasis wrong. I always thought she meant that you could count on your obsessions to show you the way, but she could have meant you don't know what's important until you've already been doing it awhile, and you've given it a chance to take hold. That sounds like self-discipline. If I have to be self-disciplined I may as well forget it." She frowned at him. "You've just screwed up my theory, anyway. I hope you're happy."

No, he thought, I just said one thing and you single-handedly destroyed your own theory.

"Who's this 'she'?" he asked.

"Dorothy Sayers. A dead writer. She wrote mysteries."

"You read a lot?"

"All the time. Don't you?"

"No. I never did that great in school. I hated it."

"I never read anything in school. I would have thought you'd read a lot."

"Why?"

"The way you write songs," she said. "The words matter. In some songs the words are just there because they needed a voice for the melody line. And to give the singer something to do besides look cool."

"I barely passed English class. I'm dyslexic. I read really slowly," he said, drawing out the last two words.

"What's that got to do with anything?" she said. "Einstein couldn't do the math for his equations. He didn't even talk until he was three. He built houses out of cards."

"Come on."

"Really. His mom knew he was okay though. She took him to one of the first schools for dyslexic kids, in Vienna."

She bummed another cigarette from his pack and stuck it in her mouth. She had a big mouth and she used it a lot. On the ferry he'd watched her eat a grape in seven bites. Sometimes when her mouth was shut her lips kept moving, following the words she wasn't saying like a sleeper's eyelids following dreams.

"Don't smoke 'em all," he said. She ignored him.

"I think Christine is like Einstein's mother. Someone who doesn't care what doesn't fit about you, but sees it as a good thing. I want to be that kind of mother."

She talked like she was planning on it. Joe wondered if she talked like this around Angel.

"I know what," she said. "I'll read to you."

"Like I'm a three-year old."

"I like reading to people. People used to read out loud to each other all the time. I've got a book I think you'd like. There's this printmaker, he was dyslexic too, and the poets in London loved him because he knew exactly how important words are. He didn't take them for granted. He didn't really learn to read until he was twenty-five."

"I'm already twenty-five. I'm twenty-seven."

"I'm twenty-eight," she said. "I'm older than you so you should listen to me. You'll like this book."

"I work all weekend."

"So I'll come read it to you tomorrow night. You won't have to be bored."

Joe thought about it. "I could show you some self-defense," he said.

He could tell she didn't want to learn self-defense. But she was going to have to if she wanted to read to him.

He sneaked her in the next night. She was supposed to come around and wait outside a side door when he did his midnight rounds. She was late. He thought she wasn't coming, and then he saw her running up the hill.

She walked with him around the warehouse. He pointed the flashlight at dark corners, checked doors and windows. Once he pushed her behind a stack of boxes, hiding her from the other guard. He and the other guy bullshitted for awhile, and then the guy went away. Alice stood perfectly still, eyes wide open in the dark, like she was playing hide and seek.

Back at his cubbyhole of an office he pushed the chairs back and showed her some self-defense. Simple stuff. How to break an elbow or a foot. She was tense and nervous. He did some warm-up Tai Chi exercises with her to get her to relax. He showed her how to do Tai Chi walking, knees bent, feet shoulder-width apart, weight shifting from one leg to the other. She was pretty good at that. Then he showed her the elbow and foot moves. She did a lot better the second time.

After an hour or so, it was time to be read to. Joe didn't look forward to it, but he'd agreed, so he sat in one of the swivel chairs, gave her the other, and put his feet up on the desk.

The book she'd brought was called *A Wizard of Earthsea*. It started slow. He hid a yawn. He shut his eyes. He could tell from her voice that she was already into the story. If he fell asleep, she probably wouldn't even notice.

He didn't fall asleep. The story caught him. It was about a goatherd who was also a magician. He didn't make friends easily. He wanted to hurt people who hurt him. He had something to prove. He reminded Joe of himself.

Alice stopped reading before he was ready to stop listening.

"You're stopping there?"

She shrugged. "My throat's dry," she said. "So did you like it?" she asked, giving up on nonchalance.

"It wasn't bad."

"Come on. It was great."

They walked the rounds again. Joe got her some water from the cooler.

"Read some more," he said when they got back to his cubbyhole. Alice read some more.

At six he sneaked her back out and told her where the van was parked. She was asleep in the back when he got there. After he dropped her off at her house he realized she'd left the book in the van.

Alice had told herself, before Angel left, that she would use the time he was gone to see her friends again. She saw them all the time at the studio, but at night she was either with Angel or she stayed home and read. She hadn't felt like hanging out.

She'd fallen out of the loop. There was a show she wanted to see at the museum. Carla and Chuck had already seen it; Matt was involved with some new guy he'd met and didn't have time. Lynn had the flu. Alice had gotten her car out of the shop, so she drove over to see Lynn.

Sitting up in bed, her thick brown hair twisted into a knot at the back of her neck, her pale face flushed along the cheekbones and her eyes glazed with fever, Lynn looked like someone from a Botticelli painting. Lynn was pleased that Alice thought so but said she didn't feel like that. She was achy and her dreams were weird. She was surprised that Alice had come over to hold her hand.

"If you're sick, you should call me," Alice said. There was nothing worse than being sick and alone. Those were the times you thought you'd die and be found a week later because of the smell.

Alice had brought orange juice and lemon-lime soda. She mixed them together for Lynn to drink with her aspirin.

"My mom always gave this to me when I was sick," Alice told her. "It was the one good thing about being sick. This and the saltines. And having her sing to me. She used to sing and tap dance, to keep my mind off my stomach."

"Can you tap dance?" Lynn asked.

Alice fake tap-danced for Lynn, making her laugh. She sang old Little Feat tunes, old Allman Brothers, old Emmy Lou Harris.

Lynn dozed. Alice washed the dishes and swept the kitchen floor. She picked up the clothes and hid them in the laundry hamper. She sang the whole time. She got into a groove with "Midnight Rider".

Lynn woke up again. She watched Alice clean the house, like this was something interesting.

"Does Angel sing to you when you're sick?" Lynn asked.

"I've never been sick around him." Alice wanted to think he would sing to her if she was sick. He probably couldn't tap dance, but he could play guitar and tell her stories about his misspent youth.

"Have you heard from him?"

"He called once. He sounded okay." He sounded far away, was how he sounded. "I've seen Joe a couple of times."

Lynn's eyes opened wide. "What?"

"He gave me a ride home from work the night Angel left and we got talking. He told me the story of his life in a cemetery."

"You're making this up."

"No, I swear. The next day we went out on the peninsula to see the trees."

"You went out with *Joe*? Get me some more juice, I gotta hear this."

"We didn't go out," Alice said, mixing the juice and soda. "It was like—would I go out with Matt?"

"You wanted to. You were hoping he was bi."

"It was like we were—like he was my brother or something," Alice said, sitting on the bottom of the bed.

"No whatchamacallit?"

"What."

Lynn shut her eyes and started moaning and groaning.

Alice didn't want to tell Lynn about Joe's admission that he'd been trying to break up her and Angel. That wasn't what Lynn meant anyway.

"It was nothing like that. I went to work with him one night, he's a security guard in a warehouse. I read to him."

"You read to him?"

"*A Wizard of Earthsea.*"

Lynn started laughing. "Oh Alice," she said. "You *read* to *Joe*?" Alice had tried to read that book to Lynn, who had borrowed it to read on her own. She'd tried to read it to Matt. It was a standing joke at the studio—watch out for Alice, she'll try to read to you.

"He liked it," Alice said. "Why wouldn't he like it?"

Lynn cackled. Thinking about the Joe she'd known until this past week, Alice laughed too. "He *did*," she protested.

"God, who would have thought?" Lynn said. "Matt should have read to him. I can't wait to tell him. So now nothing stands between you and your true love."

"Except he's not here," Alice said. "And I miss him too much. I'm too involved. I can't believe I didn't know you were sick. Don't let me wimp out on you like that, okay? That's disgusting, to forget your friends."

"Everybody does it. Before you get to the stage where you realize what's wrong with the person you're in love with and need to tell your friends about it." She sighed heavily. "Carla's in love, Matt's in love, everybody's in love but me. If I were in love, I wouldn't have the flu."

"If you were in love you'd be waiting for the phone to ring and wondering how you turned into a shadow of your former self. You'd feel like you had the flu all the time."

"At least I'm ready for the show. No love life, so I've got my three pieces ready. What about you?"

"I've got that one drawing I like, and that's it. I thought I'd get a lot done while Angel was gone, but I don't feel motivated."

They talked awhile about working when you weren't motivated, how it was sometimes useless and sometimes necessary and you never knew which beforehand. Sometimes it just showed you how stuck you were.

Meanwhile, Matt was in love with some guy no one knew; Carla was going out with a lithographer named Rick. Alice thought she knew him.

"That baby-faced guy who does super-realistic lithos of crumpled paper? He's cute, I guess, but..."

"But he looks like one of the daycare kids. Well, you know Carla. 'Get 'em young and train 'em right'," Lynn said. "He's our age anyway."

"Is Chuck in love?"

"With his dog," Lynn said. Chuck slept with everybody with no hard feelings on either side. He had slept with all of the printmakers in the co-op at one time or another. His mutt dog named Baby was the constant in his life. She ate the zinc shavings from the etching plates and then threw up in dark corners. All of them had stepped in Baby's puke at least once.

Alice spent the night on Lynn's couch. She lay awake for awhile, wondering if Angel had called. She knew he hadn't. She knew she was missing him more than he was missing her. In the morning she would be able to tell herself that that was okay. Come on, she chided herself, you've done this before. Look at Lynn. Sick and alone, and she's okay. It's only a little while more. Less than a week. Nothing.

Forever.

Alice got up early and went to the grocery store. She came back with chicken and vegetables and started soup for Lynn. Alice wasn't much of a cook, but she could manage chicken soup. She had a secret recipe—all the herbs in the kitchen, a can of plum tomatoes, and a bottle of beer.

Lynn looked better. Her face was pale instead of flushed and her eyes had lost the bright glaze of fever.

"I've got to work tonight," Alice said. "But if you want me to—"

"I'm okay," Lynn said. Daycare teachers, Alice thought. They were so into taking care of other people, they never noticed when they needed it. She said it out loud.

"You've said this before," Lynn said. "After you broke up with The Wretch." That's what Lynn called Alice's last boyfriend before Angel. "You said you were tired of taking care of weaklings. You were going to take care of the strong people, who never got taken care of because they never asked for anything."

"What if Matt came by? I could call him."

Lynn shook her head. "He's in love. There's a book I've been wanting to read. Nothing to do with two-year olds. It's a bodice-ripper. Don't call Matt. I mean it."

"You can call me at work. I'll come by after if you want."

"If I feel the need, I'll call."

"Promise?"

"Promise. But don't hold your breath."

III.

Lynn didn't call. The bodice-ripper had enthralled her or put her to sleep, or the beer in the soup had. A night spent on Lynn's lumpy couch was putting Alice to sleep at work. The owner of the Neptune, a wiry middle-aged man named Aziz, was in until midnight. He had a mournful face and a foul temper. He watched Alice to see if she'd screw up, and then she screwed up. She'd been working at the Neptune for over two years; she never screwed up except the nights Aziz was there.

At least Alice didn't have to take a bus home; the clunker was still running. It started on the third try. She hadn't been home long when the phone rang.

"Hey," Angel said. "You're home."

"Angel!" she said. "Angel!"

"Alice," he said, laughing a little at her response.

She shut her mouth on her third "Angel" and said instead, "Can you talk a little louder? I can't hear you very well."

"Wait a minute." She could hear him moving around. She imagined a shadowy kitchen, the white enameled refrigerator gleaming in the dimness, a clock ticking on the wall. "Is that better?" he said.

"Yeah. Are you in the kitchen?"

"I was. I'm in the back hall with the kitchen door shut so I won't wake everybody up. The back door's open."

Alice settled down on the floor next to the phone, ready to talk all night. "What do you see out the back door? What's it look like?"

"Backs of houses, a fence, the mountains. It's quiet out there."

She heard him breathe like he was blowing cigarette smoke. She was wearing one of his shirts; she pulled the neck of it up over her nose and inhaled, smelling Angel. She pretended he was sitting next to her and listened to him talk.

He said he'd forgotten how his mom hovered. She didn't say anything, but she watched him like she was worrying. Angel had always talked about his mother as the person who was on his side against his father. But Angel said his father was being all right. One of his old friends was in jail for selling cactus he stole from the desert, and another one was married, working in construction, and had no time at all for Angel. But some of his old friends were okay; he could talk to them about his real life without worrying what they were going to think of him. Alice wondered if these understanding friends were male or female. She didn't ask.

"What's going on with you?" Angel said. "Why aren't you ever home?"

Was he worried? If Angel worried about her like she did about him, it wasn't so bad. "Working," she said, "I've been working. Then Lynn was sick so I went over there for a night." If he was worrying, then Alice didn't want him to.

"I hear you've been hanging out with Joe. I hear you went out to the peninsula." Angel said it like he thought it was funny.

"I did," she said. "It was nice getting out of the city." She wondered if Joe had mentioned her reading to him. Angel would probably split a gut over that. She didn't bring it up.

"So you don't hate him anymore?"

"I never hated him," Alice said, although she had. But she had never said it to Angel so he shouldn't use it against her now. She wondered if Joe had told Angel why he had taken Alice to see the trees in the first place. She bet not. "I just didn't much like him."

Angel laughed.

"What," Alice said.

"Okay, you didn't much like him. Are you working on your own stuff or just at the bar?" Before he'd left, she had told him she was going to spend every free moment in the studio. It was embarrassing to tell him she hadn't.

"I'm going to," she said. "I have to now. I don't have enough stuff for the show yet. I'm feeling uninspired and dull."

"You'll be okay. When the heat's on you'll just do it." That's what she had done for the last show, back when she and Angel were first going out. She was glad he had faith in her.

"At least I got the car fixed," she said. "I can come and get you myself, when you get in."

"That's something I need to talk to you about," he said. "I'm thinking about staying over the extra time. There's no gigs until a week from Friday and it's an open ticket, no charge for changing the return date. I could come back a week from Thursday." He said it as if these were the only problems, work and money.

He wanted to stay. He wasn't worried, he wasn't missing her, he was staying in Tucson.

"Alice?" Angel said. "Are you still there?"

"I'm here," she said. And you're there, she thought. "Is that why you called? To tell me you weren't coming back?"

"I called because I wanted to talk to you. That's one of the things I wanted to talk about."

"What am I supposed to say? You've decided to stay. That's not 'talking about'."

"I haven't decided. I'm thinking about it."

She wasn't going to be like his mother, worrying and not asking. "What do you want to stay for?"

"It's like, I don't know, the time is right. To get some things straight."

"What things?"

"Family stuff, for one. You know." How would she know? She didn't have any family stuff.

She couldn't imagine his mother's kitchen anymore, the view of the mountains just outside the back door. Angel had turned into a voice on the phone.

"If it's that bad, I'll come back sooner," he said.

"No," she said. "If I have to say it's bad, you can fucking stay. If I have to beg—"

"This isn't about you begging," Angel said. "God, Alice, I just want to get things cleared up and finished with. I thought you'd understand that."

What could she say? I don't understand, and I don't care. I want you here because I miss you. What a mushball she'd turned into. What a wimp. It wasn't like she'd never had an opening before, or been on her own.

"Alice?"

"I'm tired," she said. "It's late and I've had a shitty night and I'm going to bed."

He sighed or blew smoke. "We've never had a fight," he said. "It ought to be in person. I need to see you to do this."

"I'll fight with you in person. I'd be happy to. When you get in a week from Thursday." Well, maybe it would be good for her. Maybe she'd get some good prints out of this.

"Are you sure that's okay with you? Really okay?"

"It's not okay, no," she said. He didn't say anything. "But I'll live," she added, being tough. Actually she probably wouldn't die from missing him. Although some people did, didn't they? But that was only when the other person died. If Angel was coming back, she would live.

"Thanks, babe."

"Don't thank me," she said darkly. "You make me feel like a fool."

"I'll call you the night of the opening. I'll call you and tell you to break a leg."

Tomorrow, Alice thought as she went to sleep in her bed that smelled like Angel. Tomorrow I'll go to that show by myself and get inspired. I'll be so juiced up I'll stop worrying about Angel and wondering what he's doing and be myself again.

Alice tried. She knew she was trying; she felt like Angel had been pushed to the back of her mind to lodge there like a splinter.

She went to the studio instead of the show. One print of Angel was starting to happen, another she trashed. Working on pictures of Angel eased missing him. It didn't seem to hurt the print, either. Feeling optimistic, she tried for the trees.

The trees were impossible. She wasn't remembering them right. She should have done some drawings there, or taken pictures, never mind she didn't have a camera. She knew what she was trying to do, and she couldn't get anywhere near it.

Lynn was back on her feet, but she was ready for the show and didn't come in. Carla was in the studio, so were Chuck and Baby and Matt. They all took a break together, drinking coffee. Chuck asked Alice if she wanted a puppy.

"You've gotta be kidding," Alice said. "I hardly have room for myself in that apartment. Did you breed the mutt?"

"She went into heat and all these dogs were tearing at the screen door. She wanted to go out."

"You let her out?"

"I chased away most of them with a hose," he said. "But there was this black Labrador who wouldn't quit. He seemed like a nice dog. And Baby really liked him."

"Baby was in heat," Carla said. "Baby would have liked anybody."

"I could tell," Chuck insisted. "She really liked him. More than she liked the other dogs. It would have been cruel to keep them apart."

"You better put up a sign," Matt said. "Love puppies free to good home."

Alice went to the bar with black fingernails from the ink and Aziz yelled at her for having dirty hands.

"It's not dirt," she explained. "It's ink." She didn't know why she bothered. They'd had this conversation before; there was no way to get all the ink out of her fingernails and knuckles when she'd been at the studio, and she wasn't going to stop going to the studio to please Aziz.

"It looks like dirt!" he said. "What do I care if it's ink! It looks like DIRT! Would you take a drink from a hand like that?"

"Absolutely," Alice said. "I wouldn't have any problem with it at all." Especially if the drink was tequila, which killed germs on contact.

"That is because you are a crazy person!" he yelled.

"I'll take a drink from her," said a voice Alice knew.

Aziz looked at Joe, opened his mouth, and then, because the customer was always right, did not call him a crazy person.

"What are you waiting for?" Aziz hissed at Alice. "Take his order."

Alice stepped up to the counter. "What'll it be? Sir."

"Beer," Joe said. "Whatever's cheapest."

She got him a Japanese beer. Aziz had gone back to the kitchen to fight with the cooks.

"What's this?"

"Aikido beer," she said. "Is it good? It's the most expensive beer we've got. I hope it's good."

He tasted it. "It's interesting." He tasted some more. "Not bad. Is he always like this?"

"Sometimes he's worse. He fired me and Freddie one night for doing the Tarot cards. He said we were trying to 'guess god'."

Joe laughed. "So how come you're still here?"

"The cook's his cousin. He told us to ignore being fired. We did."

"Well, he paid us for our gig. That's all I cared about."

"He must not have listened to your lyrics."

"Bar owners don't give a shit about lyrics. They just want the customers to drink a lot while you play. I brought your book back. You left it in the van. It was good."

"You finished it?"

"Yeah," he said, "I did." He looked pretty happy about it. Alice remembered the exact moment she could read, when the words stopped being separate small battles with her memory and became part of a story. She smiled back at him. But now she couldn't read it to him. Maybe she could read him the second one; it was a trilogy. She was going to suggest it but a man and woman sitting at the other end of the bar were staring fixedly at her so she waited on them.

"I've got another quote for you," Alice said when she got back to Joe. "One you can't fuck up."

"Let's hear it," he said.

"'A fool who persists in her folly will soon become wise.' It's from Lin Yutang. Actually he said 'his' folly, but I don't see why women can't be foolish, too."

Joe blew smoke and squinted through it at her. "It's the same problem. You could be dead before you got wise."

"You could be dead anyway," she argued, "spending your life trying to be smart and hiding from the foolishness that might have taught you something." He opened his mouth to say something and she went on, fast, "I don't mean obstinate stupidity. It's like the Fool in the Tarot. It can mean either thing, and you have to learn to tell the difference, but stepping off the edge is what it's about."

"If you step off the edge enough times, you learn to watch where you put your feet, or use a net. Or climb down."

"How can you say that?" she asked. "Every time you play a lead, isn't it a leap of faith?"

"No. Not like you're talking about. I know what I'm going to play. I've thought about it or worked it out beforehand."

"What about when you write a song? You don't know then. Unless you want to write the same song over and over, you have to take the risk to find out what you can do."

"Of course you take risks, but you don't have to be blind about it. You don't have to risk crashing and burning."

"Sometimes you do," Alice said, getting heated. "Dumbo did."

Joe looked at her like she was speaking in tongues.

"The baby elephant with the big ears."

"I know who Dumbo is," Joe said. "I saw the movie."

"When Dumbo was in that burning building and being forced to jump, to crash and burn, *that's* when he learned how to *fly*." Just thinking about Dumbo flying, soaring over the heads of the crowd in complete aerobatic abandon, Alice's throat closed up. "He *never* would have...*flown*...if he hadn't..." Her eyes stung. She held onto the counter with both hands, getting a grip, trying to finish what she was saying.

Joe reached out and patted her hand. "It's okay, Alice," he said, making his eyes big. "Dumbo was okay in the end."

She laughed, wiping her eyes on her sleeve. "You know I'm right," she said.

Then there was a rush of customers; Aziz was hovering instead of going home, and Alice had to stop talking to Joe.

"He is your boyfriend, right?" Aziz asked her before he left. "No one else would accept a drink from such a dirty hand."

"People have been accepting drinks from this dirty hand all night," Alice said. "From both dirty hands. I've never seen him before in my life."

"Wash them. Wash them well, or you don't work here anymore."

"Fine," she said. She meant, fire me. He knew that; he acted like she meant she would wash her hands. It was part of the ritual.

Joe was waiting when Alice got through, two aikido beers under his belt for the price of none. He wanted to see the clunker. The clunker wouldn't start. Joe couldn't start it either.

"I'll have to get it towed tomorrow," Alice said. "Fucking hell."

"You could take the plates off and just leave it here," he said.

She kicked the car. "Fucking, fucking SHIT."

"I can tow it now," Joe said. "Where do you want to take it?"

"Back to the garage. I killed myself to get the money to get it out."

"Did you pay cash?"

"Check. A good check. It won't even bounce."

"Stop payment on the check until they fix it."

"That's a good idea." Stop whining, she told herself.

Joe had chains in the van. He used them to tie the clunker close to the van's rear bumper. Alice "drove" the clunker, mostly hitting the brakes so it wouldn't bash into the back of the van. By the time they got to the garage she never wanted to see the clunker again. She wanted to torch it.

"I am so *sick* of this car! I've got better things to do than mess with fucking *god*damn, *piss*head mechanics and a dickwad *shit* of a car!"

Joe was trying not to laugh.

"It's not funny!" Alice said.

"You swear like a ten year old."

"I hate that car," she said. "I hate it. If it was a person, I'd kill it."

"You need some tequila."

"I need a car that runs. I don't need tequila." She tried to calm down, to act like an adult. "You got any?"

They went to Joe's house. Alice remembered the apartment differently. The one time she'd been here it had been a minefield of musicians. Joe had been the main mine. Now it was a place where people lived. An acoustic guitar was propped up in a kitchen chair like a person waiting for a meal. Dishes were piled in the sink and on the greasy stove. Angel must do the dishes here, too. Alice, getting a second wind, started doing the dishes.

"You don't have to do that," Joe said.

"I know. I never do them at home. It's more fun at somebody else's house. I did Lynn's dishes the other night. She was sick and sticking it out all alone. Do you remember Lynn?"

"Your friend who teaches daycare."

Alice was surprised and pleased that he'd remembered. "Lynn is one of those people I want to know for my whole life. And I didn't know she was sick. She didn't tell me." Was she making a pitch for Lynn? She sort of was. She was being a matchmaker. She didn't want Joe to notice. "She thought I was too busy with Angel. And she doesn't ask. I hate when that happens."

Joe put the glasses Alice had washed on the table, next to the tequila. Alice didn't think he'd heard a word she'd said.

"When what happens?" he said.

"When I forget my friends," she said. "Being in love has a bad effect on my character."

"It makes everybody like that," he said, echoing Lynn. "I haven't seen Angel much since he started with you."

"Is that why you wanted to cut him loose from me? You never said."

She shook suds off her hands. She'd done enough dishes. The dishtowel looked too nasty even for a dirty-handed woman. She wiped her hands on her shirt and sat down at the table, watching Joe pour tequila. He clinked her glass.

"To a decent car," he said. They drank.

"So why?"

Joe lit a cigarette. The pack lay between them on the table. Alice took one.

"Angel doesn't have good luck with women," Joe finally said. "They either want him to give up the band and get a real life or they want him to be even crazier than he is."

"Which kind did you think I was?"

"I never decided."

"Come on."

"The second kind," he admitted.

"Did you cut him loose from other women?" She felt resentful on behalf of all the women who had loved Angel.

"I didn't have to. They didn't last this long."

"You hated me right away," Alice argued. "You didn't wait to see how long I lasted."

"Hate's too strong a word. I was just watching out for him."

Alice had hated Joe right away. "No you weren't. I could have been good for him, why not? You didn't give me a chance. You just wanted to come first with him."

He smoked. His face was blank; she had pissed him off.

"So do you," he said.

"Bullshit," she said, because of course he was right, but that wasn't the point. "I didn't try to…I was willing to be friends with you. And Angel's not weak. He doesn't need to be watched out for."

Joe lit a cigarette off the butt of the other one. "You didn't know him then."

And that was true too. Angel had told her that he had needed watching, and Joe had been the one to watch. Joe had taken him to rehab. Joe had kept in touch with Angel's sister Deanna. Alice had never even spoken to her.

"I know him now," Alice said, trying to stake her own claim. Did she know Angel? She was madly in love with him, that's all. She had said to Angel once, "I wish I'd known you then." She'd had an idea she could have helped him through a bad time. But Angel had said, "I would have figured out exactly how to use you, and when I'd used you as much as I could, I would have dropped you. You should be glad you didn't know me then."

Joe would always know Angel better than she did. "Maybe it's because I didn't know him then that I can see who he is now," she said. It sounded good; she wished she believed it.

"I don't think Angel's weak," Joe said. "I never thought that."

He was following his own train of thought. He wasn't attacking her territory. He was acting like she had a real bond with Angel.

Maybe Joe did worry about Angel too much. But Angel had scared the shit out of him.

Joe had tried heroin first, which made what happened later worse. But Joe didn't like anything about it. He didn't like sticking himself with a needle, and no way was he going to let anybody else do it to him. He didn't like the company. He didn't even much like how it made you feel. It was fine when you were high, but it wasn't a high you could trust. He didn't believe it. And the hangover was a bitch.

Angel liked it fine. He ranted about people who were too chickenshit to look the truth in the face. "You're not seeing god," Joe told him, "you're just shooting up." But when Angel got kicked out of the house he lived in, he moved in with Joe. Joe let him bring his new friends home, even though Joe's girlfriend hated it. It was the only way Joe could think of to keep an eye on Angel without shooting up himself. He watched Angel shoot up stuff that had been cut with detergent, throw up, and then use the same shit until it was gone.

Angel had always been skinny, but he wasn't meant to be as thin as he got. His eyes didn't see what they were looking at;

they sank back in their sockets. Half the time he was onstage he was blasted out of his mind.

Joe never knew why Angel decided to quit. Angel told him he'd looked in the mirror. Joe drove him to the emergency room, Angel shivering the whole way. Waiting to see someone, Joe got a blanket from a nurse. He wrapped it around Angel's shoulders. Angel joked that now he looked like a real Indian, instead of a chicano boy from the low-rent section of Tucson. Angel yawned and wept. Joe didn't know if Angel was crying or if it was the drug.

Joe put his arm around Angel to help him hold still until someone had time for them. He said he was a relative so they wouldn't kick him out. They knew he wasn't; they let him stay anyway.

But that was two years ago. The first year Angel had a girlfriend who was using. Later he'd been with a woman who hated the band and was going to save Angel herself, but she hadn't lasted long. Angel's worst threat from women since then had been heartbreak or STDs. Joe had exaggerated the danger.

He worried out of habit. Angel was okay now. Joe touched wood, thinking that.

Alice stubbed out her cigarette. She was taking forever with it. "I'm so jealous of you," she said. She looked mad. "When I think of how you and Angel…sometimes I feel like I've got…just nothing." She was crying. She was still mad. "You'll know him forever," she said. "You'll know him when I'm just somebody he used to fuck." She choked on the end of the sentence and wiped her cheeks with her hands, as if she'd finished crying. It didn't work. Her face pulled in on itself and she dropped her head so he couldn't see her. She didn't make any noise.

"Come on," he said, as if it were his fault she was crying. "It's not like that."

She nodded her head, yes it is.

"Angel cares about you," Joe said.

"Then why isn't he here?" she croaked from behind her hair. Hearing herself, she laughed. It was shaky, but not hysterical. Thanking god for small favors, Joe found her a paper towel. He'd seen her reject the dishtowel earlier.

He pushed the paper towel under her nose. She looked at it, took it out of his hand, and used it to blot her face. Then she blew her nose on it. She mumbled something and headed for the bathroom. He could hear water running. When she came out her face was blotchy and her eyes were red, but she wasn't crying.

"I'm just nervous about the show," she said, although he hadn't asked. She shrugged, like it was no big deal. "And disappointed. I thought Angel would be back in time for the opening."

So Angel had let her know he was staying in Tucson. "He never goes home," Joe said, making Angel's excuses for him. "I think it's kind of important to him right now."

"I know. I know all that." Then she said to herself, but he heard, "Fuck." She stood at the sink, drinking water. Joe was glad she couldn't see his face. He'd bet his last dime that Angel hadn't said anything to Alice about his old girlfriend. Alice was probably chiding herself for being jealous; she was jealous of the wrong person, that's all. Her instincts were right.

For something to do, he picked up the guitar on the chair and started fooling with it, playing a song that he'd started. He didn't have words for it yet. Alice came over and sat down. She swiped a cigarette. She lit up and inhaled deeply. "You're really smoking that," he said.

"I remember how."

"You shouldn't start smoking again."

"Why don't you light another one off the butt of the one you're smoking," she said. "And then say that again." She blew smoke rings, showing off. "I like that," she said, meaning the song. "God that's sad."

"E minor," he said. "Always makes you cry in your beer."

She listened. "Did anybody ever do you in?"

He kept playing. "Yeah, of course," he said. What a question. She didn't follow up on it. "There was this cheerleader in high school..." Alice didn't laugh. She scratched at a place on the table where the paint had chipped, making it worse, concentrating like this was an important task. He set down the guitar and poured more tequila into his glass. He swallowed some.

"A couple years ago," he said. "We were going to get married."

Alice looked up, waiting.

"She broke up with me around the time Angel started getting really fucked up." That made Donna sound like a bitch. "She understood everything but that. She didn't understand about Angel."

"What happened?"

"She married somebody else."

Alice nodded. "But that's terrible," she said. "Do you hate her?"

"It's been two years."

"Do you?"

"No," he said. "Your turn."

"It's not my turn. I had my turn. I already cried all over your kitchen table."

"I thought that was nerves about your show."

"No you didn't," she said. "You knew exactly what it was."

He did know. Alice was crazy with love. She was howling at the moon.

"What do you have to do tomorrow?" he asked.

"Oh call the damn garage. Stop a check. Waste my day."

"I mean, what were you gonna do?"

"Go to a show at the museum. Maybe go to the studio after. There's this thing I wanted to see if I could finish for the show."

"You can stay here and I'll take you, tomorrow."

"You don't have to do that."

"I don't feel like driving you home," he said. "Besides, I haven't been to the museum since I was in high school."

"You used to go the museum?"

"Yeah, Alice, I went to the museum. It was a good place to pick up girls."

She laughed. "And it's full of naked women, some of them 3-D and larger than life."

"But it's art, so you can look all you want."

"I need to take a shower and change clothes. I smell like shish-kabob and stale beer."

"You can borrow one of Angel's t-shirts. You can use the shower here."

"Well," she said.

"What?" Did she want him to sleep on the couch?

"Can you cover up that picture in your room?"

"What picture?" Then he remembered. "The one that looks like me?"

"It doesn't really. I just said that. That kind of stuff gives me the creeps."

Girls.

Alice took a shower, dried herself on a towel that was only slightly damp, and brushed her teeth with a toothbrush that looked like it had been run over by a truck. Wearing one of Angel's t-shirts, she crawled into Angel's bed. Joe had tacked up some boxer shorts over the picture. They were printed with skulls and crossbones. He was still in the kitchen, fiddling with the song. Listening to him, she fell asleep.

She woke late in the morning. Joe was asleep in his bed. He was lying on his side in a tangle of blankets. It looked like he was working his way out of a cocoon. His hair was spread out on the pillow and across his naked back. She wondered how late he'd stayed up.

She dressed and made coffee, hoping the aroma would wake him. She rummaged in the refrigerator for something to eat. There were eggs, salsa, some English muffins curling at the edges. Huevos Rancheros, sort of. She banged around in the kitchen. Sleeping Beauty slept on.

The phone rang and she answered it. It was Dan, their drummer. He needed to talk to Joe.

"He's asleep," Alice said.

"Wake him up," Dan said. "I left a tape over there and I'm on my way to get it. I'll be there in ten minutes."

She hung up and went into the bedroom. Joe hadn't stirred. She hated waking people up almost as much as she hated people waking her up. It was always better to come back to earth on your own.

Saying his name had no effect. She could shake him by the shoulder. She didn't.

Dan woke him after all, barging in to get the tape he needed to hear immediately. He eyed Alice doubtfully, as if she were a strange dog who might bite. She didn't know if it was because he recognized her or because she was female.

"You're..." he said.

"Alice," she said. "My name is Alice." She thought about shaking his hand, now they'd been introduced. Joe came staggering out of the bedroom. He had his jeans on. He squinted at Dan, blinking in the light.

Alice turned down the heat under the mess she was mixing in a frying pan on the stove. She flipped salsa over the tops of the eggs to cook them. The joys of domesticity. All she needed was an apron.

"Hey," Joe said to Dan.

"I just came for the tape you borrowed," Dan said, not looking at Alice. "The bootleg Metallica."

"I don't know where it is," Joe said. It was in Dan's hand.

"I got it," Dan said. "See you later."

Joe watched him leave. "Huh," he said. Then he wandered into the bathroom. Alice heard the shower come on. Thinking about Dan telling Angel, she cracked herself up. Settle down, she told herself. Cook these eggs.

They got to the museum by mid-afternoon. Joe went to look at the Asian art while Alice looked at the print show, examining each print in minute detail to see how they were done. She had decided which one she would steal and was trancing on it when someone tapped her shoulder.

"Matt!" she said. "Hey! I thought you'd been here already."

"Found the one you would steal?"

"This one." It was a drypoint of the tops of buildings in a driving rain. The edges of the drypoint lines, blurred and true at the same time, looked wet.

"Me too," he said. "And this one here."

"Really?" It was a Matisse-like drawing of a face. Matt was a good printmaker, but Alice wouldn't have stolen the second print. "I don't know."

"Trust me on this," he said. "You done here?"

"Yeah." They headed out of the gallery.

"You need a ride?"

"No, I—"

"The clunker's running? At last. It was getting to be an endless quest."

"It ran for a day and died again. I came with Joe."

"Who's Joe?"

"You know, Angel's friend Joe."

Matt's face changed two or three times before he said admiringly, "You sneaky little bitch."

"Not like that," she said. "We're being friends."

"That's an interesting way to put it. As opposed to being enemies? How did that happen?"

"I'll tell you sometime," she said. "Speaking of sneaky, how come no one's met Mr. Right yet?"

"Carla's met him. You'll see him at the show."

"Aah, the show," Alice said, feeling her stomach drop. "I'm not ready."

"You're never ready, you just do it."

"No this time I'm *really* not ready."

"Hey," Matt said, not to Alice.

"Hey," Joe said behind Alice's back. She wondered if she should re-introduce them, but Joe remembered Matt, calling him by name.

Matt invited him to the show. "It'll be like a party," Matt said, "only with art on the walls."

Joe said he would try to come; he might have to work. When Matt had left, Joe wanted to show Alice this one thing.

It was a Chinese vase, porcelain, glazed red. It was a deep true red, no orange, a hint of blue. Definitely worth stealing.

It was in a case by itself. Alice walked around it, and then sat down on one of the benches to look at it some more. Joe sat next to her. They watched the vase being red.

IV.

Alice finished the second print. She had Chuck put it in the acid for her. Chuck didn't ask why she didn't do it herself; Alice was cunning. First she offered to take Baby for a walk and then she asked Chuck to watch her plate. She worried about it a little, watching the sky so Baby wouldn't have to be shamefaced while she pissed, but the plate printed up fine. It needed beefing up here and there; Alice supplied it with drypoint instead of using the acid. The fourth run was good. She liked it.

She left work early Thursday night to help hang the show. No one could afford frames, so they had decided to thumbtack their drawings and prints to cheap grey cardboard bulletin boards. The grey made a good background. They could have been done with it early.

Around one in the morning Lynn thought the bulletin boards were too bland, too formal, too something. She took a stick of black conté and drew a frame around her collage, a gaudy, museum-type frame, all curlicues and rococo. Around his prints Chuck drew the Love Story of Baby, little childlike drawings of dogs panting at screen doors, fucking, growing fat, and finally, triumphantly, popping small bloblike puppies. Matt and Alice got into bathroom grafitti, talking penises with arms and legs arguing about women's art. Carla did simple black frames realistically, with shadows where they should be.

They stood back to admire their handiwork.

"All I'm seeing is the penises," Carla said.

"That's just like you," Matt said.

"I don't know," said Lynn. "I think Carla's right. We've hidden the real work with the jokes. We can't leave it like this."

"I like it," Alice said.

"I like it," Chuck said, "but it doesn't work."

"I don't believe this," Matt said. "The first time Alice and I are on the same side of an argument, we're in the minority."

"This isn't a democracy," Alice said. "It's an anarchy. So we all have to agree."

Carla went over to her prints and started rubbing out the conté drawings of frames and shadows with her hand. "I'm exercising the prerogative of the individual," she said. "I'm not leaving mine like this." The rest of them were silent, watching her. Alice felt annoyed with Carla. "I'm not touching the penises," Carla said.

"Oh *sad*," Chuck said. It was so heartfelt they all erupted into laughter. Carla laughed so hard she had to sit down. Then they took everything down and got busy with rags and water and turpentine. By the time they finished, the grey bulletin boards were a sea of textures and washes, the artwork floating on the surface. They agreed that the bulletin boards looked better now than they had plain.

"Well," Matt said as they washed up at the sinks, "I'm glad we finally figured out a way to hang a show and get to bed early."

"If we stay until we're exhausted," said Lynn, "we feel like we've done all we can and we can let go of it. It keeps us from worrying."

"Thank you, doctor," said Matt. "For explaining my motivations so clearly."

Alice slept late on Saturday. She took a long walk and tried to read a book, telling herself she was not worrying. She wondered if Joe would come tonight. She'd invited him herself, after Matt had, on the day of the museum.

"You don't have to if you don't want to," she said when he didn't answer right away.

"I'm supposed to work that night," he said.

"Oh well, then I guess you can't."

"I'll try to switch with somebody."

She hadn't seen him since; she didn't know if she wanted him there or not. What if he didn't like her stuff?

She was changing her clothes for the millionth time when the phone rang. It was Angel making his break-a-leg call, like he'd promised.

"Hey darlin," Angel said. "How're you doing?" He sounded up, like he did when he was going out on a gig or getting ready to party until dawn.

"Hey, Angel," she said, trying to sound light-hearted instead of filled with dread. "I finished three things. I'm ready for the firing squad."

"Have a good dinner before you go," he said. He meant, don't get plastered on an empty stomach.

"Like on death row."

Angel laughed like that was funny. "Joe said he might go," Angel said, as if that made everything all right. So he had talked to Joe. He probably called Joe every night.

"He might," Alice said. "But he might be working. I think he's working. The car died again. I won't be able to pick you up after all."

"That's okay. Joe can do it."

Someone was talking to Angel. He said, "Hang on," and muffled the phone.

"What were we talking about?" he said when he got back on.

"Nothing." She should probably be glad he'd remembered to call her at all.

"What's the matter?" he asked. "Stage fright?"

She didn't say anything. Not just stage fright.

"I'm not there," he said, "where I said I'd be."

Well you're not, she thought. "I don't know what to wear," she said. "I keep changing my clothes."

"Go naked. Give them a thrill."

"Oh right. I gotta go soon. Tell me what to wear."

"Whatever feels good."

Usually Alice loved Angel's Zen responses, but none of her clothes felt good right now.

"Wear something of mine," he said, picking up on her mood across thousands of miles and a skinny little thread of rubber and copper wires. "You're always saying you can smell me in my clothes. It'll be like I'm there."

Right then she wanted him home so badly her whole body ached.

"Somebody needs to use the phone," he said. "I love you," he whispered loudly. He had never told her he loved her before. It was odd, on the phone.

"It should be in person," she said.

"Oh it will," he said, "you can count on it."

Angel called Joe too. Angel was still hanging out with his old girlfriend. She'd dumped him years ago and married somebody else, becoming Angel's bigtime heartbreak. But the marriage had fallen apart. So they were hanging out.

"What does that mean?" Joe wondered.

"I'm cheering her up," Angel said. "Ain't life strange?"

"Does Alice know?"

"It's not that big a deal," Angel said, what he always said when he was fucking someone not Alice. It had never bothered Joe before. Why did it piss him off now?

"I'm glad you're going tonight," Angel said. "Alice gets nervous about shows. She sort of loses it." What did he think Joe was, a nursemaid?

"Well, you take care."

"I will, man," Angel said. "I'm being careful." Did that mean he was using a condom, or not fucking his old girlfriend? Joe would have bet his bank account on the former. If he was wrong, he was only $50 out.

He was late to the opening. The place was jammed by the time he got there. A crappy sound system was blaring music; at least the music was good. Some people were dancing, most were getting drunk and yammering away at each other. There was a table loaded with wine bottles, beer, some cheese and crackers that looked like raccoons had been at them, a few orphaned grapes. Artists. He was glad he'd eaten dinner.

Alice came pushing through the crowd, her cheeks flushed, and pitched herself into his arms. He caught her, staggering back a step. He was glad his reflexes were good or they would have been on the floor.

She wriggled free and stood back, grinning from ear to ear.

"You made it," she said, like it had been a major undertaking, crossing the continent in a covered wagon or discovering the North Pole.

"It wasn't that hard," he said. "The roads are pretty well marked."

She laughed. "No but I thought you had to work," she said.

"I got off." He was thinking, you idiot, and didn't know if it was aimed at her or at himself.

"Get something to drink and I'll show you what I did."

He got a beer and followed her around as obediently as a dog trained to heel. She was wearing a short skirt that flipped around when she walked, black tights, and boots to her calves.

He'd never had a good look at her legs before. He was looking when she stopped so fast he bumped into her.

"Maybe I should let you check out the whole show," she said.

"Just show me what you did," he said. She was wearing another one of Angel's t-shirts. Once it had been black. Now it was blue-grey and the writing on it had faded to hieroglyphics.

She pointed from her hip. "Those over there," she said out of the corner of her mouth, like a spy. Joe went over to look. There was an ink and wash drawing of Angel. It wasn't a portrait, only a piece of his face, and then his shoulder and arm, but Joe recognized Angel immediately.

There was also a print of Angel leaning over a coffee cup, looking out at the viewer. The steam from the cup obscured part of his face, shadows the other. It was all light and dark, more than it was Angel.

The last piece was a print of water and sky, low mountains dark in the background, clouds coming in over the mountains. It was all shades of grey from light to dark; she had caught the silvery quality of the light on the water. He recognized it from their day on the peninsula. "I remember this," he said.

"I tried for the trees and couldn't get anywhere near them. This one just happened. Do you like it? Nobody else has said anything about it."

"I want it."

"You do? It's yours."

"How much is it."

"Come on."

"Really," he said. "Don't you want to sell your work?"

"It's a print. There's more than one. And I wouldn't have done it if you hadn't taken me that day. I wouldn't have seen it."

"Would you give it to me if there was only one?"

She frowned. "I'd think about it more."

Lynn appeared at Alice's shoulder. Lynn didn't want to show Joe her collages. She wanted to dance with him. He obliged. Then he wanted another beer but all the alcohol was gone.

A group of them were going to a club to hear a blues band. Alice and Lynn and Matt and some other people Joe didn't know piled into the van. It looked like Joe was going too. It looked like he was the designated driver. At least he could get a drink at the club.

He was catching up on his drinking when some woman who had been in the van asked him to dance. She had wild-woman hair, eyes outlined in black, blood-red lipstick. Her skirt was short and tight and her scoop-necked t-shirt kept slipping down over one round shoulder. Above the scoop her breasts were tattooed with dragons and flowers. She took hold of Joe's hand and did the jitterbug.

Joe knew how to do that. He skinned the cat with her.

"Your mouth is hanging open," Lynn screamed into Alice's ear.

Alice shut her mouth.

"You still don't see it?" Lynn yelled.

Alice shook her head no to the music, then she nodded her head yes to the music.

Carla had taken one look and honed right in on Joe, leaving Rick forlorn on the sidelines. Alice had always been in awe of Carla's move-straight-in-on-the-babes attitude towards the opposite sex. Carla and Joe were a pair. Carla would get a response out of him if anyone could. Alice should be interested and amused. She should wait to see the outcome, or hear about it. So why did she grab Rick and drag him out onto the dance floor?

Alice knew some old dances too. She knew the dirty dog. Her foster mother had taught all the kids the old dances. She'd called it therapy.

Rick nearly passed out from astonishment when Alice pretended she was going to hump his leg. At least he stopped looking forlorn.

"What are you doing?" he yelled at her.

"It's a sixties dance," she said. "The dirty dog."

Properly done, the dirty dog came from your back, not your butt. It should have been called the dirty snake, it was supposed to be elegant as well as lewd, a flexible spine was everything. Rick did an Elvis thing, simple and obscene. At least he was enthusiastic.

Carla was not oblivious. She nabbed Rick for the next song, a medium-slow tune impossible to dance to. She wrapped herself around Rick and showed him how to dance to it. Deserted, Alice watched the band, listening to the song. She knew the exact moment when Joe was next to her.

Joe had on his wearing-sunglasses face.

"What was that about?" he said. He didn't yell; he leaned down and spoke below the noise, into her ear. His breath tickled.

"What?" she said. She didn't speak into his ear. He heard her.

Joe shook his head, never mind.

The next song was more kick-ass; it started Alice moving where she stood.

"Come on," Joe said, and they pushed out onto the dance floor, which was filling up fast.

There was barely room to dance. Some guy was dancing wildly to Alice's left. She moved away from him, closer to Joe, who took hold of her arms, to get her out of the guy's way, she thought. But no, he wanted to do the dirty dog. He even knew how. No stiff-backed pelvic thrusts for him. Knees bent and legs apart, like a Tai Chi exercise from heaven, he moved in on her. He knew how to do what she had tried to do with Rick. She didn't actually hump his leg; it only looked like that. She turned her back to him and leaned forward with her hands on her knees. He came up behind her. His head leaned close to hers, his hair fell forward onto her shoulder. "We're clearing the floor," he said in her ear. He was laughing. There was a little space around them, some people looking shocked. Matt could barely contain his hilarity and Carla looked impressed.

Alice took a step away, turned to face Joe, and started headbanging insanely, which always made her giggle. Joe imitated Alice's imitation of himself, which was headbanging for someone who's had too much to drink. For awhile they had room to dance. Then the other dancers, with nothing to watch, seethed back in.

"Who taught you how to dance?" she shouted at him.

"My uncle," he shouted back. She thought his uncle must be pretty hot. "Who taught you?"

"Christine," Alice mouthed. Joe raised his eyebrows in surprise.

In the bathroom line between sets, Carla wanted to know the same thing. "That was something," Carla said. "I wanna learn how to do that."

"I'll show you how to do it," Alice offered. "You can teach me how to jitterbug."

"Angel can show you that," Carla said.

"Angel doesn't know how to jitterbug. At least, I don't think he does."

"That guy's not Angel?"

"That's Joe. Angel's at his sister's wedding in Arizona."

"That was Joe? The *creep*?"

"He hasn't been such a creep lately," Alice said. "We're getting to be friends."

"I guess," Carla said, staring at Alice as if Alice were a life form she hadn't met with before, which was how Alice often felt about Carla. "I gotta hand it to you," Carla said and went into the next empty stall.

Back at the table, Lynn was with some guy who had been at the show. He and Lynn were talking each other's ears off. Chris something. Rick knew him; when they started talking to each other Lynn moved closer to Alice.

"I saw that dance," she said.

"So did god and everybody," said Alice. "Carla wants me to teach her the dirty dog. I would have thought Carla was born knowing how to do the dirty dog."

"You won't be able to get away with that for long," Lynn said.

"Get away with what? What's with you guys? It's just a dance. Angel wouldn't care."

"I don't mean Angel."

"Well what do you mean?"

"Maybe you should stop drinking," Lynn said. "Your brain's on hold."

"Come on, Lynnie. I've had two glasses of wine. And we already decided to drink abusively tonight. That's what show openings are for."

Joe sat down on the other side of Alice. "What are they for?" he asked.

"Drinking abusively," Alice said.

He had a beer and the tequila she had asked for. It was a tequila sunrise, not what she'd wanted, but what the hey.

"You've had more than two," Lynn said.

"You were counting?"

"I can just tell," she said, and Joe said, "More than two what?"

Alice turned to Joe. "Do you think I'm drunk?"

He looked at her judiciously. "You're definitely getting there," he said.

"How much have you guys had?"

Lynn shut her eyes and started counting on her fingers. Joe said, "Too much," and swallowed beer.

"Well, then," Alice said, and sipped the tequila sunrise. It didn't taste like alcohol at all. "Is there any tequila in this?"

"Some," Joe said.

"You told the bartender to make it weak." Joe lit a cigarette and didn't answer. Alice guessed that was a yes.

Lynn looked at her. See? her look said.

Alice squeezed out from between them. She was furious. She wished she'd never told anyone about her father. Everyone was a shrink nowadays, they all knew what was good for you. Except Angel. But she never drank much around him. She was trying to follow this train of thought but it didn't seem to lead anywhere. Her mouth was parched. How many glasses of wine had she had? She shut her eyes briefly; she didn't have the whirlies, she could still dance, her lips were totally numb. Waiting in line she thought of her own reason not to drink. She got a glass of carbonated water with ice cubes and limes from the bartender.

The music had started again, last set. Joe waited alone at the table. She was gulping the water before she reached him, defiant. She sat down. "Just what I needed," she said.

She leaned back in her chair, waiting for him to say something. He reached for her glass. Before she had time to move he had raised it to his mouth and taken a swallow.

"Hey!" she said.

"Water," he said. "Good."

"Why good? So I don't get drunk?"

"You're already drunk. You're shitfaced, Alice." He rubbed his hand across his mouth. "So'm I. Jesus. Artists are as bad as musicians. Worse."

Okay, so it had been more than two glasses of wine. Closer to three, and then she'd stopped counting.

"Let's dance," she said.

Joe was great to dance with. He was loose and fierce, an aikido dancer. Alice wanted to keep going but the band was through for the night. At the end of the set they looked around for everybody.

Matt and Mr. Right, some guy Alice had met at the beginning of the show, had left. Lynn was getting a ride with Chris, and Carla and Rick were going with them, so it was just her and Joe.

Waiting for a cab in the street, Alice shut her eyes. The drizzle on her face was an interesting sensation; she thought it would sober her up.

The cabbie had a plastic Jesus on his dashboard, god on his side. That could mean he was driving on blind faith. Alice watched to make sure he knew how to drive. He stayed on the right side of the yellow line, he stopped for red lights, but he hadn't figured out the accelerator yet. She leaned back in her corner and stopped watching the road. Joe was leaning back, but his eyes were fixed on the road. His hand moved restlessly on his knee, shifting an invisible clutch.

"You're worse than me," she said. "I never realized you were a back seat driver."

"That's because I never ride in the back seat."

"Don't you like being a passenger?"

He turned toward her so he couldn't see the road anymore.

"Not much." His fingers drummed on his knee. "No control," he said.

Alice laughed. He smiled a little.

"At least the opening's over. Talk about no control. I can never figure out if I'm more afraid that no one will look or that they will look and say something awful."

"I looked," Joe said.

"Yeah, you did," she said. "You made my night. I can't believe you liked that print. I sort of love it, myself. But nobody else said anything, so I wondered if it was one of those things not meant to go out into the world."

"Why wouldn't I like it? You liked the red vase."

She stared at him. "It's hardly the same."

"I don't know," he said, his attention on the road again. "It felt the same to me."

He wasn't flattering her. He meant it. She wanted to throw her arms around him again. He was sitting too far away. Besides, he was working hard, keeping the cab on the road.

"I've got coffee at home," she said. "I can take these tights off and we can watch the late movies. You want to?"

Joe walked around the apartment while Alice went to the bathroom to change her clothes. He had never been in her apartment before. The front door opened into the kitchen and the bathroom was off that. The kitchen opened into another room with windows along one side of it, bookshelves to the ceiling and a bed on a low frame. There was a door in the wall that used to go someplace; it was covered with drawings, postcards, a couple of photographs of people, one of them Angel. A small dresser regurgitated clothes, mostly ratty t-shirts, and the overflow covered the unmade bed and the floor. Books lay open, flat on their bellies as if gut-shot, all over the apartment. A couple of plants on the windowsill looked healthy. He thought it was homey.

He heard the toilet flush and Alice came out of the bathroom in Angel's t-shirt, faded jeans, and bare feet. "Your turn," she said.

He needed a turn. All that beer, and then whiskey. Pissing made him feel more sober, as if he'd lowered the alcohol content in his blood.

Back in the kitchen, Alice was making coffee. A double row of pills was set out on the kitchen table, and two big glasses of water.

"What's this?"

She pointed. "B-vitamins, emergency C, pain reliever, and Chinese herbal remedy for hangover. You have to drink all the water. Dehydration."

Joe took his pills. Alice took hers, watching him over the rim of her glass.

"Are you really drunk?" she asked.

"Are you kidding? I've been drinking all night," he said. "But not as bad as I was an hour ago."

"How come you don't act any different?" She frowned at him like he was a print in the museum and she wanted to see how he'd been put together.

"The coffee looks ready," he said.

She poured the coffee, taking aim from too high and hitting each cup dead center, looking pleased about it. She was definitely smashed. She put the cups on the table and plonked herself down in a chair.

"Remember that party you guys had?" she asked.

There'd only been one that she came to. "What about it?"

"Were you drunk then?"

"Pretty much, yeah."

"Huh." She drank coffee, thinking.

"So?"

"I don't know." She looked at him again; this time like he was a math problem. "Everybody else was drinking to extinction and you just watched. It's kind of a weird way to get drunk."

Well he did watch. That's what he was like.

"You're watching me right now," he said. She kept on doing it. "What are you saying?"

She looked surprised. "Me? Nothing." She gulped coffee, not even wincing. She must have a mouth made of asbestos.

The coffee was hot, black, and strong. The caffeine was starting to take effect, enough so Alice knew something was up. Joe had a funny look on his face. Was he insulted? She tried to explain, in case he was. "It's just, I've never seen you do anything—"

"Spontaneous? Impulsive?"

He was insulted. Maybe she should shut up until she sobered up. She patted her mouth with her fingertips. Still numb. She downed her coffee and got up. She put the cup in the sink and ran water on it. The sink was full of dishes. She started washing them.

Joe brought her his cup. He leaned against the counter. She kept her eyes on her job. "What are you doing the dishes for?"

"They're dirty," she said. "And I feel like it. I have to take advantage of the impulse when it strikes." Then she wished she hadn't used the word "impulse". She bit her tongue.

"So what did you mean?" he said.

She placed dishes in the rack. She could try to soothe his wounded feelings. He would know right away. "You don't lose it ever. That's all." She scrubbed a pan furiously. He was standing right next to her. He was wearing a dark blue sweater. She could see it out of the corner of her eye. "Well maybe you do," she said. "You probably do. I've just never been around to see it."

"You think I should be more like Angel."

"No I don't," she answered, sounding angrier than she felt. "I don't think that at all."

She finished the pan and dried her hands on a dishtowel over the sink. Then she had to look at him. He looked...she didn't know how he looked. Then she did know.

Uh-oh, she thought, finally understanding what Carla and Lynn had been talking about, much too late. It was time to do something else, and to do it fast. Like right now.

She didn't move.

He leaned towards her. She watched him come. His mouth barely touched hers. He moved back a little, and she stopped breathing. Then he did it again, not so tentative this time. It was like cat paws, pat, pat, pat. Or a butterfly landing on a leaf, fluttering up, lighting down again, checking out the space. Or it was Joe kissing her, and Alice kissing him back.

The butterfly landed, spread its wings in the sun. Joe and Alice moved up against each other. Someone groaned. One of his hands was in her hair and the other one on her back. She felt his sweater under her hands, and his back underneath that, and his mouth that was sweet and dirty at the same time. He put his tongue between her lips and a zizzing heat raced down her belly.

She turned her face away, into his neck. They stood still, breathing hard. Joe rested his chin on top of her head. His hand made little circles on her back, over and over. She could feel his heart, pounding away.

She should tell him to leave. She was in love with Angel. This couldn't be happening. It wasn't real. She wanted it to last longer. She shut her eyes and breathed him in.

Joe was breathing her in, too, but he was thinking. She rubbed her face against his neck and sighed. Did she think he could stand here like this forever?

What a weak point this would have made, back when he was looking for one. He had been so angry at Angel on the phone, angry at him for fucking with Alice. That was no excuse for Joe doing it. What would he say to Angel? I was just cheering her up? Christ. If he'd been thinking, he wouldn't be here now. He'd gotten drunk instead, so he wouldn't have to think.

"Alice," he said.

He looked down at the top of her head.

"This isn't good," he said. Meaning just the opposite.

She let go of him. She rubbed her forearms, looking at them instead of him. He knew how her arms felt, empty. The whole front of him was aching.

"Tell me to leave." He should just go.

She opened her mouth, drew a deep breath, and let it out. She cleared her throat. Then she lifted her head and looked at him. Her pupils dilated and her whole face went soft. "No," she said. Then she looked surprised, as if someone else had said it.

He reached out and pulled her back against him. He wasn't so nice this time. He kissed her with his tongue, showing her what he wanted, trying to scare her. He lifted her shirt. He ran his hand up across her ribcage, over her breast. Her breast fit neatly into his hand. Her nipple was hard.

"Ohhh," he said. "Oh honey." Her arms went around his neck. "Tell me," he said. "Tell me, Alice."

"Don't go," she said. "Don't go, don't go, don't…"

He picked her up. She wrapped her legs around his waist and started doing things to his ear that were going to make it difficult for him to walk very soon. He moved fast. She was pulling his sweater up over his back, getting a head start. When they got to the bed they let go of each other. They needed their hands free to take each other's clothes off. She got his sweater off and then fumbled at the laces on his high top sneakers. "I'll do it," he said. He knew exactly how few to unlace to get them off. "Do you have any condoms?" She knelt on the bed, bare to the waist, and rummaged in the bookcase behind the bed. She found an empty box, made a small despairing noise, and flipped it onto the floor.

Then she found another box, shook out a condom, and dropped the box on the bedside table. Angel's condoms, but Alice didn't seem to be thinking of that. In the light from the kitchen he could see her face, intent on the task at hand. Now that he had his sneakers off, she got to work on his jeans. She was careful with the zipper in spite of her haste, for which he was truly grateful. While she did that he tore the condom wrapper and reached back to set it on the table; then he went after her zipper.

They were like two firemen working side by side in a three-alarm fire to control the blaze. Once they'd put out the first fire, smaller ones kept flaring up. They worked diligently throughout the night, but it was hopeless. There was an arsonist loose somewhere, who didn't give up until the last condom was used.

Alice woke in the late morning. Joe lay on his back, his arm making a pillow for her head. She was stretched out against his side, her arm across his chest. He was asleep, looking peaceful. He should. There had been four condoms left. Now there were none.

He wasn't watchful in bed. He said things, he groaned, he didn't care who came first. She didn't know whether to call it fucking or making love. With Angel she always knew which was which.

She moved against him a little. Whatever it was, she wanted to do it again.

She should feel guilty. Sooner or later, she figured she would. For now she pretended that she lived with the Senoi tribe in Malaysia and had two husbands.

She got out of bed being careful not to wake him. He didn't stir. He looked like he wasn't going to wake up for awhile. She went to the bathroom, took a five minute bath, brushed her teeth, and threw some water on her face. Her eye make-up had smudged under her eyes; she washed it off. She didn't look any different than usual, except for that bruise on her neck. It wasn't too bad; she slapped some homeopathic cream on it. Then she put on the kimono that was hanging on the back of the door. It was full of holes, but it was silk.

The phone rang in the kitchen, shrill as an alarm. Oh god! She knew it was Angel. What if Joe answered it? She came out of the bathroom so fast she stubbed her toe on the doorsill. She grabbed the phone and held it up to her ear. "Hello?" she said.

"Hi. Are you up?"

It was Lynn. Alice breathed a sigh of relief. So much for being a Senoi.

"Just barely," she said.

"Should I call back?"

"No," Alice said. "That's okay. What's up?"

What was up was Chris, the guy Lynn had met last night. They had talked until dawn. They were going out for dinner tonight.

"Hey that's great," Alice managed.

"You sound like you're still asleep," Lynn said. "I'll call you tomorrow. I'll tell you how it went." Then she laughed. "God you were so out of it last night. Are you hungover?"

"No. I took my hangover pills," she said.

"At least you made it home okay," Lynn said.

"Yeah," Alice said. Did she? "Have a good time."

She hung up. Guilt was moving in on her. She hadn't lied, but she'd felt like she was lying. She always told Lynn everything.

Joe was standing in the doorway. He was wearing his jeans, nothing else. She'd seen him with no shirt on plenty of times. So had a million other people. So why was she feeling like she shouldn't look?

"Who was that?" he asked.

"Lynn."

"Oh," he said. He went into the bathroom, sleepwalking.

Alice unplugged the phone. The outside world could stay where it was for now—outside. She had enough to think about with what was inside.

She started water for coffee. What would Joe be like when he came out of the bathroom? She and Lynn and Carla had compared notes once on the morning after. There were guys who gloated over you like now you were their own private sex machine, and ones who avoided your eyes because they didn't want you to fall in love with them or because you had made them sin, and ones you stared at in the broad light of day and wondered what had come over you.

Joe wasn't like anything; he came and watched her pour boiling water over coffee grounds. He yawned. He smelled like toothpaste and sex. Alice concentrated on what she was doing so she wouldn't spill the water all over herself. He put his hand on her neck, rubbed it, felt along her shoulders.

"You're like iron," he said. He kneaded her shoulders, trying to get her to relax. "What happened to your neck, Alice?" he said, touching the bruise.

"Someone bit me," she said, sounding grumpy.

He kissed her neck where he had bitten her. He got into it. Well, she was the one who had wanted him spontaneous. She pulled away before she melted into a puddle.

He licked his lip. "What's that taste?"

"It's a healing cream. So it'll disappear fast."

"Mm," he said. He went and sat down at the kitchen table. His cigarettes were there, and he lit one. She brought the coffee over and sat down across from him. In the broad light of day she knew exactly what had come over her.

"I thought it was Angel, on the phone," she said.

"Angel isn't awake yet."

"You know what I mean."

Joe smoked.

"Say something," Alice said.

"You want to forget about last night?"

"Yeah, I'm gonna get a lobotomy," she said. "No I don't want to forget about it. I want to talk about it."

"Then come over here," he said. She went. It was harder to think, sitting on his lap. "What do you want to do?" he asked her.

She told him about the Senoi, who lived according to what they dreamed. They were peaceful, and the warlike tribes who lived around them were terrified of them because of their magical powers.

"Aikido," Joe said.

"Yeah, like that," she said. "But it's because they were taught from childhood to listen to their dreams. They dream strong. They learn how to fight enemies in dreams. By the time they're teenagers, they don't have nightmares anymore." She reached across the table for her coffee. She was wandering from the point. "They get married according to what they dream," she said. "They accept all forms of marriage—group marriage, monogamy, gay and lesbian marriage. Sometimes one man will be married to more than one woman, and sometimes one woman will be married to more than one man."

Joe was still listening.

"So what do you think?" she said.

"You're telling me you're with Angel," he said. "But the sex was good, so you're letting me down easy."

He was angry. His body felt tense. Where was his aikido control? She couldn't believe it. They were already having a fight. After six months she couldn't get a fight started with Angel.

"I'm not letting you down easy. I'm telling you what I feel." And you're not listening, she thought. "If I wanted easy sex I sure wouldn't choose you." She got up out of his lap and pulled open the bread drawer, muttering under her breath, "You're the *last* person...I'd have to be out of my fucking mind." A heel of dark rye lurked in the corner of the bread drawer. Alice pulled it out. Halved, it was not much, and she was starving. She examined the refrigerator. In the freezer was some lasagna she'd made a while ago and saved for an emergency. She pulled the foil back. It looked okay.

She turned the oven on and put in the lasagna. She sat down at the table and tore the bread in half, pushing Joe's half at him.

"What's that?"

"Food," she said.

He did some refrigerator-rummaging himself and brought out butter and jam. They applied butter to bread in slabs. They didn't talk, they ate. They scraped jam out of the bottom of the jar with a knife and smeared it on the bread. They sucked their sticky fingers.

"What's so funny?" she said.

He shook his head, nothing. Why did she feel like laughing? This was serious.

"I guess we should talk about Angel now," she said.

"No," Joe said.

"What do you mean no?"

"I mean no. I'm not going to."

"He's coming home on Thursday."

"We'll talk about him on Wednesday then."

Alice was impressed. "Okay," she said.

Alice's talk about the Senoi didn't convince Joe that what they were doing was going to work out. They did not live in the jungles of Malaysia and listen to their dreams every night. He didn't think his dreams were the same as hers anyway.

He sneaked her into the warehouse that night, late, after she got off work. She sat on his lap this time, reading out loud to him. He closed his eyes, listening to the story of a man and a woman lost in a dark labyrinth. When they walked the rounds, he held her hand. He drove her home at dawn, and they made love until they fell asleep, even after they fell asleep.

They both had to work all week; Alice came by when she was finished at the bar and he sneaked her into the warehouse. He should have worried about getting caught; he needed this job and he could have been fired if anyone found her there. He should have worried about Angel.

The second morning, riding home in the watery dawn, he asked her, "Do you do this a lot?"

"Do what?" Her voice was hoarse from reading to him. She was half-asleep and starting to yawn and she had no idea what he was talking about. He almost let it go.

"Screw around with one guy when you're supposed to be with another," he said.

He kept his eyes on the road. When he stopped for a light he glanced over at her. She was watching a delivery truck, a man unloading papers at the corner.

"I thought you didn't want to talk about Angel," she said.

"This isn't about Angel," he said. "It's about you."

She'd be right not to answer him, to get mad and clam up. He was the one who'd refused to talk about what they were doing. He'd wanted to do it and not think about it; he'd wanted to have an idyll.

"I've fucked around on people." Her voice was hard, her face trying to be. "How about you? Do you screw around a lot with women who are supposed to be with someone else?" she asked, returning the knife he'd just stuck into her. She kept watching the delivery man, as if Joe's answer didn't interest her.

The light changed and he put the van in gear, thinking about those minor dramas that seem major when they're happening and funny when you remember them. Luv omelettes, Angel called them. But that wasn't what they were talking about now. "Once I did," he said. "But I was only seventeen. I had an excuse."

"You want all the dirt?" she asked. "The whole litany?"

"What litany?"

"The Litany of Past Loves. You know," she said, bitter, "when you talk about how fucked up all your relationships have been and try to make it sound like it was the other person's fault." Now she was talking about Angel, who wasn't a past love, not at all.

"No," he said. He wasn't going to drag Angel or luv omelettes into this. But they couldn't go back to taking it as it came, and they sure as hell couldn't talk about the weather or sweet nothings instead, neither one of them could. Then he had an inspiration. "What do you think about death?" he asked.

She didn't answer.

"I'm not bullshitting you," he said. "I want to know." Even without a delivery man to watch, she stared out her window. The view must be riveting. "Come on, Alice, we've got to talk about something."

"Well it's a good idea," she finally said. "Big questions. Better than the litany." She shifted in her seat, leaning back and putting her feet up on the dashboard, getting comfortable now that they were talking about something besides Angel. "Why do you think you're here on this planet?" she asked.

"It better be to make music," he said, without even thinking once. "If it isn't I'm fucked."

Being with Alice for those few days was like swimming a long distance underwater. Sometimes he felt dazed from the lack of air. He surfaced to go home and check the messages on his answering machine for gigs. He kept that together. Then he took a shower, changed his clothes, and ate something, functioning on automatic. He went to see Alice at the bar for a couple of hours before he had to work. She came to the warehouse as soon as she was off.

In the warehouse she read to him or they talked. They asked each other big questions, and then tried to answer them. Peeling down to the bone, breathing water instead of air, they could leave Angel and the future alone.

"Who takes care of you when you need it?" she asked him one night. "You take care of the band, you took care of Angel, who takes care of you?"

"Me?"

She pinched his arm, not very hard. "Ow," he said.

"Well, you feel pain," she said. "I just proved it."

"Angel takes care of me," he said. Who did she think? "My brother Frank, his wife Michelle." When he asked them for help. Mostly he just waited for the bad times to pass. "You should meet them," he said. "You'd like them."

They were lying in bed, Alice's head on his shoulder. Outside the windows the pearly night was fading into a grey, featureless dawn.

"Who are you going to tell them I am?" she asked. He didn't say anything. He ran his hand up and down along her upper arm. She didn't seem so skinny, naked. She had a layer of roundness all over her, suitable for a water creature.

"It's like being underwater, this," he said. "It's making me stupid."

"I'd like to meet them," she said. They both knew she never would.

"Maybe it's time to talk about Angel," he said.

"No. You said Wednesday. I want to stay underwater and be stupid with you for as long as we've got."

V.

Alice went to the studio on Tuesday afternoon. Joe had pushed "talking about Angel" up a day and she felt like she needed a reality check. She wandered into rooms that had been the scene of frenetic activity the week before the show; her footsteps echoed.

She finally found Carla in the room with the presses. Carla was working on a plate with the radio on for company.

"Hey," Carla said. "Another person."

Alice pulled up a stool and stared out the window while Carla caught her up on the gossip. Lynn was seeing this guy Chris all the time, and Matt was still with Mr. Right, which was some kind of record for him. Chuck was out of town, visiting an old friend on a farm to give Baby the chance to run free.

"I can't believe you're working," Alice said. "I can never work after a show. Takes me a week at least."

"This is an old one," Carla said. "I just got an idea for it last night." It was a huge plate, abstract, like all of Carla's work. If Alice worked abstractly she could draw Joe.

"What do you think?" Carla asked. "Should this here go darker? I think it should. Or maybe I'll pop this other thingy out by making it lighter."

Alice looked at the plate. "I don't know," she said. "I feel totally blank right now."

"That's understandable."

Alice thought she was talking about the show.

"Did he fuck as good as he danced?" Carla asked.

Carla wasn't a sex goddess in the studio. She was wearing overalls and a t-shirt that covered her tattoos. She had glasses on instead of purple contacts. She eyed Alice over the tops of her glasses like a librarian examining a rain-damaged book.

"Don't tell me all that juice was for nothing?"

"I guess not," Alice said, thinking how Joe had been right, living underwater made you stupid.

"You don't have to talk about it."

"I don't know what to say. I'm getting over the shock that you knew."

"It was fairly obvious."

Carla poured oil on the plate, working on it with the burnisher. Matt appeared at the door silently and made both of them jump.

"This place is like a tomb. I don't know why I'm here." He pulled up a chair. "Can't stay away, I guess…is this a private conversation?"

Carla glanced at Alice.

The world of air-breathing creatures. Alice took a deep breath, hoping the oxygen would have some effect on her brain. "We're just gossiping," she said.

"Oh good," Matt said. "I could use some gossip. Is it good?"

"It's good gossip," Alice said. "I don't know if it's good."

Matt made a face to signify he was all ears.

"I've been sleeping with Joe," she said, trying it out. Although sleeping was only one of the things they'd been doing. Keeping each other awake was more like it.

"I *knew* it," Matt crowed. "I knew it."

He could at least have the grace to be surprised. "How did you know it?" Alice said. "I didn't know it."

"Well, Alice, when you freak out because he's dancing with Carla—"

"Freak out! I did not freak out."

"Yeah you did," said Carla. "You moved right in. I thought you were jealous, the way you moved in. I thought he was Angel. I was just being sociable."

Matt patted Carla's shoulder. "You're always misunderstood. It's the tattoos."

"I was jealous," Alice said, realizing it as she spoke, amazed that she hadn't seen it earlier. How long had she been underwater, anyway? "Shit." She felt like a fool.

Carla shrugged. "If I'd known he wasn't Angel, I wouldn't have backed off so fast," she said.

Matt and Alice went out for Mexican food. She didn't work that night, Joe had an early shift and would be by later. "Oh to be a fallen woman," Matt said. He sort of sang it. It was easy for him; he didn't have to live with it. Over his combination plate he rhapsodized about the endless permutations of love.

"You must be in love yourself," Alice said, "You usually call it lust."

"What are you calling it?"

"I'm not calling it anything. The part of my brain that makes words has been struck dumb. Mr. Right is still Mr. Right, I take it."

"Yes, he is," Matt said, biting off a flauta neatly. He went on awhile about Mr. Right, how he was smart, funny, an artist himself. Matt prophesied great mutual artistic inspiration from their union. "But why are you looking so morose? Isn't Mr. Right Mr. Right?"

"Matt! Joe is not Mr. Right. He's Mr. Wrong as can be. He's Angel's best friend."

"Well, yes, but he must know that himself. You didn't have to drag him off by his hair. Or did you?"

"I just made a spectacle of myself," she said.

"That's never bothered you before. It was fun to watch. Alice going after her man. It was so country-western."

"I hate country-western," she said.

"And you were so sweet together at the museum. I kept waiting for you to hold hands."

"*What?* Nothing was happening then."

Matt smiled. "Lynn said you were reading to him. God, Alice, you finally found somebody to read to. How can this be Mr. Wrong?"

"Look. He gave me a ride home from the airport because Angel asked him to. Then he took me to the peninsula. He was nice. He was being real nice. And then he told me he was being nice because he was trying to figure out a way to break up me and Angel."

Matt frowned. "That's…vile," he said. "Do you think that's what he's doing now?"

Alice, who had made her point better than she'd hoped, lost her appetite entirely. "It never even occurred to me."

"Don't look stricken. Think about it."

Alice thought. "No," she said. "It's too surreal for that. And he's not smug. I think I would know."

Matt nodded once, okay. He paid her the compliment of believing her intuition and not calling it gullibility.

"So Angel's Mr. Right?"

"Yeah. Of course he is. What is this? I thought you liked Angel."

"I like Angel. Angel's fine. I'm just asking. I'm trying to get it straight in my mind. Angel comes home, you dump Joe, and everything's okay, right? Unless you plan to keep two going at once. Like juggling plates."

"I can't do that," Alice said. "I *love* Angel." Matt's face blurred. Tears burned her eyes and then her cheeks. She sobbed once and covered her face.

"You can't do this here," Matt said, passing her a napkin.

"People will think I'm breaking up with you. Alice, please. I'll pay for your meal. Stop."

She wiped her face on the napkin. "I'm not very good at this, am I?"

"Terrible. If you want to succeed at a life of crime you have to plan carefully. Being totally oblivious to what you're doing only works up to a point."

"I guess this is the point."

"Does Joe know you're going to dump him?"

"I'm not dumping him. I just can't...I think he knows. We're supposed to talk about it tonight." She sighed. "Besides, I think I'm pregnant," she said.

Matt put down his fork. "How late?"

"About a week. More or less."

"More, or less?"

"More."

"Well," Matt said after awhile, "At least you know who the father is. You and Baby."

Alice started to laugh. She stopped before it got out of hand.

"Abortion's still legal," Matt said.

"I did that once already," she said. "I don't know."

"Oh lord. I thought you hated country-western."

"Don't tell anybody. I haven't told anybody but you."

"Don't tell anybody which thing?"

"None of the things. I'll tell them myself. Only not yet."

"There's those over-the-counter tests," he said. "You should do one before you make yourself crazy."

Alice had a moment of hope. Her periods weren't that regular. They came in their own time, and didn't follow the calendar. "Are you really paying for dinner? If you are, I want dessert."

On the way home she bought a pack of cigarettes for Joe and a pregnancy test for herself. As soon as she got home she used it. If she was pregnant, there would be two dots on the little stick instead of one. She set the stick on the bathroom windowsill and went into the kitchen so it could do its thing in privacy. She washed the dishes and scoured the top of the stove. If she worked extra hours she could afford an abortion, especially if she junked the car. Should she tell Angel? It would be stronger and braver not to, but she knew she'd blurt it out anyway; she may as well decide to tell him. Maybe there'd be nothing to tell. She'd been ten days late once, and it hadn't been anything.

But there were two dots. One for her, and one for somebody else.

Alice sat down on the edge of the tub. She had another look at the stick in her hand, the magic wand. Then she set it back on the windowsill.

The bathroom shelf on the wall across from her was littered with odds and ends—a dusty red candle, an abalone shell filled with cotton balls, a rolled-up comic book, a spool of gold thread. She stared at these things until their names went away. Without names they lost their hard edges. They pulsed with color, with the vibration of light. The color hummed.

Voices floated up from the street, a group of kids talking all at once. Their voices mingled, broke apart, and faded as they moved on down the block. Outside the window the evening had gone blue as a periwinkle; in the house next door, a light went on.

She looked down at her hands cupped over her belly. The smile that had been creeping up her throat came out of hiding. She had her message from the universe at last.

"Hi," she said. "Hi there, you."

Later, she thought about calling Angel. But she didn't want to tell him on the phone. He'd be home soon enough; she'd tell him then.

She should call Lynn. She hadn't talked to her in days. What was she going to say? Maybe Lynn wouldn't be home and she wouldn't have to say anything.

Lynn picked up on the first ring. She was waiting to hear from Chris. They had been together every night since the show and he was wonderful.

"I guess we should call him Mr. Wonderful," Alice said, "to keep him separate from Mr. Right. Matt's already got dibs on that name."

Lynn laughed. "Mr. Wonderful!" she said. "Oh that's so sick. I love that." She laughed again. Giddy. She had it bad. "So when does The Missing Link get home?" she asked.

"Day after tomorrow," Alice said. She took a deep breath. "I just did a pregnancy test and it looks like The Missing Link hit the bull's eye. Although I guess a link can't hit anything. Maybe Angel's the missing arrow. Like Cupid."

"Wait a minute, Alice. Are you saying—what are you saying?"

"I'm saying I'm pregnant," Alice said.

"Omigod, what are you gonna do?" Lynn asked. I'm going to get fat, Alice thought, but Lynn was still talking. "You don't have to decide anything right away. You've got some time to think about it." Lynn was trying to sound calm, to give good advice so Alice could get grounded and not freak out.

"I know," Alice said. She wished Lynn would just be happy for her. She wanted to tell her it's all right, don't worry, I greeted the baby this time. This one's coming in loud and clear.

But nobody was going to understand that. Matt and Lynn were acting like it was another one of Alice's disasters. They were girding their loins to be stalwart, to see her through. "Listen," she said, "we should get off the phone if Mr. Wonderful is calling." Lynn told Alice to call if she needed anything; she'd call Alice this weekend no matter what.

Alice hung up and unplugged the phone. She'd chickened out on telling Lynn about Joe. Carla had guessed, taking it as a matter of course that Alice would sleep with Joe, and Matt loved complications. But telling Lynn would be hard. Lynn would want to know why Alice was sleeping with Joe when she was in love with Angel. Alice didn't have a good answer. She was going to keep doing it anyway. She was going to hold onto Joe as tight as she could until she had to let go.

Two more nights. Tears came to her eyes, but that was the hormones, crocodile tears. The deep, dark truth was, Joe scared the shit out of her. If she hadn't been with Angel, she never would have messed with Joe.

She threw away the pregnancy test and the box it had come in and took out the trash, covering her tracks.

Joe talked to Angel in the afternoon. Angel had called to give him his flight time. A lot had happened in Tucson. Angel would tell Joe all about it when he got home. Joe told him about the work they had lined up, trying to sound enthusiastic about the work and bored in general, like nothing much had happened here.

"Have you seen Alice lately?" Angel asked.

"Not lately," Joe said. He hadn't seen her for at least two hours. "Why?"

"I can't reach her. Maybe her phone's on the blink." Joe knew Alice unplugged the phone when he was there, which covered most of the time when she was there. She plugged it back in when she left, which, since she had no answering machine, meant she never had to return her calls.

He spent his work shift rehearsing what he would say to her when she said all the things he thought she was going to say to him. He had gone over all the arguments he could make. He was still going over them when he parked the van on her street.

Standing outside her door he thought about Angel coming home and his mind went blank.

Alice didn't buzz him in, she came down. "You want to go for a walk?" she asked.

"Sure," he said. "You want to talk about terrible things, it's better to keep moving."

"Better not to sit in the kitchen," she agreed. "With the tequila and the knives."

He put his arms around her, like he had a right to. She pressed her face into his neck, hugging him hard. She didn't let go. Her hair smelled like his shampoo. They would have to do something about that. "Come on," he said. "Let's go for a walk."

The sky was clear, the moon huge. They came to a playground. They swung in the swings. They talked about how when they were kids they'd swing as high as they could before they jumped off.

"I used to think if I just got high enough, I'd learn to fly before I hit the ground," Alice said. "I'd wave my arms like crazy."

"You should have waved your ears," Joe said. He was thinking about Dumbo.

Alice laughed. "Did you ever try to fly?"

"I spent an entire summer jumping out of my treehouse."

Alice put her toe out, touching earth, slowing herself down. She drew breath, as if she was getting ready to say something. Then she stared at the moon. Procrastinating.

Joe lit a cigarette, sitting in his swing. "You're staying with Angel," he said, getting it over with.

Alice traced signs in the dirt with her foot. "Yeah," she said.

He passed her his cigarette, lit another for himself.

"Say something," she said.

He blew smoke into the air. The night air was chilly on his face. "He called me today. He said he's been trying to reach you. He thought your phone wasn't working."

Her arms were hooked around the chains of the swing; she held her hands together in front of her, holding the cigarette like she was praying with it. She leaned her head down to the cigarette. The ash glowed red. She blew smoke, watching it like she was blowing bubbles. "I feel like a shit," she said.

"Because of me, or because of Angel?"

"Angel. I'm not lying to you."

He walked the swing back as far as it would go and lifted his feet from the ground. Pumping with his legs, he went up into the sky. He swung back, his hair blinding him, flew up again. At the top of the arc, he jumped. The bones of his feet protested loudly when he landed.

Alice clapped.

"You want to do the seesaw?" he asked.

"Naw. It doesn't go anywhere."

"Like us."

"I hate metaphors," she said.

"But that's what's happening." The moonlight made her look like she was wearing dark lipstick, when she never wore any. "We should have talked about Angel up front," he said.

"I'm glad we didn't. It didn't have anything to do with him."

"It does now."

She didn't say anything to that. Her mouth was probably moving. "You want to go back?" he asked her. "We could get out the tequila and the knives."

"We could watch a late movie," Alice said. "We never got to do that. What do you want to do?"

Steal you away from Angel, Joe thought. See if I still feel like this in a month, or a year. See what happens. Be a shit.

"Let's find someplace and look at the sky," he said.

They lay on their backs in the grass, staring into the deep ocean of sky. The grass was cool and itchy. There was a small, faint star winking at the center of the sky, the deepest, farthest one. Alice watched it until she felt like she was falling into the night. Hands pressed flat against the earth, she held on. She watched the star until she felt it coming towards her. She was reeling it in. Swimming so deep with Joe, she had hooked a star.

"What happened to the Senoi?" Joe said. Alice turned her head to look at him. He was watching the sky.

"You thought that was crazy," she said.

"What do you think about it?"

She tried to imagine living with Joe and Angel. They could take turns cooking dinner, passing the baby around. Three parents for one child; there would always be a lap. But did either of them want a baby? She didn't want the baby to be rejected before she was even born. "I think they live a different life from us," she said. It sounded meaningless as soon as she said it out loud.

Joe turned on his side, propping his head on his hand. "What if I don't want to stop?"

Well, what if he didn't? Why did she think this was going to be easy?

"You could meet me at the warehouse. Say you were visiting a friend."

"You mean, after Angel gets back?"

"Yeah."

"No," she said. "I can't do that. That's...I can't."

"I could tell him," Joe said. "What would you do then?"

"I was going to tell him anyway. I wasn't going to lie about it."

"You were going to tell him?" Joe asked. "You think he won't *mind*?"

Alice sat up. The star, left to its own devices, unreeled itself back into the sky.

"I didn't say that. But I think it's better to tell him."

"Why? If you wanted to be with me instead of him, it makes sense. Otherwise it's fucking nuts. You'll just hurt him for no reason."

"I don't want to lie. That would hurt, too. What he didn't know would change everything. It's already changed, but how can he deal with it if he doesn't know what it is?"

"So you think he'll understand."

"I think he'll..." What? Not understand. She didn't understand it herself. Forgive her? She didn't much want to be forgiven. "Trust me I guess," she said. "Trust me again." That's what she hoped for.

Joe grunted and sat up. "I shouldn't say anything. I should let you do it."

"You don't want me to."

"I don't think he's going to trust either one of us anymore if you tell him."

She hadn't thought about how it would affect Angel and Joe. If it had been Lynn and Angel instead of her and Joe, how would she react? She might decide to trust Angel, but how would she feel about Lynn? Stabbed in the back, totally betrayed.

"I guess it's not fair," she said. "Me telling him when you don't want to...okay, I'll wait."

"For what?"

"For you to change your mind."

"What if I don't?"

Alice got to her feet. Joe reached up his hands and she grabbed them, leaned back, and hauled him up. "Then I don't know. I'll warn you or something. When I can't stand it anymore."

"Before the shit hits the fan. That'll be a big help."

"Well what do you want me to do?"

"I already told you," he said.

"Lie and sneak," she said.

"You're doing it now," he argued.

She started walking. He walked with her. "It's different and you know it," she said.

"Yeah? Then let's go to a club. Let's go see somebody we know and hang out. Let's plug your fucking phone back in."

"You're trying to make me mad," she said. "You want to fight with me and get it over with."

"You're the one that wants it over with. What were you going to tell him, anyway? It was just a phase you were going through?"

What a shit! She wasn't going to get angry; she was already so enraged her head felt light. She wanted to say something scathing, and fury was making her incoherent. She stuffed her hands in her pockets and her fingers touched the cigarettes she'd bought. She pulled out the pack and looked at it. Then she held it out to him. "Here," she said.

"What's that?"

"They're for you. To pay you back."

He looked at her like she was offering him poison. She guessed she was.

"You can't pay me back," he said. He turned away from her, turned on his heel and walked away, back straight, head up, moving fast.

She put the cigarettes in her pocket. She watched him until he was out of sight. He didn't look back.

She turned around and walked back to the swings. She didn't feel that great; her heart hammering under her ribs, her chest heaving. Tomorrow she would begin her life of crime in earnest—wash the sheets, go through the apartment and remove all the evidence, quit smoking again.

She sat in the swing. Some teenage kids came into the park. They had a radio with them. They sat on the jungle gym, since she had the swings. They were talking and laughing, smoking cigarettes.

Alice walked the swing back as far as she could go and then lifted her feet, pointed her toes, and leaned back to push herself up, up, into the sky. When she hit the top of the arc, she jumped. For one long second she flew.

Her landing was okay. She looked around the playground, at the kids, who hadn't noticed, didn't applaud. No one else was there. Well, who did she expect? She started walking home. She knew he wasn't going to be there. She looked for him anyway, flinched every time a car went by.

The van was gone. Her front steps were empty. The phone was ringing. She ran upstairs, caught the phone in time. It was a crank call, it sounded like a slumber party of gigglers. She slammed the phone down so hard it jumped back off the hook. She slammed it down again. "That does it," she said out loud. "That just does it." She brushed her teeth, went to the bathroom, and left the apartment.

VI.

It was a long walk to Joe's house. It felt good to be walking alone at night. It made Alice feel free. If he wasn't there she would turn around and walk back home, and be tired enough to sleep instead of pace and swear and fixate on the phone.

Joe's house was dark, the van gone; Alice leaned on the bell anyway. No one answered. She sat down to wait. She hadn't been there long when his neighbors came home, two guys who were musicians too, who didn't mind loud music at late hours. Alice recognized them from the party at Joe and Angel's. They eyed her with curiosity and said hello.

"I'm waiting for someone," she said.

She thought they looked at her pityingly, but it could have been her imagination. "You want to wait inside?" one of them asked.

"What time is it?"

"Almost two."

"I guess I'll go." She had a vision of Joe coming home with one of his friends who knew Angel. They would act like strangers, only not polite. Now she wanted to get away, fast.

"Hey," one of them yelled after her. "You need a ride anywhere?"

Her feet hurt; he seemed okay. "You been drinking?" she asked.

"A couple a beers, hours ago," he said. "Want me to walk in a straight line?"

"Yeah," she said. Both guys laughed. Then one sat down on the steps, watching with Alice while the other one walked a straight line.

Straight Line drove her home. They talked about music. He was nice, a nice, normal person. On the surface, anyway. If he had any deep dark secrets he didn't share them with Alice.

"Thanks for the ride," she said.

"No problem," he said. "I don't feel sleepy tonight."

"I know what you mean," she said. "It must be the full moon." She shut the car door and watched him drive away.

The moon was setting, its face changed, like it did sometimes, from woeful to shocked. A car door creaked and slammed shut somewhere down the street, loud in the stillness of early Wednesday morning. Nobody could sleep.

Alice felt better. Joe had cut loose from her, and Angel—well, she had no faith anymore that Angel wouldn't do the same. She had never felt sure of Angel; it was part of his appeal, and it left her out in the cold. But she was okay on her own, and there were other people in the world. People she would probably never see again, but could remember with friendliness.

"Hey moon," she said low, hearing footsteps across the street. She couldn't talk to the moon with people walking around. She glanced over, hoping they would go on by.

He crossed the street, watching for cars. No it wasn't...yes. It was.

Joe came up to her and said, "I got home a little while ago. My neighbor said there'd been some girl waiting for me."

The moonlight made his face a mask of light and dark, she couldn't read his expression. She couldn't tell anything from his voice, whether he was still angry or not.

"It was me," she said.

He waited. She waited too. "So what did you want?" he asked.

"You pissed me off," she said. "I wanted to say something wounding."

"Here I am. Now's your chance."

"I never thought of anything."

He nodded, as if this made sense.

"Do you want to come in?"

He had to think about it. "What the hell," he said.

In the kitchen his face looked bleached except for the dark circles under his eyes.

"Where'd you go?" she asked.

"Drove around. Went to the cemetery."

"Are you okay?"

He looked at her then. "What am I, the man of steel? No, I'm not okay."

"We could just go to sleep," she said. "Unless you want to talk."

He shook his head. "I'm tired," he said. "I don't have the energy to argue with you."

But you've got the energy to guilt-trip me, she thought. The trouble was, she did feel guilty. Guilty and miserable and happy to see him. "You want the bathroom first?"

He did.

She went in and shook out the sheets while he was in the bathroom. Last night they'd slept in this same bed and talked about his brother. It felt like another geologic age.

He came out of the bathroom and she went in. She washed her face and brushed her teeth. She took off her clothes and put on a t-shirt. By the time she came to bed he was asleep, lying on his side facing the wall. She climbed in next to him. He'd left her plenty of room. She lay on her back, trying to relax. He snored a little. After awhile, she slept.

In the night he turned and threw his arm over her; she woke enough to grab his hand and hold it trapped under her breast.

When she woke in the morning he was already dressed, kneeling by the side of the bed, saying her name.

"What?"

"I'm going now," he said.

"No," she said, "no wait." She reached out and touched his arm. It didn't feel like it had when he was asleep. She pulled her hand back and sat up.

"You don't have to get up," he said.

She put her elbows on her crossed knees, her head in her hands. She was dizzy from sitting up too fast.

"I'm up," she answered.

"Don't go yet, okay?" she said.

There was no point in staying. Neither one of them was going to say anything different. "Okay," he said.

They sat in the kitchen, eating what was left of some strawberries from the day before. The ones that were left were green. They ate them anyway.

He had watched her sleep this morning. That night at his house, when she'd cried about Angel at his kitchen table and slept in Angel's bed, he'd come in late and she had the covers pulled over her head. All he could see were strands of dark hair on the pillow. How could she breathe like that? He lifted the blankets away from her head and she mumbled and groaned, burrowing deeper into the pillow. She was curled up as tight as a new fern.

Sleeping with him, she let the air touch her face. She kicked off the blankets and slept stretched out against him. She probably stretched out with Angel, too. Angel slept crosswise, his pillow under him like it was a woman he'd fallen asleep on. There was no way Alice could curl up and hide, sleeping with Angel.

The kettle steamed and she got up to make the coffee. "You're not going to be friends with me anymore, are you," she said, her back to him.

"No," he said.

"It's all my fault then," she said. He could barely focus his eyes and she was having this burst of energy. He lit a cigarette.

"I've been thinking, maybe this isn't about me, anyway," she said.

"Who's it about? My mother?"

"No. Angel." She poured the water through the filter. The coffee aroma filled the room. "The only reason you wanted to know me in the first place was to get rid of me. But sooner or later Angel's going to find somebody to be with, and you won't be as close to him as you were. Fucking me was a way to be close to Angel. You could pay him back at the same time, for being someone who was going to leave you for some woman."

"Did you stay awake all night thinking this up?"

"But it's easier to be mad at me than at Angel. So you give me this line about wanting to fool around behind his back, and then you can be pissed off at me because I don't want to." She wasn't angry, she was being a lawyer, presenting her case. She brought the coffeepot over and sat down, waiting for the defense.

He drank coffee and smoked, thinking. "In the first place," he said, "all that about Angel leaving is what you feel. You're the one who can't deal when he's gone. You're the one who can't get close enough. You could have been using me to feel closer to Angel."

Let her chew on that awhile. It was mean to use it against her, but he didn't feel like being nice.

Her mouth pulled sideways. "Well I wasn't," she said. "What about the second place?"

"I can't remember the second place."

"How you're setting up something you know I won't do so you can be pissed off at me. Besides, if you really wanted to be with me you wouldn't say let's fool around behind Angel's back. You'd say, forget Angel. If I said okay, you wouldn't be fucking me, you'd be fucking Angel's girlfriend. I could be anybody."

"Forget about Angel," he said. "Break up with him."

She didn't understand at first. Then she got mad. Her face turned red. "That's easy to say," she said. "You already know I won't, you're perfectly safe saying you want to. So you can hate me with a clear conscience."

"The first thing you said about Angel was that you were sticking with him and I should take a hike. Why would I say anything about you and me after that?"

She leaned back in her chair, all the lawyer knocked out of her. "But you knew about that," she said. "You know more about what I feel for Angel than anybody does. Even Angel."

"Well I didn't think about it," he said. "It was easy."

She pressed her lips together. Her eyes filled with tears. Oh no, not again. She lifted her feet onto the chair and pressed her forehead into her bent knees, going fetal. How could he be hung up on someone who cried so much? She cried about every single fucking thing. She got weepy over road kill. She cried over the news, for chrissakes. He'd asked her once why she cried so much and she said to keep her tear ducts clear. "They must be there for something," she said. "You must be supposed to use them."

Now she was crying to win an argument, doing the girl thing. It wouldn't work on this boy. He was glad she was miserable. He moved to the chair next to her to enjoy it.

She said something into her knees.

"I can't hear you," he said.

She turned her face sideways. He pushed her hair back behind her ear and watched tears slide along her nose. She was getting into it. Her nose had turned red and her mouth was all twisted up.

"I said, what about what I feel? I can't say anything, once I've said I want to stay with Angel. I have to bite my tongue and let you abuse me."

"Say whatever you want."

"I don't want to meet you in secret," she said. "I want to be with Angel." She cried harder. He wished she would shut up. "I miss you," she said. "I miss you so bad."

He half-scooped, half-hauled her onto his lap. The chair creaked ominously. She held onto him like a shipwrecked sailor holds onto the idea of land. She cried all over his shirt.

"You're glad I'm crying," she said.

"I'm glad you're crying about me," he said. "You should. You should miss the hell out of me. I hope it hurts."

She relaxed a little, unbending her knees and rubbing her wet face on her sleeve.

"You're not crying, though," she said. "You're fine."

"I'm a guy," he said. "I'm tough. Besides, I cried last night in the cemetery."

"Really?" She craned her neck around, slitting her eyes at him as if that would make it easier to tell if he was lying or not.

"After I yelled and kicked things. I nearly broke my foot on a gravestone."

"Good," she said.

"That's why we can't be friends, Alice. If you're not with me, I want you to be miserable. And you're just as bad."

"I didn't even want you dancing with someone else," she said. "And that was before." She wiped her face with the back of her hand. "But we could try. It would be better than this."

"I don't want to try. It sounds like torture."

Seeing her with Angel was going to be bad enough; he didn't want to be "friends" with her. They'd been friends anyway, and look what happened.

"I wish we'd never had sex," Alice said.

He thought about that for a second. Then he laughed. "You're so full of shit."

"I mean it. If we hadn't, we could still do stuff together. I could read to you some more. We could get to know each other."

"We know each other. That's one of the ways."

They sat still for awhile. In his arms she felt like she was going to sleep.

"We can do something tonight," he said. "I'll take you out. I'll take you on our one and only date."

"I've got to work tonight."

"Call in sick."

She chewed the back of her lower lip, thinking.

"We can go to a movie," he said. "That way we can't fight. And I'll leave now, so we don't start fighting before then."

"What movie?"

"What do you want to see? No love stories," he said.

"You probably like a lot of blood and guts. I want to see something funny. Like the Marx Brothers. Stupid and funny. Or a detective thing. Can we do that?"

"If you wear a skirt," he said.

For some reason she smiled at him. "Okay," she said.

Alice wore the dark skirt she'd worn to the opening. The only difference in her outfit was the shirt; instead of Angel's ratty t-shirt, she had on a boxy white thrift store blouse with a big collar and pleats and little buttons all down the front. She wore a funky leather jacket over it. She'd washed her hair, put on eye make-up with a heavy hand, and no lipstick. She looked about fourteen.

"Hm," he said, walking around her.

She gave him a beady eye, put a fist on her hip. "What."

"I like it," he said. "Like the girls who went to Catholic school."

They went to an early show. There were no Marx brothers movies, but *The Blues Brothers* was showing at a place that ran old movies. He hoped Alice wouldn't cry because John Belushi was dead.

Alice had never seen the movie. She thought it was hilarious. At the scene in the restaurant, the dishwasher picking up a sax and starting to play behind Aretha, she laughed herself sick. Joe was pleased; it was one of his favorite movies.

When they came out it was still early. "What do we do now?" she said. "I haven't been on a date in a million years."

Joe knew what he wanted to do. It must have showed.

"Oh, that," she said.

"Yeah that."

She took hold of his hand. "Well, come on."

Joe wanted to unbutton her blouse, which she was going to pull off over her head. He wanted to unpeel and unbutton and unzip and unlace everything, even her boots. He wanted to go slow, to make it last.

She took off his clothes, too, slowing things down more. When he entered her, he lay still, held her still. She came anyway, without a sound. Her whole body tensed, her head arched back. He didn't move.

After awhile he whispered, "Move when you want to. I'll follow you."

"I already—"

"I know. I could tell."

"You could?"

"Yeah."

"Can I kiss you?" she said, starting on his neck.

"No, don't." He sort of gasped it. She pulled her head back, looking at him. He kissed her carefully. Carefully, she kissed him back. She started to move, just a little, and then stopped. Then he did. They made it last until she couldn't stand it anymore. She bit her lip and tried to pull away.

"Go on," he said, and she went. He was right behind her. It was like following her off a cliff. She gave a seagull cry, short and ecstatic, discovering flight. He let go. He jumped off the cliff too.

He was asleep, lying across her, pinning her down. She stared at the jumping candle shadows on the wall and tried to get a breath without waking him. She wanted to feel his sleeping weight on her. She said something to him inside her head. As if her unspoken words had penetrated his skull, he stirred and woke.

He shifted sideways. "Can you breathe?"

"No," she said.

He moved off of her. His face, smoothed by candlelight, was peaceful and triumphant. She was proud for him.

"It's never been like that before," she said.

"No," he agreed.

"Has it for you? With other women, I mean." Just thinking of the next woman he was going to do this with filled Alice with helpless fury. "I guess this is just normal for you," she said.

His eyes widened. "You're jealous," he said. He looked like he thought it was funny.

"Pretty disgusting, huh."

"Yeah, totally." He was teasing her, that's all. She didn't have to disintegrate. She should be cool and tough, so he would remember her with yearning. She only had a few more hours she had to fake it.

She was going to cry, she could feel it coming. Damn it to hell. She couldn't say, "I'm not really like this; it's the baby hormones."

She got out of bed fast and went to the bathroom. She drank water from the tap. She splashed water on her face, as if she already had cried, and put on a big t-shirt hanging on the back of the door. On the way back, she snagged the tequila.

Joe was sitting up in bed, smoking. He was looking at her like he'd never seen her before. At least he hadn't run out the door when he had the chance.

She sat crosslegged on the end of the bed, uncapped the tequila, and took a very small swig from the bottle. It tasted great. If she only had one more night of being bad and weak and disgusting, she was going to make the most of it.

"You want some?" she asked.

He raised his eyebrows. "Yeah, sure." He drank some and set the bottle on his belly. "Why are you sitting so far away?"

She got up and moved back next to him. The tequila was over there anyway. "Did you ever finish that song?" she asked.

"The words aren't working." He looked at her sideways. "Are you going to get drunk now?"

"No. Are you?"

For an answer he capped the bottle. He passed it to her and she set it on the floor.

"Are you ashamed of being jealous?" he asked.

She took a deep breath. "Yeah," she said. "And I hate how it feels. I hate it worse than anything."

He blew smoke into the air, watching it. Then he put out his cigarette and set the ashtray on the bookshelf.

"Why are you looking at me like that?" she asked. "Are you psychoanalyzing me?"

"It's that ugly thing," he said. She thought he meant her jealousy until he started tugging at the t-shirt she had put on. "There," he said when he had gotten it off. He put his arm around her and leaned back against the pillows. He shut his eyes. She knew what that meant. It meant, let's be quiet and not talk. Alice was full of things to say; they were bouncing around in her head like bumblebees in a jar.

"I feel like I can tell you things I haven't told anybody," she said. "I was thinking, maybe I feel like that because I know we aren't going to last long enough for you to use it against me."

"Do you sit around thinking up the worst possible reasons for everything?"

"No, it just now came into my head…so what do you think?"

"In a few days we've used practically everything we know about each other against each other. I think your theory's wrong."

"Would you have come back last night if I hadn't gone over to your house?"

"No," he said.

"Why not?"

He started laughing. "What?" she said. He kept laughing. "What?" she said again, but now she was laughing too. They laughed until they ran down. Then Alice said "But what's so funny?" and set him off again. Still laughing, he pulled her down against him. Before the water closed over her head she had a thought that was also an illumination; it floated away like seaweed.

They didn't sleep until the sky had started to lighten, and then Joe startled awake in the late morning. He didn't know what had wakened him. No sirens, no phone, no car alarms going off. Hissing rain, Alice asleep in his arms, he should be asleep. It must have been a dream; he couldn't remember it. He raised himself cautiously to see the clockface; it was only eleven. They had eight hours until Angel's plane came in, six until Alice went to work. Not enough time for anything; too much time.

They didn't make love, or fight, or ask each other big questions, or put forward theories. Alice didn't smoke; she said she had to begin her life of crime, clean up the evidence. She had it backwards, but he didn't point it out to her. If she didn't think he was the crime, but hiding him was, then she was giving herself away. She didn't notice.

They took turns in the shower, starting with the primary evidence. Wrapped in a towel, he went through the apartment, taking his shampoo (how had that gotten here?), crawling around on the floor looking for stray condom wrappers and cigarette butts. Alice burned incense and opened all the windows to get the smoke out of the house. Angel smoked, so he might not notice, but there was no sense in risking it. The bruise on her neck was almost gone. Only a smudge was left, nothing you'd notice unless you knew where to look.

They went to the laundromat. They sat in hard molded plastic chairs watching two women fold their clothes. When the women left Joe put his arm around Alice and she leaned her head against him.

"Will you do something for me?" she asked.

"I don't know," he said. "Ask me."

"Can you leave me out of your litany?" She turned her head up under his arm to watch his face. "You can say whatever you want about me to anybody," she said, "only not to a lover." He didn't see what difference that was going to make.

"Then you can't talk about me to a lover either," he said. He meant Angel. He didn't care what she told anybody else.

"I wasn't going to."

The dryer stopped before the towels and jeans were dry; they unloaded the lighter clothes and Alice went looking for change. The change machine was empty so she went to the convenience store next door. While she was gone, Joe took a pair of her black cotton bikini underpants. She had an underwear uniform and that was it. She wouldn't notice one pair missing. He folded them small and stashed them in the inside pocket of his jacket.

When she came back he was decorously folding t-shirts. She put the change in the dryer and came over and started folding.

"What?" she said.

Either his face was getting away from him or she was learning how to read it. "What?" he said back.

"I don't know. You don't have to do that."

"Nothing else to do."

He wanted to drive her to work. He could drop her off before he went to the airport to pick up Angel. Alice wanted to get to work on her own. "Won't it be harder anyway, going straight to the airport from dropping me off?"

"I want to," he said.

She gave in. She stared out the window the whole way to work, nothing to say, like the time he'd driven her back from the airport. He pulled over and killed the engine.

She put her hand on the door handle. "You sure you don't want to be friends?" she asked.

"Kiss me goodbye."

She crawled over and knelt on the floor next to him. She steadied herself with her hand on his knee, bent over and kissed his thigh. She moved her head down and used her teeth between his legs so he would feel something through his jeans. He put his hands on her head. He turned himself towards her, leaned back in the seat and groaned out loud. Across the street, a man mailing a letter stared at him. It was a good revenge.

He hauled her up and she put her arms around his neck. They were laughing. "You bitch," he said, kissing her. "I'm not sorry about this," she said, kissing him all over his face, "I'm not," and then, her mouth on his ear, "I've gotta go." She untangled herself, was out of the van, slamming the door hard, and gone.

VII.

Angel's flight was late. Joe had time to get a beer in the bar and chain-smoke. He had time to feel guilty and arrange his thoughts, make them suitable. He tried to feel like someone who'd done nothing much but write songs and get gigs while Angel had been gone.

Angel saw him first, was up next to him while Joe was still scanning the crowd. Tucson had turned Angel a different color—his rain-belt pallor had given way to an overall bronze tone, his hair had reddish highlights. He looked like he should have a knife in his belt and be riding a horse. Alice was going to fall in love with him all over again; he would put her in front of him on his horse and they would ride off into the sunset. Except they would be right here where Joe, pale as a supermarket mushroom, could watch them.

Angel hugged him. "Hey man. You look so white," he said, echoing what Joe was thinking.

"I am white," Joe said, hugging him back. "I'm not multi-cultural, like you."

Angel laughed. He was wearing faded jeans and a black t-shirt with no sleeves. "It's fucking freezing here, you know that? Where's Alice? Couldn't you get a hold of her?"

"She had to work," Joe said. It came out sounding normal, like nothing. "How was Tucson?"

Angel was full of stories, the traveller returning home after adventures. At least he didn't expect Joe to have any adventures to tell. Angel had finally made peace with his father, finished old business with his ex-girlfriend. He couldn't wait to start gigging again. He'd written a new song. He wanted to try it out. He wanted to go see Alice.

"So you guys finally got to be friends," Angel said.

"Sort of."

"Let's go see her at the bar."

"I'll drop you off," Joe said. "I've been working a lot. I need to catch up on my sleep."

That was fine with Angel. Joe drove him. Watching Angel's back as he went into the Neptune, Joe was so jealous he felt ill.

Seeing Angel come into the bar alone, looking for her, looking happy, Alice wanted to tell him everything. She couldn't lie to Angel. She couldn't tell him either, because she had told Joe she wouldn't.

Angel looked like a different person from the Angel who had left, not just his tan, but the expressions on his face. His arms around her felt like a stranger's. She thought it was because of all the secrets she was keeping.

She told him what she could. As soon as they got home, in the middle of a story he was telling her about his sister's wedding reception, she said, "I'm pregnant."

The wash was all done, put away. She didn't know if Angel would have been able to smell Joe all over her clothes and bed, but she had.

"What?" Angel said. She didn't know if he'd heard what she said.

"I did a pregnancy test. I never got my period."

Angel looked around at her apartment as if he'd never been there before. "Is that why you're cleaning the house?" he said.

No, she thought, that's because I've been fucking your best friend and I'm planning to lie to you about it.

He looked at her, seeing her. She didn't know what he saw.

"You've decided what to do," he said.

"I want to have her."

"Her? It's already a girl?"

"I don't know why I said that," she said. "I hope she has your mouth."

Angel looked blank. "How long have you known?"

"I thought maybe, last week," she said. "But I'm late all the time, so I wasn't sure. I didn't know until a couple days ago, when I did the test. It wasn't like when I had the abortion. This time I was glad."

"Are you sure you want to?"

"I do want to. I'm going to. You don't have to."

"It looks like I already did. You got anything stronger than coffee to drink around here?"

She brought out the tequila. Angel poured himself a shot. He knocked it back, set the glass down, and poured himself another. Then he didn't drink it. He stared at her belly.

Alice drank water. Now that she was admitting things, now that she was back in the real world, she had to be good. "I shouldn't have told you right away, I guess." He had gone into shock. She should have worked up to it slowly. What if he fainted? Thinking that, Alice wanted to laugh. She suppressed it.

"There's really a baby in there?" he asked.

She nodded. He started to smile. It came up slow, but it stuck. It was the same smile that had been on Alice's face when she saw that second dot. It was the smile of the Fool in the Tarot, stepping blithely from solid ground onto thin air. Even if there hadn't been any other reasons, she would love Angel forever for that smile.

Angel got home from Alice's in the afternoon, in plenty of time for the gig. Joe was still asleep. He hadn't slept until dawn, and then he'd wrapped himself around his pillow, pretending it was the woman of his dreams, the babe on his wall, long blonde hair, big breasts, legs wide open. But she loved him. She didn't love anyone else.

Angel was unpacking noisily to wake Joe up. Joe took a shower. He washed his hair. He soaped himself all over. When he was clean he came out. Angel was doing the dishes. He frowned at them, concentrating on getting all the grease off.

Joe made coffee and sat down to drink it, watching Angel sweep the floor. "You're such a fucking slob," Angel said. "I go away for a couple weeks and it's like a pig sty around here." He sounded pleased.

"It's always like this," Joe said. "You just forgot."

"Maybe it's the nesting instinct," Angel said.

"Tucson was that bad? It made this place look like a nest?"

"No." Angel swept crumbs into the dustpan and emptied it into the trash. "I'm a father," he said.

Joe thought of Angel's old girlfriend, married to someone else and having Angel's baby. It was the kind of thing that would happen to Angel. The kid must be five or six by now.

"Jesus," Joe said. "Did her husband know?"

"Husband?" Angel said. "Alice doesn't have a husband."

"Alice?"

"Who'd you think I was talking about?" Angel laughed at Joe's face. "You're still asleep," he said.

"You said you were a father. I thought you got your old girlfriend pregnant before you broke up and met the kid in Tucson."

"What a disaster that would have been. A dizz-ass-ter." He grinned, sharing a huge joke. "I got Alice pregnant."

It couldn't be Alice.

“She thinks it’s a girl. She says she’s hoping she has my mouth.”

“Alice,” Joe said.

“Her period’s so weird I never even think about it anymore. And we were careful. I can’t believe she didn’t tell me on the phone.”

You bitch, Joe thought. You lying bitch.

“I had to tell someone,” Angel said. “Don’t tell the guys. She’s going to the clinic next week.”

Well, she’d won. She had her hooks into Angel as deep as they would go, and Joe so bollixed up he didn’t know his ass from a hole in the ground. And he’d been teaching her self-defense. He should have asked for lessons.

“You want a kid?” Joe asked, being a shit, being himself again.

Angel looked at Joe from someplace far away. “You know, I kind of do…” You dumb fuck, Joe thought.

“Surprise,” Angel said. He pretended like he was giving Joe shit for being so dull and stodgy that he couldn’t imagine Angel as a father. Angel acted like he didn’t care what Joe thought, like he didn’t want or need Joe’s approval. He did though. It showed in his eyes, and in the skin around his eyes.

“Well congratulations, man,” Joe said. It sounded so wrong he got up and hugged Angel. He tried to relax, to hug Angel as if he meant it. Angel hugged him back, a real hug.

“What are you going to do for money?” Joe asked.

“Get a lot of gigs,” Angel said. “Get rich and famous.”

Joe got them a lot of gigs. It reminded him of the time just before Angel crashed and ended up in rehab. Everybody wanted them.

They even got a manager. Joe had been sending stuff around forever, trying to get someone interested, and then this woman showed up at a gig and gave him her card. Her name was Cynthia. Joe studied her card, trying to remember what he knew about her. She had gotten them some work, but that was over the phone. He'd never met her. He shook her hand, since she seemed to expect it.

She had blonde hair cut to the exact same length all around her jaw and her face was so perfect she was almost plain. She was wearing a black leather jacket that would have cost Joe a month's rent. She looked to be in her late twenties, Joe's age. He had to remind himself of that a couple of times. Joe bet no one ever called her Cindy.

She was from L.A. and had moved here to get out of the city. This isn't a city? Joe wondered. She was doing fine as an agent, she said she had quite a few local bands "under her belt" besides them. But she felt like the time was right to "get her hands dirty"; she was ready to be a manager. Either she had no sense of humor or she was better at deadpan than anyone he'd ever met. She thought she could do something for the band. She said she liked their sound. She could get them a regional tour by next month, if they wanted it.

Joe said he wanted to think about it, talk it over with the rest of the band. Cynthia had no problem with that. She would come back tomorrow night, which gave him a whole day to think.

She came by the next night to meet the band. Stringer put himself out to be charming. Cynthia was polite. She didn't seem especially charmed, a point in her favor. Angel made some vaguely rude remark about not wanting to tart up or tone down and relaxed once she said she didn't want them to change a thing. Dan hadn't wanted a woman for a manager in the first place. There was no second place. She could get them work, she wanted to get them into a studio to do a new demo tape, and she had the contacts to get it listened to. But first a tour. That would be their trial run, straight percentage but no strings. They could see how well they worked together.

After she left, Dan said he'd like to have a trial run in private. Stringer couldn't wait to get home and tell his wife they were finally going to make it.

Angel didn't say much. Joe asked him what he thought about their possible new manager.

"She knows her stuff, but I kept wondering why she liked us. I felt like I had to watch my language."

"The 'sound'," Joe said. "She likes 'the sound'. She's done good things for us as an agent. She doesn't try to screw you over and she doesn't let anybody else screw you over either."

"Yeah?" Angel said. "Then what's your problem?"

"No problem. What do you mean?"

Angel gave him a look. "Stringer's pissing his pants, but you're the one who wouldn't have to deal with all the business anymore. If she's as good as she says she is, we could be recording. And you're not that excited."

"I know," Joe said. It had puzzled him, too. He'd been working for this so long, it ought to cheer him up. "I just want to make music," he said.

"Don't you want people to hear it?" Angel asked. He wasn't arguing, he was listening.

"Yeah, of course. I like performing. It's great when people like what you're doing...but all that other shit, I don't know." He named a band they both knew, old friends of theirs who had made it big. Everybody seemed to want something from them, money or to rub up against success. "It fucks with your head," Joe finished. "Sometimes it seems like more trouble than it's worth."

"Being broke all the time is trouble, too," Angel said. "Or working a job you hate. That fucks with your head." Angel was basically unemployable. He worked a series of jobs until he got fired or quit. He had been a dishwasher, a bicycle courier, even worked a security guard gig Joe had gotten him until they found him asleep on the job.

"Yeah," Joe said. "But I know how to deal with that."

"You worry too much. Look on the bright side. Maybe she won't be able to do a thing for us. Maybe she's not that good. Maybe we're not. We could find out that we suck." Well, that was the other thing Joe was worrying about. Believing in yourself against the odds was one thing. But if the odds were in your favor and nobody wanted to listen to you, what did that mean? What were you supposed to do then? Be a security guard for the rest of your life? But Angel had laughed, saying it.

"So how do you feel about it?" Joe asked.

"I just keep thinking of the looks on the faces of the people I owe money to, when I pay them back," he said. "Like my dad. I'd love to tell him we had a recording deal. I'd love to play Tucson."

So Angel was into it, too. Angel would be able to afford a baby, if Cynthia came through. Alice could quit working at the bar and grow large in peace. If she got large enough Joe might not even mind seeing her. Joe called Cynthia and told her to go for it, try to get them a tour, and they would see how it went.

Angel's euphoria about being a father started to wear off after a couple of weeks. He said Alice was moodier than shit, driving him crazy. He had just mentioned her getting an abortion, waiting until they were in a better place, which could be soon. Then she could have as many babies as she wanted. He would marry her now. Alice didn't care about getting married or having other babies. She broke all the glasses in the house, yelling and screaming that Angel could do what he wanted, she was having this baby and if he didn't like it, he could leave.

Another time, when they were out walking, she picked a fight with a drunk. The drunk was being obnoxious, acting as if they owed him something. When he asked them for money, Alice told him to go fuck himself. That started a real pissing match. They were yelling at each other on the street, Alice right up in the guy's face. He finally threw a punch at her; Alice got out of the way and then made fun of him for being too drunk to hit what he swung at. She was urging him to try again when Angel pushed the drunk up against a wall and told him that if he moved a muscle Angel was going to beat the crap out of him. The guy was terrified, which made Angel feel like shit. Later, when Angel asked Alice what the fuck she thought she was doing, she blew up at him. And cry? God, she'd gotten so good at crying she could do it in her sleep. She didn't even wake up.

Angel told these stories to Joe as if Alice was some kind of natural disaster, like a tidal wave or a volcano, something to watch with awe. The baby was due in mid-December.

Angel had told the other guys in the band about the baby. They didn't have much to say, less than Joe, though Stringer, usually such a jerk, tried to get into the idea for Angel's sake. Stringer sort of worshipped Angel for being his own self and not caring about any of the things Stringer thought were important, although Angel had never noticed it, he couldn't stand Stringer. Dan was funny about women in general and, since finding Alice with Joe, Alice in particular. Hearing the news, he didn't say congratulations, he said "good luck". He looked at Joe, hard. Joe looked back, harder, daring him to speak.

Joe worked as a security guard most nights they weren't playing. Angel was never home anyway; Joe figured Angel would move in with Alice as soon as they could afford a bigger place. He didn't ask Angel about it.

One night the guy Joe worked with at the warehouse asked him what had happened to his girlfriend, how come she never came around any more?

"How'd you know?"

"Your windows are always open. I could hear her talking when I took a break out front. How'd you get her past me?"

"Side door. When I was making my rounds." Joe wondered if he was about to lose his job.

"I used to sneak my girlfriend in. She got sick of me being gone nights. It was kind of romantic."

"What happened to her?" Joe asked. "I've never seen anybody here with you."

"We got married," the guy said. "Now she works the late shift at the post office. We meet at home, in the morning."

"How's that? Being married."

"That's fine. It's great. You thinking about it?"

"No," Joe said. And then, feeling like the guy deserved more of an answer than that, he said, "It didn't work out."

"That's tough," the guy said. He sounded like he knew how tough it was. Joe thought that this was something he would have shared with Angel, but here he was telling somebody he hardly knew what he hadn't told anybody.

He tried reading the last book in the trilogy. It wasn't the same. This book was sadder, anyway. It was about the meaning being sucked out of the world by a cowardly shit who couldn't face the end of things.

Joe knew about that on his own, he didn't need a book. He finished the song he'd played for Alice, finally finding the words for it. At first he tried it as a bitch-fucked-me-over song. He could drop a few hints, clue Angel in to what was really going on. For one long evening he was happy, working on his song, imagining the havoc he would wreak.

By the next day he was thinking the havoc wasn't worth it. Besides, the music was all wrong for that kind of song.

Sticking to the music he wrote a song about being alone, cut off forever from what you wanted. The lyrics were so obscure they could be referring to anything from lost love to seasonal affective disorder. He gave his song to the band.

They loved it. Angel said he wished he'd written it; he played a bass line that sneaked up on you, smashed you flat, and left you gasping. Dan abandoned his speed-metal roots and turned the song into a dirge, leaving Joe plenty of room to let the guitar wail its guts out. Stringer, who seemed to have never had one moment in his life when he doubted his inherent wonderfulness, sang the song like self-hatred was about to propel him off a bridge. It sounded great.

One night when they were performing Joe looked out into the crowd and saw Alice. He hadn't seen her in three weeks.

Her face was thinner than he remembered. She looked tired. Hearing Joe's new song, her expression changed. He didn't look at her anymore. He wished he'd written the bitch-fucked-me-over song instead.

She was hanging around after, waiting for Angel. Angel was talking to a couple of people backstage; he could be talking all night. Alice sat at a table out front, her eyes closed, wearing a too-big jacket and looking out of place.

She looked up when Joe pulled out a chair and sat down. She started to smile, she looked glad to see him. "Hey," she said. Like they were friends. That made him angrier than anything else she'd done.

He didn't smile back. He looked at her like she was a snake. He waited until she got it, until the smile on her face died and went to hell. Then he said, "You did a good job, Alice. You were major league."

She made her face blank. It took some effort, her mouth twitched. He wanted to shut up, and he wasn't about to.

"Angel thinks he's the father. Who is it really? Some guy you were fucking before you got around to me?" He didn't believe it, he said it to hurt her.

Alice shifted in her chair. He thought she was getting comfortable but she stood up and walked away. She was going to find Angel. Joe followed her. He grabbed her and strong-armed her into the bathroom, the one amenity they had backstage. Dan was coming out; he looked surprised when he saw them, but he didn't say anything. Joe shut the door on himself and Alice and held it shut with his foot. He shoved her up against the wall.

"Is it mine?"

"No," she said.

He pushed his face up close to hers. "So what was I for?" he hissed.

She didn't say. But she looked at him like she thought she was saying something.

"It was all the free rides, right?" he supplied. "While your car was in the shop. While Angel was gone."

She blinked fast. She stared at a spot beyond his ear.

"Look at me," he said.

She took a deep breath and looked at him. This time her eyes weren't trying to tell him anything. She stared at him like she was memorizing his face for a police line-up.

Say something, he thought. Do something. Fight back.

She covered her ears with her hands. She reminded him of a kid on a playground, about to get beat up and refusing to let it matter. Shutting him out.

He wanted to take hold of her wrists, pry her hands away from her ears, and make her listen. He could do it easy. It felt good knowing that, it was a rush. He could pay her back, even the score.

He let go of her.

She pushed past him, out of the bathroom. He locked the door after she'd left and stayed there.

By the time he came out, Alice was gone. Angel explained that she wasn't feeling good; Dan looked over at Joe and didn't say shit. They packed up. Stringer did his usual song and dance about how it wasn't on the way for him and he didn't play an instrument anyway, did they really need him to unload a mike and an amp. Joe said no. Angel looked disgusted behind Stringer's back.

Joe drove the van full of equipment home. Dan and Angel followed him in Dan's car and helped him unload. Nobody felt like sticking around. Joe could hardly wait until they left.

Alice couldn't make love to Angel anymore. At first it had been all right, then it wasn't. He wanted to keep using condoms. Alice didn't see the point since she was already pregnant, but Angel said it was a habit too old to break. Ever since he'd been a junkie he got tested for AIDS twice a year.

At first she thought it was funny that Angel had a phobia about something. Then she started worrying. There was a six-month lead time for AIDS testing, if she'd gotten it from Joe it was too soon to tell. Joe and Alice had always been careful, but so had Angel and Alice, and Alice was pregnant. She started to be terrified that she had AIDS; it was her punishment for being unfaithful. Sometimes she thought Angel knew deep down that she had betrayed him and that that was the real reason he insisted on safe sex. Then Angel started talking about abortion, like he thought she had no business having a child. She wondered if she did.

Alice went and got tested. She was HIV negative, for now anyway. Her terror retreated a step. But she never got around to telling Angel she'd been tested, and she didn't ask him if he had been.

Sometimes when he was on top of her, his hands on either side of her head, she was attacked by claustrophobia. He left her alone, puzzled and hurt. He thought it was because she was pregnant. It was only by pretending that Angel was on the verge of leaving her forever that she could make love to him at all.

It distressed her, not only for herself and Angel, but for what this feeling, or lack of feeling, would do to the baby. The baby wasn't growing in her head or her hand or somewhere removed from all this other stuff; she was right at the center of it, floating in Alice's belly that should have been warm and had turned cold.

One night a couple of weeks after Angel got home, Chuck picked her up in his cab after work to give her a ride home. Alice asked him to drive her to the warehouse. She swore him to secrecy first but Chuck was good that way, he wouldn't tell anybody, he didn't ask her was she out of her mind. Joe never locked the van; Alice could wait in the van for him to finish work. If she could just talk to him she would feel sane again, that was her fantasy. She knew it wouldn't happen like that and she still wanted to do it. But they couldn't find the van anywhere. Fate had saved her from making a total ass out of herself.

She wanted to cry. She swore instead. Chuck drove her around until she had calmed down. He asked questions, he shook his head and said "Um" sympathetically at her answers, he offered no advice.

Once, in the bathroom with the doors locked and Angel anyway gone for the night, gigging out of town and not due home for hours, she turned on the shower as hard as it would go and lay down under it. She turned her body this way and that under the warm stream of water, letting it strike her belly and the insides of her thighs. Lying on her back in the bottom of the tub, knees apart and hands cupped over her breasts, the hot water felt like a tongue licking her, a tongue or a finger, like Joe that first morning when they had used all the condoms and he said he would make her come anyway, don't be shy, Alice, don't be shy, he said, I want to see you…lying over her, two fingers inside and his thumb on top, he made her come. He came too, her hands on him, her tongue in his mouth. "You're so sweet," he said, but she denied it because what they were doing was not sweet, she didn't want any credit for it. "Sweet?" she said, making fun of him. He put his fingers in her mouth, "Taste," he said...she came now, in the shower, saying the wrong name. She knew she loved Angel. She felt like a crazy person, crazy and wicked.

Sitting in the bottom of the tub, watching the water rush down the drain, she told herself she was not going to think about Joe anymore, it was too dangerous.

Angel had written a new song; he talked about it but he wouldn't play it for her. She was no musician, she couldn't hear it without a band and know what it was going to sound like. He wanted her to hear it. She had a night off when he was playing in town.

She didn't have a good reason for refusing. She got to the club late so she wouldn't be right up front. The place was packed; Alice wondered if the possible-new-manager was there. Joe was there. Well of course he was. He didn't see her; she could look all she wanted. At first she didn't; then she did.

Angel's new song was still rough, but she could already hear how full of meat it was. Something about his dad, she knew that much, but Stringer was howling it, she couldn't make out all the words. The refrain rushed along, full of energy, Angel going free. He looked for her when the song finished; she gave him a thumbs up, smiling all over her face. He grinned back, breaking his stoneface onstage pose.

Later in the set the band played Joe's song. She'd heard bits and pieces of it before. It had been a sad song with just the music. With the words it was a killer. The lead guitar started it out, quiet as water dripping from the trees. By the second verse it was wailing like a lost soul, it was gut-wrenching. It was wrenching Alice's gut, anyway, unless she was finally getting morning sickness. Joe had spotted her. He looked away.

She didn't want to go backstage with Angel; too crowded, she said, too claustrophobic. Angel asked her how she could be claustrophobic and sleep with blankets pulled over her head? "It's different," she told him. "I'll wait for you out front."

"It might be awhile," he said.

"That's okay."

She was nearly asleep when Joe came over to where she was sitting. The sound of the chair being dragged back from the table woke her up. Seeing his hand on the chair back she realized that he was the one person bad enough to trust with her own evil self. She forgot that he'd looked away from her onstage. She was so relieved to see him she didn't notice the expression on his face.

Then he started talking, telling her what he thought of her. Whatever had prompted that song, it wasn't her. Or his feelings had changed drastically since then. Listening to him was like drowning in dark water. She tried to get away from him, and he pushed her into the backstage bathroom so he could tell her some more. So he could cover all the bases.

He wasn't the person to trust, unless she wanted to hate herself. He wasn't any help to her at all.

Alice needed the company of her own species. She had talked about starting a Ladies' Night back when Lynn was sick. She'd mentioned it to Carla at the studio in the distant past, a few weeks ago, when they were getting ready for the show.

Carla liked the idea. Matt wanted to know if he could come too, as an honorary lady.

"What about me?" said Chuck.

Behind their backs Carla shook her head at Alice, and the discussion of Ladies' Night was shelved.

Alice phoned Lynn and Carla now, to call an emergency Ladies' Night.

They met at Lynn's the next night. Carla borrowed Rick's car and picked Alice up; they all brought food and drink. Lynn had made a conception day cake for the baby, Carla made tabouleh and a tossed salad, and Alice splurged on salmon that they grilled in Lynn's backyard. Carla and Lynn had wine, which seemed more ladylike than tequila. Alice drank tonic water with limes and pretended it was gin. She didn't drink gin, so it tasted right.

They sat in the backyard under a cloud-swathed moon, their jackets on against the chill, talking. Lynn was in the first throes of mad passion and had to get it off her chest. Chris was a Taurus. That meant more to Lynn than to Alice or Carla. He was also funny, in a laid-back sort of way, smart in an intuitive way, and he knew how to listen. He had steady work as a carpenter. He loved to cook. They had the same taste in music and he was building some boxes for Lynn to make her collages in.

"Sounds like a relationship," Carla said.

"That word," Lynn said.

"We should make up different words," Alice said. "Boyfriend sounds so lame. Significant other doesn't work either. Significant other what?"

"Honeylamb. This here's my honeylamb," Carla said, introducing an invisible male with a wave of her hand. They laughed but Alice would never introduce anyone that way. Joe had called her honey. Her nemesis.

"Nemesis," she said. "This here's my nemesis."

Lynn and Carla thought that was funny. Alice did too, but she wasn't joking.

"So is Rick still your honeylamb?" Alice asked.

Carla leaned back in her chair like a gambler ready to put down her hand. "He's not my honeylamb or my nemesis," she said. "I give it two more weeks, max. Then it's back to the salt mines. How about you? Have you decided who's your honey-lamb and who's your nemesis?"

"Decided?" said Lynn, who still had not been told about Joe. Alice had kept her up to date on everything else, but she had never gotten around to telling her about Joe. It was easier to keep it secret from Angel if Lynn didn't know either, for some reason. "What do you mean *decided*?"

Carla placed a finger over her mouth. "Oop," she said.

"Uh," Alice said.

Lynn was looking back and forth between the two of them. "What?" she said. "What?"

"You tell her," Alice said to Carla. She felt funny talking about Joe. She had felt guilty about Joe ever since Angel came home, but after the scene in the club, she felt ashamed. It was humiliating to have felt so much for someone who thought you were dirt.

Carla looked at Alice.

"Tell me what?" said Lynn.

"Alice had a...what do you want to call it?" Carla asked.

"An experience," Alice said.

"An enlightening experience," Carla said, "with Joe."

At Lynn's face they started laughing. It was no laughing matter. Laughing felt good.

"After the show?" Lynn asked.

"God!" said Alice. "Are you guys all psychic or what?"

"You weren't very subtle," Carla said.

"It was that dance," Alice began, but Lynn cut her off.

"It was before that. I saw the way you guys were at the show. Something was going on. That's what I was trying to tell you."

"Well, I finally figured it out."

"I can't believe you didn't tell me," Lynn said.

"I didn't tell anybody at first," Alice said. "I didn't know how to say it. And you were with Chris."

Lynn looked at her. "So what?"

"I guessed," Carla said, trying to smooth things over. "And so did Matt."

"We should have had this Ladies' Night sooner, I can see that," Lynn said, getting up and going inside.

"Shit," Alice said. She didn't want to be hurting Lynn's feelings on top of everything else. Maybe she should go in and talk to her. But Lynn came back out with the cake and the bottle of wine.

"I couldn't think of a good way to bring it up," Alice said while Lynn cut huge pieces of cake. "Oh, by the way, I'm not only pregnant, I'm fucking Angel's best friend."

Lynn handed her cake. "There's twelve eggs and four sticks of butter in that sucker," she said. It was pound cake. "At least you told me you were pregnant."

Nobody said anything. Lynn sat down with her cake on her lap. She took a gulp of wine. "Will you tell me things from now on, please? This is worse than me not telling anybody I was sick."

"I felt like if I told anybody I would have to think about it like it was real, instead of it being like this dream I was having." If you had known, I wouldn't have been able to stop thinking about it, Alice thought at Lynn. She couldn't say it because Carla was here. She hoped Lynn would pick it up from her mind; she would tell her later anyway.

Lynn took a huge bite of cake. Carla was demolishing hers.

"So go ahead," said Lynn, her mouth full. "You have to think about it now. About this dream you had. Was it a good dream?"

"Yeah," Alice said. Then she heard how she sounded. Carla and Lynn had heard too. They laughed at her, spitting cake, really whooping it up. Alice watched them, being the sober person among drunkards.

"Come on," Carla said when they had settled down. "Give us the gory details. That's what Ladies' Night is for."

Alice felt a stirring of panic. Chuck was the only person who really knew the gory details. Driving her around the streets down by the warehouse, looking in vain for a parked van, he'd had a front row seat to the spectacle of Alice chewing her own entrails. But he'd never tell anyone except Baby. Her secret was safe with him.

"Yeah," Lynn said. "Last I heard, Joe was like a brother to you."

"Well he was," Alice said. "That's probably why—"

"Not like my brothers," Lynn said.

"I could tell him stuff," Alice said. "I even told him why I was jealous of him. We argued about life." There was a beech tree in Lynn's backyard. Alice stared at the leaves against the sky to help her organize her thoughts. "You know, how when you meet somebody you want to know, there's always a kind of infatuation? I thought that's all that was going on."

"For who?" Carla asked.

"Me," Alice said. "I thought he was just giving me a break, thinking I wasn't so bad for Angel after all."

Carla made a noise with her mouth full.

"What happened when he stopped being like a brother?" Lynn asked.

"Oh, you know," Alice said. She made a circle out of one hand and put the first two fingers of her other hand through it, in and out. "The usual." Carla snickered; Lynn smiled, but she was waiting for Alice to answer the question.

"You want to know something funny?" Alice said. "It didn't feel wrong. I mean, I knew I shouldn't do it, but it didn't feel like I shouldn't. Especially when no one else knew." Lynn was frowning at her, concentrating. Carla was concentrating on the cake. "That sounds terrible," Alice said.

"Not to me," Carla said, licking her forefinger to pick up crumbs. Alice was grateful to Carla for being such an odd duck.

Lynn was still frowning, but not in a judgmental way. She was trying to understand.

"Well, I wanted to do it," Alice said. "And I did. I'm not going to be sorry about that. Only...I guess I thought he'd stay friends with me. I mean, he practically promised me he wouldn't, but we were friends right up to the end. I didn't think he'd just turn around and hate my guts."

"I missed something," Carla said. "Why do you think he hates your guts?"

"I saw him. Night before last. He made it really clear."

They both stared at her. Now that it came down to it, she didn't know if she wanted to talk about it. But she'd started this. So she told them about seeing Joe at the club, how he'd said that she just fucked anybody who came her way. "He thinks I'm a schemer. He thinks I was using him for sex."

"Guys," Carla said. "It's okay for them to fuck around, that makes them studs. But if a woman does it, she's a bitch from hell."

Alice wished she'd thought of that. It would have given her something to say to Joe in the bathroom. She told them how he'd locked her in the bathroom so he could hate her in privacy.

"I was so glad to see him again and he was like...like he wanted to cut out my heart with a dull knife and gnaw on it."

"Uck," said Carla. "Alice, please, I'm still eating."

"Did he want to break it off?" Lynn asked.

"Well, no," Alice said. "Neither did I. But he knew why we had to. He seemed to know, back then."

Lynn looked confused. "He knew you were pregnant?"

"No. I couldn't tell him before I told Angel. And he wasn't around to tell, after."

Lynn opened her mouth to say something and changed her mind. Carla cut herself another piece of cake.

"Being pregnant wasn't why, anyway," Alice said. "Angel was why."

The cake smelled great but she had a lump in her throat. She sipped quinine water to make it go away. "And the worst thing is, I can't tell Angel. I told Joe I wouldn't. But I can't get, I can't...I still..."

"You can't finish a sentence," Carla said.

"You can't what?" said Lynn.

"I can't sleep with Angel. I mean, we try. But there's this big secret between us, like a wall. I feel like I'm not really there. Like I can't be there until he knows."

"Then you should tell him," Lynn said. She looked relieved that something was finally clear.

"But that's going to totally fuck up his friendship with Joe. It'll make Joe look like the bad guy."

"I don't know," Carla said. "Angel might hate you instead."

"That's heartening," Alice said.

"But you really love Angel, right?" asked Lynn.

"Of course I do," Alice said. "But I hate feeling like he's this sweet dummy. He's not dumb. And I hate feeling like the fallen woman. I want to tell him so he can just yell at me and get over it, so we can be close to each other again."

"You could sort of tell him," Carla said. "Tell him you slept with somebody and don't tell him who it was. Although why you're protecting Joe is a mystery to me."

"If I tell Angel that much he's going to want to know who it was," Alice said, ignoring the part about Joe.

"Make up someone," Carla said.

"Tell him it was Matt," Lynn said. "Tell him you talked Matt into being bi for a night."

That was so evil; Alice had never told anyone but Lynn that old fantasy of hers. And what if it got back to Matt!

The ladies were rolling in the aisles. Carla wheezed "Oh god," every time she looked at Alice's face. Lynn had to put her plate on the ground. She laughed into her knees.

"Ha ha," Alice said, which only made them worse. Oh well.

Carla got Alice home sometime after three. Alice drove, since she never got to anymore and missed it. After an evening of telling-all and decent food, Alice was euphoric. Her friends were still her friends, even though they knew the terrible truth about her. Most of it, anyway.

"It's such a weight off me," she told Carla as she drove home. "Now that I can tell Angel."

"You haven't told him yet," Carla pointed out.

"But I feel like I finally can. It's like seeing the light at the end of the tunnel."

"As long as you don't forget the tunnel."

When they turned into Alice's street she saw the van double-parked in front of the house.

"Oh shit," she said, hitting the brakes. "Shit fuck." She flattened herself on the seat. "It's Joe."

Carla hit the floor. She reached over to turn on the flashers so they wouldn't get rear-ended. "Why am I hiding?" she whispered loudly. The two of them giggled hysterically. Alice was terrified but she couldn't stop laughing. She pushed her face into the plastic upholstery to muffle the sound. She gritted her teeth.

They could hear Angel's voice, and the van door creak and slam. "I feel like I'm in high school," Carla said. The van sounded like it was pulling away. The front door to the house banged shut, Angel going inside. Carla peered over the top of the dashboard. "All clear," she said. Alice sat up, watching the taillights. Then the van turned a corner and was gone. Now that she was safe she felt disappointed.

"I wonder if he's got a girlfriend yet," she said.

"I doubt it," Carla said. "He wouldn't hate you so much if he did."

"I don't know. I think he could manage both."

"Maybe I should go after him. It would be a good cover for you and it would give me something to do besides the salt mines." She laughed. Alice didn't. "I'm kidding," Carla said. "After what you told me I wouldn't touch him with a ten-foot pole."

"Why not?" Alice said. "What's wrong with him?"

"Too crazy."

"Crazy and mean," Alice said. "A cold-hearted fucker."

Carla raised her eyebrows. "If you say so."

"God, you sounded just like Matt. What are we going to tell Matt and Chuck? If they find out we had a Ladies' Night without them?"

"We'll have an anarchy night to placate them," Carla said.

Angel was in the shower when Alice got in. She had brought the remainder of the quinine water home. She felt disgustingly sober so she drank it with ice, pretending the medicinal taste was alcohol. Angel came out of the bathroom as she was tilting the last of it into her mouth.

"Hey babe," he said. "Should you be drinking?"

Angel asking didn't make her angry the way anyone else asking would have. "It's okay. It's a virgin," she said.

"How was Ladies' Night?"

"Good," she said. "The ladies made a cake for me."

His hair was wet, black on his shoulders. He was still dark from his stay in Tucson; the towel wrapped around his waist made a nice outfit.

"You look fetching," she said.

He smiled, taking it for a come-on. His smile made her realize it was a come-on. She felt like she had before she saw the van, like she had already told him the entire unexpurgated truth, and he had accepted it. She felt like they could go the way they had been going. She stood up and went over to him.

"Let's be bad," she said.

Making love to Angel, Alice felt like she had finally made it to a safe harbor.

"About time," he said after. "You've been a million miles away."

"Well, I'm back," she said. Now was the time to tell him? But she fell asleep. For the next few days she put it off. They both worked nights; during the day he had rehearsals and she went to the studio, but when they were together it was like it had been at the beginning, only better. Angel was working on a couple of new songs, Alice was making charcoal drawings of landscapes with bits of people in them; faces in the trees, bodies in the clouds. Some of them worked. They made plans for finding a bigger place, buying a car with all the money Angel was going to make when the band had a manager. They could take their trip through the desert. Angel would rig up a hammock in the back seat for the baby. Alice thought: this is how we were meant to be together. Like people.

Angel finally had a chance to tell her, now that he had her attention, about his trip home. He had had only one major fight with his dad, and they had talked it out, staying up all night.

"What was the fight about?"

"I can't remember what started it," Angel said, "but it was the usual fight. About when am I going to get serious about life and do something real. I told him this is as real as it gets for me."

"And then what?"

"It took all night, but he finally said okay, good luck. He meant it, too, he wasn't bullshitting me."

The next day before he went to work she said she had something to tell him, it wouldn't take long.

"Good," he said. "I don't have long. Dan's picking me up soon."

"I slept with somebody else while you were gone," she said.

He looked at her like he thought she was making a joke. "What?" He was ready to laugh.

She had rehearsed it in her head; she had slept with the guy she had met months ago at the art opening, that time Angel had not come home for two days. What the fuck was his name? Brian. Only she decided he should be visiting from Minneapolis and gone home now—out of the picture, kaput, finished. No threat.

"You're serious," Angel said.

She was getting ready to lie through her teeth, but she was serious. She nodded.

"You slept with somebody else? As in 'had sex with'?"

Alice went into her spiel, how she'd met this guy from Minneapolis at an art show and they'd gotten into a "thing". He was an artist, they sort of went crazy, but she'd realized…Angel wasn't listening. He had gone pale.

"I don't want to hear about him," Angel said.

He wasn't reacting the way she'd thought he would. "I thought if you knew, it would be better."

"You thought you were pregnant then, you said."

"I thought I might be. But I wasn't really—"

"And you made it with some guy you met at an art opening? The first night you met him?"

"No. The next night," Alice said. As if that made a difference.

"I don't believe this," he said. "You were horny, you missed me, what?"

"I liked him," she said, feeling like a fool. It was hard to tell the "truth" about Brian. "A lot," she said.

"You liked him a lot. How much is a lot?"

"A whole lot," Alice said, feeling desperate.

"Enough to fuck him, anyway," Angel said. "Is he gone?"

"Gone?"

"You said he was from Minneapolis."

"He's gone," she said.

"So you didn't want to go to Minneapolis?"

"What? No, it's not like that. I never wanted to go anywhere with him. It was—animal attraction. That's all." But that was true about Brian, and she hadn't followed up on it. Now she sounded like an airhead, a horny airhead. "No, that's not true," she said. "But I want to be with you."

"You didn't want to leave town," he said.

"He didn't go anywhere," Alice said, changing stories in midstream. "He lives here now. He was from Minneapolis before."

"You just said he left."

"He left as far as I'm concerned. I haven't seen him, I don't want to see him, I want to be with you."

"Does he want to see you?"

Alice opened her mouth and shut it again.

"He found out you're pregnant and that was it, right? So you stuck with what you could get."

"No!" Alice said. She sat in her chair, watching Angel pace. "I didn't tell him I was pregnant," she said. "That's got nothing to do with it." Angel punched the wall. Alice jumped.

"Christ!" he said. "I guess all your friends know."

"What's that got to do with anything?" Alice wondered.

"Did he come to your art opening? Is that where you met him?"

Sticking to the truth as much as she could, Alice said yes. Mad as he was, Angel's instincts were working.

"So Joe knows, too," Angel said. "And he didn't tell me."

"No he doesn't."

"Joe's not stupid. He would notice something like that."

"Well he didn't," Alice said. "I'm not stupid either. I didn't do anything Joe would notice." Except for the something that he had noticed. But he surely hadn't noticed the invisible Brian.

"I've gotta go," Angel said.

"Now?"

"Dan's here," he said, and Alice realized a horn had honked in the street.

"But Angel—"

"Save it," he said. He slammed the door on his way out.

VIII.

Something had happened. Angel was drinking too much and Dan kept giving Joe measuring looks. They were talking, or Angel was drinking and Dan was talking. "Fucking bitch," Dan said, looking right at Joe.

"What's going on?" Joe said.

Angel turned around. "Did you know, man? Just tell me."

"Know what?"

"About that guy from Minneapolis."

What guy from Minneapolis? Stringer joined them just then. Joe had never thought he would be grateful to Stringer for anything. Life was full of surprises. Minneapolis?

"What the fuck, Angel?" Stringer said. "You get trashed, you'll miss your cues."

"Who gives a shit," Angel said.

"I do," said Stringer.

"Alice has been fucking around on him," Dan said, filled with righteous indignation.

"Tell the world," Angel said.

Stringer turned to Joe. "Can you sing his back-ups?" he asked.

Joe just looked at him. Stringer took that for assent. He said to Dan, "If you can hold yourself together we don't have to sound like a garage band. At least Cynthia's not around to hear us." This was his parting shot as he went off to find better company; himself, probably, since his wife Julie wasn't there tonight.

"What's wrong with sounding like a garage band?" Dan asked no one in particular.

"Is it his band?" Angel said, looking at Joe.

"He's a good singer. He's an asshole," Joe said. "What guy from Minneapolis?"

"She said she met him at her art opening. You were there. Who was it? I'm going to find him and kill him."

"I don't know," Joe said. "I didn't see her with anybody in particular. There were a lot of people there."

It was time to go on. Joe talked Angel into drinking water for one set. Joe sang Angel's back-up vocals; at least he knew his own songs. They made it through okay; the Saturday night crowd seemed to be drinking as much as Angel, so no one minded, if they even noticed.

Angel had slammed the door so hard Alice couldn't get it open until he was already out the downstairs door and gone. She called Lynn, who wasn't home. She kept calling. She damned-to-hell the clunker, which would have at least gotten her to the club where Angel was playing. At the thought of walking the five miles there to confront him, and Joe there too, she turned cowardly. She paced and said, "Oh Angel" and startled herself once by laughing out loud. Brian from Minneapolis! She was the worst liar on the planet.

She kept calling Lynn. Around midnight, Lynn picked up the phone.

"Thank god you're home."

"We just walked in," Lynn said.

"We, as in you and Chris?"

"Yeah, wait a minute." She muffled the phone and said something. "Okay. What? Did you tell him?"

Alice told Lynn the whole sorry tale. Lynn groaned in the right places.

"Do you want us to come and get you?"

"No, no that's all right. I'm not afraid of Angel. I'm just afraid he won't come home. And I'm too chicken to go the club and find him. That's what I should have done, huh."

"I don't know. Maybe he needs time to absorb it and be mad at you."

"I think I should go," Alice said. "I'm going now. Thanks, Lynn. Thank you for coming home and being a sane person."

"Alice wait, don't hang up. Do you want us to come get you and take you there?"

Alice was tempted, but why should Lynn and Chris have their evening spoiled? Besides, "I had enough trouble keeping a straight face with all the lies I was telling," she said. "I couldn't do it if you were there. I lie better when I'm surrounded by enemies."

"Maybe you should wait. Wouldn't it be better to talk to him alone? You don't want to talk to him with Joe standing there and those other guys. Angel won't be listening to you, he'll be thinking about what the guys think."

"You're right," said Alice. "But I hate this waiting. Okay, I'll wait. I'll wait by the door and by the phone."

Joe and Dan and Stringer did most of the breaking down and loading up of equipment, Stringer bitching the whole time because they didn't have roadies yet. Joe finally told him to stow it. He told him if he wanted roadies, he should go find them and pay them himself. Stringer shut up. Everyone looked sideways at Joe. Angel grinned to himself.

Joe drove the van and Dan followed him, bringing Angel. Joe, finally alone, had time to think. Alice had wanted to tell Angel, and she'd said she'd keep Joe out of it. That's what she'd done.

Stringer actually came too, in his own car, without any comments about how it was out of his way. He helped unload and then he left. "See you later," he said.

"You wish," Angel said, but after Stringer was out of earshot.

Angel wanted to go look for a party. Joe and Dan talked him out of it. Rooting around in the pantry for something to distract Angel, Dan found a bottle of tequila. Angel was laughing about Stringer.

"Did you see how he shut up when you told him to go find a roadie himself?" Angel said. "You should have done that months ago. Let the fucker know he's dispensable."

"We should look for another singer," Dan said.

"I don't know," Joe said. The message light was blinking on the answering machine. He pushed the playback button for something to do.

"Angel, if you're there please call me," Alice's voice said. She spoke in a rush and hung up. They all heard it.

Angel poured tequila into his glass. "Fuck," he said, and Joe remembered Alice, standing at the sink.

"Are you gonna call her?" Dan asked.

"I don't know...I don't think I will. I don't feel like talking to her."

Joe got himself a glass, poured tequila, sat.

"You call her," Angel said to Joe. "Tell her not to wait up."

"I'm not going to do that," Joe said.

Dan went to the phone and lifted the receiver. "I will," he said. "What's the number?"

Angel gave it to him. Alice must have picked up on the first ring. "Angel says not to wait up for him," Dan said, and hung up. That task done, he downed his tequila in one gulp. "I'm beat," he said. "I'm going home. You don't need a ride?" he asked Angel.

"Go ahead," Angel said.

With Dan gone, Joe felt like he should ask Angel about Alice. He didn't want to know. Angel told him anyway.

Joe had no trouble acting surprised and disbelieving. It sounded like such a cock and bull story, Brian from Minneapolis, that Joe wondered how Angel could have swallowed it. He was glad Angel believed it, and irritated with him for being so upset about nothing, about a fictitious guy. Which was nuts of Joe. He should be believing Angel right now, not knowing better. He knew he should keep his mouth shut, but he said what he was thinking.

"What about your old girlfriend? Weren't you fucking her?"

Angel looked at him. "Yeah, I was. But it didn't get in the way of me and Alice. It didn't have anything to do with her. I didn't need to *tell* her about it."

"You're pissed off because she told you?"

"No, man," Angel said, "I'm pissed off because she *did* it. She was pregnant for shit's sake! And she went out and—" He made a fist and hit the kitchen table. The glasses jumped. Joe didn't. "I can't believe she would do this. It's like she turned into somebody else while I was gone. She's been so fucking weird, and just when we get it straight she dumps this on me. Like it's *nothing*. Like she's surprised I think it's anything."

Joe felt a pain somewhere in his body, he didn't want to figure out where. He drank tequila. He lit a cigarette.

"She's lying," Angel said, out of nowhere. Of course she was. What she hadn't told him was worse. What would Joe say if he didn't know that?

"What do you mean? You think she made the whole thing up to make you jealous?" That sounded good, a little nuts but exactly right. Angel wasn't even listening.

"She could be meeting him somewhere. She was home later than me the other night, almost four in the morning. Ladies' Night, she said, no men allowed, not even Matt. She came home in a real good mood, for once."

Joe went cold. Was there really a guy from Minneapolis? He thought he knew her, but Angel had thought that, too. Had everything he'd accused her of been true? Then he shook himself, holding onto what he did know.

"But why would she tell you about it if she was still seeing him? Why would she tip you off? It doesn't make sense."

"I don't know," Angel said. "I can't think straight. It's like a bad joke." He stared at his hands on the table. "I get the feeling..."

"What?" Joe asked, because that was in line with who he was pretending to be. A friend would ask.

Angel shook his head, never mind. He reached out for the glass, picked it up, and held it in his hand like he was trying to decide whether or not to drink it.

"When did you start drinking tequila?" he asked.

Joe looked at the tequila. When Alice was here. Was that okay to say? Dan might have told Angel already about finding Alice here. And that time had been innocent enough. "When Alice was here," he said.

Angel looked at him.

"The night her car broke down," Joe said. "I towed it. Didn't she tell you?"

"No," Angel said, watching him, being the Indian tracker, reading fleeing footprints and murder in a bent blade of grass, a chipped stone.

"It was the same night you told her you weren't coming back for the show. I gave her a drink and had to listen to her crying over that."

"She cried in front of you?"

"After accusing me of trying to keep you for myself," Joe said, skating near the edge because Angel was getting too close, only the edge would do.

"She said that?" The tight watchfulness left Angel's face and he half-laughed. "What did you say?"

"I don't remember," Joe said, like why would he remember what he'd said to a crazy person. "I let her sleep in your bed. That calmed her down." He sounded a little bitchy, like a worn-out nursemaid. He lit a cigarette off the butt of his other one. His hands were perfectly steady.

Angel drank off the rest of his tequila. Joe wished Angel would stop drinking and go to bed. Then Joe could go to bed. He could pull the covers over his head. Alice wanted to wake up in a different world; Joe wanted to wake up a different person.

With no change in his face Angel said, "It was you, wasn't it."

He knew. Joe hadn't been good enough. But he looked at Angel like he didn't understand what Angel meant. Then he let light dawn. "What was me," he said, cold and hard. Like he didn't appreciate what Angel was thinking. Like Angel better watch his step.

"There's no Brian from Minneapolis. That was made-up shit. Alice was fucking you." Angel lifted his chin, a sharp little gesture, the fox at the henhouse door. "Go ahead. Say it."

Adrenalin was making Joe dizzy; he kept sitting there, like he'd been turned to stone.

"Say it," Angel repeated. His eyes had gone flat.

"It was me," Joe said.

Angel smiled, as though he were pleased. Then he hurled the bottle at Joe's head.

Joe ducked; the bottle hit him on the tip of his shoulder and popped up into the air, baptizing him with tequila. Before it hit the floor Angel was on top of him. He had Joe by the hair, yanking his head back, ready to punch him.

Joe didn't wait for the punch; he threw himself backwards, in the direction Angel was pulling him, grabbing for Angel's wrists. They rolled on the floor. Angel came out on top, his hands around Joe's throat, his hair dragging across Joe's face. "You couldn't stand for me to have anything," Angel was yelling, something like that. Joe was concentrating on not getting killed. He couldn't break Angel's elbow because then Angel couldn't play bass. He dug his thumbs into the bones on Angel's wrists. Angel yelled and let go. Joe lay still, trying to breathe. Angel got off of him slowly, like an old man.

Joe got up, too. His throat felt like hell. His cheekbone ached. He guessed Angel had punched him after all. He hadn't even felt it. They faced each other, breathing hard.

"My friend," Angel said. His face was wet and he didn't try to hide it. He stared his betrayer in the eye. Joe was the one who couldn't look.

The tequila bottle hadn't broken. What a miracle. "I tried to get her to leave you," Joe said. "She dumped me."

"Oh that makes it okay."

"No."

"Keep away from her," Angel said, with no particular inflection.

"She doesn't want me," Joe said. "She wants you."

"Just keep the fuck away."

Alice came awake, Angel's pillow still clutched in her arms. A candle was burning on the windowsill and Angel was sitting on the floor, staring out the window. Behind him the sky was getting light. How long had he been there?

She sat up slowly. He turned his head to look at her. The pillow slid onto the floor. Angel leaned over, picked it up by one corner and tossed it back on the bed. They both looked at it like it was a lost rune they had to decipher. Failing, they looked at each other.

"I have to go to the bathroom," Alice said. In the bathroom she brushed her teeth and threw water on her face. She pulled on some leggings and a sweater, feeling the need for armor. When she came back Angel hadn't moved. She sat down next to him on the floor.

"Why'd you do it?" he said.

She looked at his hands. The knuckles of his right hand were bruised.

"What happened to your hand?" Then she remembered he'd punched the wall before he left last night.

He looked at his hand, flexed the fingers. "I hit him," he said.

"Hit who?" Brian from Minneapolis didn't even exist. Did Angel find someone named Brian and punch him?

"Joe," Angel said.

Joe. That made sense.

No it didn't. Joe wouldn't tell Angel, and Alice hadn't. Unless she talked in her sleep.

"You're a lousy liar," Angel said. "Joe's a great liar, but I know him."

She had been right. Angel was no dummy, he'd found the trail and followed it.

She wasn't really awake. Half-asleep, in a room turned into a cave of jumping shadows by candlelight, smelling the alcohol on Angel and his own scent underneath that, she asked the question that had been there all along.

"How about you?" she said. "Are you a good liar?" An expression ran across his face, gone too fast to read. "How many women have you slept with since you met me?" she asked.

"He told you," Angel said, bitter.

She picked at a loose thread in the rug. "You did," she said. "Just now." She pushed the thread back down into the weave. It was an old faded Oriental, left in the apartment by the person before her. She'd always liked this rug, wished it weren't so worn. "How many?"

"I don't know," Angel said. "I don't keep track. It's not that important."

More than three, she thought. "In Tucson?"

He didn't say anything. She looked at him and he moved his chin down, yes.

"Your old girlfriend," she said. Alice had blanked on the woman's name; what she remembered was that Angel's old girlfriend was the reason he had left Tucson, or one of the reasons.

"Yeah," he said. Like it was just a simple fact.

Alice couldn't sit there anymore. She got up and opened the window, fished around behind her art books and pulled out the pack of cigarettes she'd tried to give Joe. She lit one on the candle, taking smoke into her mouth, no further, and blowing it out the window. It tasted like shit.

Angel was looking at her like she was a real person again, someone who might do anything.

"She didn't want to leave town?" Alice said. "She wanted to stay in Tucson?"

Angel reached for the pack of cigarettes. She handed them to him, thinking he wanted one. She hadn't let him smoke in the house since he'd been home. He held the pack in his hand and looked at it. Joe's brand, not Angel's.

"It didn't come up," Angel said.

Alice took another drag. Why had she never noticed how smoking diffused pain, made it bearable?

"I thought you knew," he said.

"Maybe I did," she said, stubbing out the cigarette on the sill and flipping it out the window. "Not really," she said. The baby couldn't smoke, that's all there was to it.

"It's different for me," he said.

"Oh it always is."

"It is. That's who I am. I always have other women. You came first." She noticed the past tense. She wanted to tear her hair and howl. Before she did that she wanted to kill him.

"Until you find somebody else who's first," she said. "And then it's goodbye Alice, it's been fun."

"That's just jealousy talking," he said. "Don't be stupid."

It was so unfair she sputtered. "You're the one that hit Joe. Don't talk to me about jealousy."

"Mine makes sense," he said, grim.

"Give me a break."

"You couldn't stand for me to touch you when I got home. You made me feel like a rapist. I *never* did that to you." He was outright angry, not sitting on it anymore. That was good; she was furious.

"No, you weaseled around on me, sticking it to every babe who looked like a good time. I was just at the head of the line."

"I said I'd marry you."

"People get married all the time, it doesn't mean shit," Alice said. She meant her mother.

"It would have to me," he said, so quiet it stopped her in her tracks. She hadn't thought about him meaning it; she'd thought he was offering marriage as a consolation prize, no baby, but a ring. If he'd really meant it, it must have hurt, the way she'd said no. He must have felt like she didn't take him seriously.

She wanted to say she was sorry, but it sounded too dumb. Besides, he had slept with other women, and he wasn't sorry at all.

"Would you have stopped fooling around?" she asked, trying to find her way back to solid ground.

He sighed. "You're not going to change me, Alice. It's something I do. I don't do it to hurt you. It's got nothing to do with you and me."

"Then what does it have to do with?"

"It's friendly, it's fun. That's all."

Fun! "Well I did something 'friendly' too, and you freaked out. And I'm not saying, 'it's who I am, you have to accept it.' I said, it's over."

"I've been with women who fooled around," Angel said. "Women who were like that, like me. You're not. If you did it, it meant something."

"It did mean something. If you're going to do it, it ought to mean something. I counted," she said. "One." She watched that sink in.

"So what did it mean?" He looked awful, asking that.

"I don't know."

He gave her a look, you can do better than that.

"I don't," she said. "If I knew, I'd tell you."

"Sure you would. Like you told me before. Brian from Minneapolis."

"I didn't..." she said, and stopped. What could she say? I didn't want to lie, it's all Joe's fault?

Angel watched her trying to find an answer. He looked like he was daring her to. Take your time, his face said. Make it good. But underneath all that she sensed a kind of hope. He wanted her to have an answer, that's what he was waiting for. For a moment she couldn't look at him.

"God*dam*mit, Alice," he exploded. "Why *him*? Of all the fucking guys in the fucking world—Why'd you have to do that to me?"

"It just happened," she said, too fast. "It didn't have anything to do with you." Then she heard herself using Angel's reasoning. She wanted to tell him the truth. It did have something to do with Angel. But she couldn't tell him about the Senoi and their dreams. Not anymore she couldn't. If she'd told him the truth as soon as he got home...but she hadn't. And now the truth had changed, because she'd lied to him.

"Come on, Alice, you're the one who's so moral, I'm just dicking around, right? You gotta know why."

"I don't," she said again, knowing that wasn't enough.

"Was it a one-night stand? This thing that 'just happened'. Or more than that?"

"Angel—"

"Or don't you know that, either?"

"More," she said, faint.

"But you don't know why you did it."

"No."

"Well god, I hope he was good."

Alice burst out laughing. Angel watched her. That was even funnier. She laughed so hard her belly ached. She wound down. Angel hadn't moved.

"What was it," he said, with the ghost of a sneer. "You fell in love?"

"Oh shut up, Angel," she said, exhausted.

He raised his eyebrows.

"I mean it," she said. "Stop badgering me. If what you do is okay then what I do is okay."

She put her elbows on her knees and leaned her forehead on her hands, staring at the rug. She thought about sitting at Joe's kitchen table, how she'd been crying over Angel and Joe had known, the whole time, about Angel running around on her. She hadn't acted any differently than Angel, though, in the end. But she wasn't calling it love. Lust was more like it, blind lust. And she'd been blind twice. Blind in both eyes.

"So what I do is okay?" Angel said. "I guess it has to be, doesn't it."

All those times he hadn't come home because he was "drinking" she'd worried that there was more to it and chided herself for being too possessive, too anxious, too suspicious to accept him as he was, to accept a relationship that was flawed, but basically good. She should have trusted her instincts instead of calling them names.

She peered at him slantwise through her fingers. He was a stranger. She had been in love with him all this time and he wasn't real. It made her feel sick. "No," she said. "It's not okay."

She headed for the bathroom. Leaning her elbows on the sink, she turned on the tap and held her hands under the water. If she concentrated on the water, she felt better.

Angel came around behind her. He put his hands on either side of her head and moved her hair away from her face, being nurse to her sick person. All the muscles in her face pulled hard into a grimace. He was going to make her cry. She rested her forehead on her wet hands and didn't cry. He reached around her and turned off the water.

"Now you know how I feel," he said.

She pushed up on the sink and looked at him in the mirror. Backwards, Angel had an eyebrow that slanted upwards in a way she'd never noticed before. It made him look pleased and malicious.

"You shit," she said.

She turned around. She checked his face for the upslanting eyebrow; it was still there, but it looked different, the only sign of life in a frozen landscape. She had hurt him, that's why he looked like that.

She could smell the alcohol on him, stronger now he was close. She wasn't afraid, she could break his foot, Joe had taught her how…

Angel kissed her, first on one side of her face, then on the other. It was soft and nice, all over her cheek and on her eyelid and then her ear. He wouldn't kiss her mouth. He kept his hands on her shoulders, holding her away from him.

"Angel," she said. Please come back, she meant, this one last time. He kissed her neck, he said something she didn't hear. She put her wet hands on his face, turned his head toward her, and kissed his mouth.

He let go of her shoulders, ran his hands down her back, and pulled her in.

"Last dance," he said. She heard that. She was shivering all over. In spite of everything. Because of everything. It felt like dying, like coming undone, like she shouldn't. But she wanted to. This once, it would be real.

"Not here," she said. Angel never cared where he was, the bathroom floor would suit him as well as anywhere.

"Not here," he agreed.

They made it to the bed, fumbling for the condoms on the bookshelf, never mind she was pregnant, they'd both been fucking other people, they'd both been lying. They held on to each other like they never wanted to let go, like a cruel fate was driving them apart, and not themselves.

Afterwards Alice listened to Angel breathing. For once she had nothing to say. She was trying to soak him in through her skin. A strand of his hair lay across her mouth; she tasted it with her tongue. She heard her neighbor across the hall, going out. It was morning; it was raining. She was glad of the rain; it blurred all the sharp edges. She propped herself up on one elbow to look at Angel. She wanted to fix him in her memory.

He put up his hand and touched her mouth. All at once she did have something to say. She'd better say it now or it would never get said. Because he wasn't who she'd thought he was and she would hate him tomorrow. She would have to.

"Anyway," she said, because right now none of that mattered, "I love you."

He tapped her mouth with his fingertip, as if he could sense the truth that way. "That's a start," he said. A start for what? This was the end, wasn't it? She couldn't read his face.

"But Angel, I can't deal with you running around with other women. I wish I could, I wish I was—but I can't."

"I know."

He'd already said she wasn't going to change him. Were they saying goodbye? She stared at him hard, trying to figure it out.

"Anything else?" he asked.

"No," she said, surprised. What else could there be? "You're hetero, right?"

Angel actually laughed, although she had been serious. "So far," he said. "But I've got one for you." She had a moment of hope. Did he mean—?

She waited to see what he meant.

"I don't want you even thinking about Joe." He was watching her intently, half-ashamed because it sounded so nuts, but sticking to it. "I want you to forget him," he said, "like he never existed."

That was no problem. Since the last time she had seen Joe she couldn't stand thinking about him. The things he'd said to her, like she was somebody else—and that was not who she was.

"Okay," she said. It was Angel's turn to look surprised.

"You mean it?" he said.

"Yeah I mean it. Do you mean it?"

"Yeah," he said. "I do. If it's the only way, then I do. I want to."

She was close to tears, but she held onto them. He shook his head at her. "You're supposed to be happy," he said.

"I am," she said. "It's the hormones."

"Well bring those hormones here."

IX.

Joe's cheekbone and the outer edge of his eye turned purple. He looked like he'd been given a black eye by someone with a bad aim.

The guys next door asked him about it. They'd probably heard the fight with Angel, and they would know soon enough that Angel had moved out.

"I walked into a wall," Joe said.

By the time the next gig rolled around, Joe's eye had turned yellow and green.

"What happened to you?" Dan asked.

"Angel," Joe said.

"Figures," Dan said, and went back to setting up his drum set.

Angel took a long look at Joe's black eye. He didn't look pleased or remorseful, just interested. Stringer didn't ask. Joe thought he didn't notice until, between sets, he made a point of telling Joe what a shit he was. So someone had given him the news.

Joe would take that from Angel. He told Stringer to go fuck himself.

The other guys in the band didn't have a lot to say to Joe for awhile. At least Dan still took his cues from Joe. Angel ignored him, and Stringer followed Angel. Joe thought they should change their name to Two Heads.

Now that the band was on the verge of breaking up, they had more gigs than ever. They had a following. People requested songs. One of the songs they wanted to hear was the one Joe had written about Alice. Stringer didn't want to do it, but Angel did. Joe had a feeling it was a comfort to Angel, playing a song about Joe's misery.

One night Cynthia came to hear them, unannounced. She asked Joe, in the others' hearing, if the band was getting tired from playing so much. After that, Stringer followed Joe's cues.

At night when he wasn't playing or doing the warehouse Joe went to clubs to hear what other bands were doing, catch up on the rumors and gossip, make himself visible. He hadn't done that in too long. He forced himself to, going through the motions.

He paid special attention to the singers. Stringer annoyed him more than usual. Jeannie was a good singer, and a friend of Joe's besides, but she was already in a band. They weren't very tight yet, but the energy was good. Joe envied them.

"I heard you guys were breaking up," Jeannie said. Joe remembered Jeannie and Angel had had a thing for awhile, a few years back.

"Where'd you hear that?"

"I don't remember," she said. "Around."

"Did you hear why?"

"Something about you and Angel having a fight." She made a face over the unbelievable things people said. "I guess it was you and Stringer."

Joe hated people knowing his business. But Jeannie was okay; if he told her it wouldn't go any farther. He still didn't want to. She was staring at him like she'd figured out it was him and Angel who were fighting.

"The band's not breaking up," Joe said. "Not yet, anyway. Spread the rumor that we're not, okay?"

"Should I also spread the rumor that you're looking for a singer?"

He guessed he hadn't been circumspect enough. "No," he said.

She looked like she had a couple of questions to ask, but she didn't ask them.

After a couple of weeks Dan started talking to Joe again. He sat down and had a beer with him during a break one night. Joe tried not to look surprised.

"Stringer wanted to kick you out of the band," Dan said, straight to the point as usual.

Joe sipped beer, wondering if they'd given Dan the job of telling him they had found another lead guitar player.

"Angel didn't go for it," Dan said.

"How about you?"

"Shit no," Dan said. "But Angel, you know. It was always your guys' band. Stringer knows that, but he's such a stupid fuck he thinks that's going to change because Angel thinks you're pond scum."

"Thanks for telling me," Joe said. Dan frowned at the sarcasm.

"I didn't tell Angel anything," Dan said. "About you and her."

"You didn't have to," Joe said. "He figured it out on his own."

"Yeah, well," Dan said. He fiddled with a matchbook, rolling it up tight and then unrolling it. "Women are poison," he said. Dan said this so often it had become a joke. For a while women had not been poison. Joe had noticed Dan mooning around Cynthia—for Dan, mooning around meant he listened when she spoke and focused on her face instead of her "lungs"—but Cynthia didn't respond to this exceptional treatment. So women were poison once more.

"This whole fuck-up with you and Angel would never have happened if she hadn't been a dick-chaser."

"Alice didn't chase me," Joe said. "I chased her."

"I'll bet she didn't put up much of a fight." Joe couldn't argue with that. "Sometimes I think a blow-up toy would be just as good," Dan said. "A lot less trouble, that's for sure." He was trying to get Joe to laugh.

Joe had always wondered how Dan found so many women, thinking like he did. "How come you're not gay?" he asked, curious.

"Who, me?" Dan looked startled. "You ever go with a guy?" he asked, taking a long time to light a cigarette from a limp, half-unrolled match.

"Once."

"Angel," Dan said, as if he'd known all along and wasn't shocked.

"Before I knew Angel."

"What happened?"

Joe shrugged. "It didn't work like that for me. We stayed friends."

"Not like with a woman," Dan said, moving onto safer ground.

Joe didn't ask him if he'd ever tried a man. He figured he'd tested Dan's goodwill enough for one night.

He was glad Dan had decided to talk to him, but in a way it made him feel worse. The person who really knew what to say to him when he hit rock bottom wasn't speaking to him anymore. Trying to cheer him up, Dan depressed the hell out of Joe.

Joe got Alice's print in the mail. It came sandwiched between two pieces of cardboard, wrapped in brown paper, no return address. At first he thought it was a joke. Who would send him cardboard? Then the print slithered out and fell on the table onto a pile of bills and junk mail, face up.

After that disaster at the club, he didn't know why she'd sent it. He wondered if she knew why she'd sent it. There was no note, nothing written on it anywhere except his name and address on the brown paper. He could tear it up. Then he wouldn't have to think about it. Picking the print up by a corner, he put it in a drawer, and then he shut the drawer. He thought about taking her underwear out of the lefthand inside pocket of his biker jacket and storing that in the drawer too. He left it where it was.

He watched Angel that night. Did Angel know she'd sent the print? Joe didn't think so.

Angel didn't look so hot. Alice was probably making his life hell. She'd sucker-punched Joe, that's all. He didn't have to live with it. He'd escaped by the skin of his teeth, he was lucky. She never came to gigs anymore; at least he didn't have to see them together.

Joe started going to the library. He needed something to do at home besides stare at Angel's stripped bed and write songs he was never going to let anyone hear. At the library he looked through the science fiction section for books by the same author Alice had read to him. He found one that looked interesting, about a man whose dreams came true. It sounded like a good thing, but it sucked. Worrying about this guy in the book, Joe could forget his own troubles for awhile.

Alice and Angel had their starting place; everything was finally clear. And Angel had moved in with her, like she'd wanted. Except not like she'd wanted.

Dan had helped Angel bring over some cardboard boxes of clothes and tapes, but Angel wouldn't unpack them. They sat on the floor and got used as an extra set of dresser drawers. Alice was glad when he finally opened them; closed, they felt like a constant reminder of her betrayal.

Angel didn't go to parties anymore; Alice suspected there weren't any, as far as the band was concerned, but that wasn't Angel's fault. She was supposed to be taking him at his word, like he was supposed to be taking her at her word.

Alice kept her part of the bargain. To finish old business she mailed Joe the print he had liked. She had said she would give it to him and she wanted him to have it. He would probably throw it away.

After that she didn't think about Joe except when Angel brought him up, which he did regularly. At first it was done too casually, Angel watching her sideways. "I gave Joe a black eye," was his first installment. Alice had nothing to say to that.

"Aren't you worried about him?"

"Did you damage his eye?"

"Just his looks," Angel said.

"Then I'm not worried about him," she said. Angel let the subject drop.

One night Angel went to a band meeting at Stringer's house. Stringer had been mysterious about it; he said it was important but he wouldn't say why.

Angel told Alice the whole thing when he came home. Julie had been there, saying hello and then disappearing into another room, probably to eavesdrop. Angel thought the two of them had cooked it up between them, this plan to kick Joe out of the band.

"Stringer was trying to kick Joe out?" Alice asked. She figured she could say the name, since Angel had brought it up and they couldn't have the conversation otherwise. "But he can't, can he? And why does he want to?"

"Because the *feeling* in the band is so bad. And that's Joe's fault, right? Basically, he said that Joe's such a treacherous shit, who knows what he'll do next? It didn't make a lot of sense. He must have thought I was such a wreck he could flatter me by badmouthing Joe and then take over himself.

"Dan freaked. He told Stringer the only reason he was still in the band was because Joe didn't want to kick him out."

"Is that true?" Gossiping about the band was so much like old times with Angel she felt safe asking.

"Oh it's true all right. Stringer sure didn't want to hear it. He never asked me if it was true. Dan told him we could find a singer as good as him in a couple weeks, but we could never replace Joe. Just ask Cynthia, Dan says, because Cynthia is like god to Stringer. 'Ask Cynthia how long she'd work for us without Joe.' And Dan's right, Cynthia pretty much talks to Joe, nobody else. Joe found her, for chrissake."

"What were you doing all this time?"

"Sitting there watching. Keeping my mouth shut and trying to figure out what was going on." Being Joe, Alice thought, since Joe couldn't be there himself. "Then Dan says to me, 'It's your guys' band, not his. What do you say?' So I said getting rid of Joe was a poor idea, and if I could deal with him, I didn't see why anybody else should give a fuck." Angel started to laugh. "You should have seen Stringer's face. Like I'd stepped on his sand castle. Then Dan called Stringer a dumb cunt, and Stringer went berserk. He tried to throw Dan out of the house for being such a sexist jerk or something. He kept yanking on his arm but he couldn't move him an inch, and then Dan gave him this little tap on the chest and sent him flying. Then Julie comes charging out of the other room to save Stringer, and I had to get between her and Dan and talk them both down. I had to keep a straight face through the whole thing." He laughed again, in pure enjoyment. "What a scene."

Angel's reaction gave Alice hope. Maybe they would make it through this mess. She was glad Angel hadn't tried to kick Joe out of the band, or even thought of it, apparently. If Cynthia got them the tour Angel kept talking about, he would have a real chance to "deal" with Joe. Three weeks on the road together: she wondered if they would become friends again. If they did it would be tricky for her, but at least she wouldn't have to feel like she had ruined a lifelong friendship.

But that was one of the good times. Alice and Angel, who had been together for almost six months without fighting, couldn't get through a week anymore without three or four skirmishes and one major uproar. They made up in bed, but out of bed they were wary and raw with each other. Starting over didn't mean they had nothing to fight about, just the opposite. They didn't fight about other women or Joe, but they fought about everything else they'd let go by. It was almost a relief to go to work and spend a few hours fighting with Aziz instead of Angel.

"Every time you went to those parties," Alice might say, heralding another round. This was her main problem with Angel, that he had wanted to spend so much time away from her. Why had he needed to be gone for days on end when he wasn't even gigging?

"Well I'm not doing anything but being with you, now," he would say, and she would tell him he was acting bored and dragged down, why didn't he go out and find something to do.

Angel had his own bones to pick. Alice made some innocuous comment about the baby one day and started a whole new war.

"Yeah, it's always been your baby," Angel said.

"What does that mean?" They had taken a walk, as much to escape the apartment, which was now definitely too small, as for the exercise. They ended up at the playground, on the swings, Angel smoking and Alice wishing she could.

Angel blew smoke like he was spitting it into the air. "You decided what to do on your own," he said. "You didn't even ask me what I thought about it."

"I'm the one who's going to have to do it," Alice said. "You aren't."

"Right," he said. "It doesn't concern me at all. I was just the sperm donor, now I can go to hell." He swung hard in the swing, getting away from her without leaving.

"But Angel," she said, watching him sail up and back, "part of why I wanted to have this baby is because it's yours." He wasn't impressed. "What was I supposed to do," she said, exasperated, "ask you if it was okay?"

He let the swing slow down to make his point. "Why's it got to be one way or the other? Why couldn't we be in it together? You could at least let me have feelings about it; you could have listened instead of breaking glasses and yelling at me."

"No I couldn't," she said. "I've got my own feelings and they're hard enough to deal with. I can't deal with yours too."

"Who's asking you to deal with them? I just want to be able to have them. It's like if I'm not this totally strong, totally together person, I'm going to wimp out on you like your father did."

Was that true? It sounded true.

"Okay," she said. "What are you feeling?"

Angel didn't answer right away. Alice was patient, or pretended to be. She didn't want to have to listen to him talk about her getting an abortion. It wasn't too late.

"Like I don't want to turn into my dad," he said.

She almost laughed with relief. Angel was serious though.

"Not very likely," she said instead.

"Why not? You started acting like your mother as soon as you got pregnant."

He meant Joe. He wasn't saying it because he wanted to talk about it, though. He wanted her to listen. He was watching her, waiting for her to give him her attention.

"How are you going to turn into your father?" Does he say mean things that are true when you least expect it? "Wanting the baby to be like you instead of having her own thoughts?"

Angel relaxed a little. "That's one way," he admitted. "What if the kid wants to be Catholic? Or gets into disco oldies?"

"This child doesn't have any disco genes. You don't have to worry about that," she said.

"And then there's money," Angel said. "I worry about money."

"But you're making money now," Alice said. "Or you're going to."

"Who knows how long that will last? And you don't make shit."

"A breastfed baby doesn't cost that much," Alice said, stung. It was true, she didn't make enough to support a wreck of a car. She'd had to scrape to get the money to have it towed to the boneyard. How was she going to support a baby?

"You can't breastfeed until the kid can go out and work to feed itself," Angel said. "I never cared about money for myself, but when I think about a kid…maybe that's how my dad got like that. All us kids, and our broken arms and new shoes."

Alice swung slowly.

"I think the money will show itself, I think we'll find it," she said.

"Show itself?"

"Yeah."

"Jesus, Alice, you sound like an old hippie. Where are we going to 'find' it?"

"Heroin's not cheap," she shot back. "You found the money to do that, because you wanted to. How'd you manage?"

He looked at her. "I sold it to other people for more than it was worth," he said. "I cut it."

She had never thought about the logistics of that part of Angel's past, about Angel dealing heroin. She didn't want to think about it now.

"The point is," she said, "you find the money, when you want something badly enough."

"So if I don't find the money for a baby, it's because I don't want to? That's nice and simple—make it my fault. But it was your idea to have a baby. What were you going to do for money if I said, no thanks Alice, I'm outta here?"

"I don't know. I hadn't figured it out yet," she said. "I'll think of something now, since it's my idea and you're doing me such a big favor by sticking around."

"That's not what I said. You won't let me say anything—"

"Well what are you saying? You keep saying the same thing, you don't want to, you don't want to—"

"Oh forget it. I can't say a fucking thing to you."

"You feel trapped. That's what you're saying. I trapped you. And since I already turned into my mother, I'll probably take off as soon as I have the kid, and you'll be stuck with a kid you don't even want."

Angel started swinging again, his face calm and blank. It was infuriating. He was much better at this kind of fight than she was. She thought it was because he had grown up surrounded by people to fight with.

"At least you won't be able to take off with Joe," he said. She stuck out her tongue at his back when he was on an upswing.

"He's going out with Cynthia now, did I tell you?" Angel asked.

"Gee I don't think so," she said, sarcastic. "And you're usually so good at keeping me up-to-date." He kept swinging. "What am I supposed to do now? Cry?"

"Go ahead," he said.

She watched him swing, and then she got up and walked away. She wanted to drag him out of the swing, knock him down, and punch him until he begged for mercy. She wasn't big enough.

"You fucking asshole," she muttered under her breath. She wasn't crying. What did she care if Joe and Cynthia...Angel probably wished he'd gotten to Cynthia first. The way Angel talked about her Cynthia sounded like someone who knew how to make tons of money, besides being incredibly beautiful. Angel would never have to worry if he was with her instead of Alice.

Alice kept walking. Angel didn't follow, he had too much to think about, how she'd ruined his life, how he couldn't be a free spirit anymore.

The problem with walking was that Alice didn't have anyplace to go. She didn't want to go back to the apartment; it was making her feel trapped, too. If she went home, Angel would be there, and they would keep fighting, or he wouldn't be there, and she'd start worrying. She walked. She was raging; it gave her a lot of energy. Her thoughts circled like hamsters on a wheel, squeak, squeak, squeak.

She wished she could call Christine. She wished she could see her. Alice was grown up now, she didn't like calling Christine when she was down. She thought it would make Christine feel like a failure; also, she was afraid Christine wouldn't have time for her anymore. Well, Christine had other things to do, new kids, who needed her help more than Alice did.

Christine was a bad letter writer. She sent cards on Alice's birthday and at Christmas and sometimes out of the blue, every couple years. Maybe Alice should take the train and go see her, help out with the kids. Make herself useful. She'd done that before. She didn't have to be so needy.

Thinking that, she headed home. Her stomach growled. Suppertime. It was a nice evening. It had been a nice day; she and Angel should have gone somewhere, instead of sleeping late and then hacking away at each other. One of her old boyfriends used to hate it when she wanted to talk about their problems. He wanted things to be "nice". Alice couldn't relax until things were straight, she didn't care about nice. But this with Angel was wearing her down. She wanted time out.

Angel was sitting on the front stoop, smoking and drinking beer, reading the paper. She sat down next to him. He didn't seem angry any more. He put his arm around her shoulders.

"What're you reading?" she asked.

"Want ads," he said. "We need a bigger place." He was letting go of the fight; he was already on to the next thing.

"I was thinking," she said, "we should have gone somewhere today. Just had a day when we forgot about being scared and not knowing what we're doing."

Her stomach growled again, loud. "I got take-out," he said. "There's some left upstairs."

She wanted barbeque. Take-out anything would still be great.

"I didn't know you were scared," he said.

"I thought it was obvious."

"It was," he said, "now I think about it. I've been too pissed off at you to think."

"We should take a day off," she said again. "When we give each other a break. When we're just together without all that other stuff."

"We'll have to do it soon," he said. "The tour came through."

No wonder he wasn't angry anymore. He was leaving. She didn't know if she was sad about it or glad. "When do you go?"

"Next week," he said.

Next *week*. She was definitely sad.

At least she didn't have to worry about not being turned on anymore. She had always liked it that Angel was so light-hearted in bed, even while she wished it wasn't so easy for him. It wasn't easy now. When Angel entered her he groaned aloud, as if it hurt. Afterwards he held her tight, like she was the one who might escape. It was like they cut each other to the bone and then pressed their wounds together. If they'd been trees, they would have grafted by now. But they were people, and they weren't any closer at all.

Maybe it will do us good to be apart, Alice thought the night before he left, maybe we can heal a little.

"You're worse than junk," Angel said, half-asleep, speaking into her forehead.

She couldn't get her breath for a minute.

"Don't," she said. Don't think that, she meant. Don't talk like that. Don't let it be true.

He didn't say anything else.

The band used to sleep in the same room on the road, when they had a room. Sometimes they slept on couches and floors, or in the van. Once they'd slept in a bar, everybody twisted like pretzels to fit into the padded booths except for Angel, who stretched out on the countertop of the bar itself.

They had a manager wooing them now; no more sleeping in bars. But after a couple of nights when they had all bedded down in one room, Dan came to Joe and told him that he and Stringer had decided they should rent an extra room whenever they needed it. Or they'd never make it through the tour.

"You and Angel in the same room, it's like a fucking war zone," Dan said. Joe pretty much agreed. Angel wouldn't speak to Joe, so Joe didn't speak to Angel. If Dan or Stringer said anything to either one of them, it looked like they were choosing sides. Joe could have solved the problem by sleeping in the van, the nights were warm enough now. He didn't want to.

So they forked out the cash for an extra room, an investment in their future. Joe roomed with Dan, and Angel got stuck with Stringer. Angel didn't seem to mind. He and Stringer seemed to get along all right.

Joe had a brief fantasy of Stringer and Julie with Angel in tow, Ken and Barbie with an exotic and dangerous pet. They would give dinner parties and Angel and Alice would come and eat, not food, but "cuisine". This part of the fantasy faltered. Joe couldn't imagine Alice getting along with Stringer or Julie. But he'd never imagined Angel getting along with Stringer either. People changed.

Angel started taking cues from Joe again. He spoke to Joe, too. When it was absolutely necessary. He had no suggestions for the set lists, which he and Joe used to decide on together. Stringer was full of ideas for the set lists. He acted like he'd never tried to kick Joe out of the band. Did he think Joe didn't know? But Joe didn't really care. He couldn't get excited about Stringer, he couldn't take Stringer seriously enough to feel vengeful. Joe ended up keeping the set lists pretty much the way they were.

Dan disappeared with a different woman nearly every night. Once he brought a woman back to the room; she didn't have a place of her own yet. Joe wondered if she was the age of consent. Neither of them minded Joe being there, trying to sleep with a pillow over his head. Joe ended up sleeping in the bathtub with the shower curtain drawn for privacy.

The next day Joe told Dan, no more women in the room. "If you can't find someone with a place of her own, beat off," Joe said. He had a sore neck from sleeping in the tub.

The next time Dan had two women. He took Joe aside and told him one was for him.

"No thanks," Joe said.

"She likes you," Dan said. "She thinks you're hot."

"No."

"It'll make you feel better."

"I'm not interested." If all that was wrong with him was random horniness, Joe would be in good shape. Besides, he had slept with enough strangers in his life.

Dan left with both women. He came back late the next day, dragging his ass, eyes glazed over.

"How'd it go?" Joe asked him.

Dan shook his head. "Unbelievable," he said.

"Both?"

"They were so…athletic," Dan said. "If they hadn't been bi, they would have killed me." He put his hands on his crotch and groaned.

Joe started laughing, and then he couldn't stop. For awhile after that, Dan left women alone and Joe had some peace at night.

Halfway through the tour, Angel and Stringer had a fight. Joe didn't know what it was about, and no one told him. Angel moved in with Dan and Joe was left with Stringer. Stringer mostly talked about food, only to complain. He was used to beautiful food, lovingly prepared and arranged, dainty bits of this and that. Road food was killing him—he would die for a grape, some rosemary chicken, a vegetable that hadn't been cooked to extinction. At least Stringer went to sleep at night, only throwing Joe out of the room so he could have privacy for his nightly long distance phone conversations with Julie. He talked in his sleep, probably the result of his unquiet digestion. Joe couldn't tell if he was saying "Julie" or "zucchini".

Angel, who'd stayed pretty sober, started drinking again. Dan, his sperm count replenished, was back to a different woman every night. From what Joe could tell, Angel was keeping up with him on that score.

Joe stopped feeling guilty and started feeling jealous. Why should Angel have everything, Alice waiting at home, probably throwing up, while he was out carousing? Joe had never thought like that before; one of the things about their friendship had been that there was no rivalry in it, they didn't begrudge each other anything. Angel was Angel, and you took him as he was or left him alone, unless you were a fool. Joe had always thought the women who got upset over Angel's behavior were fools. Besides, what did Joe care if Alice suffered? It served her right.

But what had Angel been saying the night he punched him, about Joe not wanting Angel to have anything of his own? What had that been about?

Joe watched Angel, since he couldn't ask him. Angel caught him at it and snarled, "What're you looking at?"

"Nothing," Joe said, realizing too late that Angel would take this as an insult.

Angel stared at him. It was like a contest between fifth graders. Joe let Angel outstare him. Angel was satisfied with that. So was Joe. It was better than Angel being polite and looking right through him.

As the tour wore on Stringer's complaints about road food and the state of his bowels became constant. Grease and starch were making him ill. If Joe had wanted revenge, this revenge would have been perfect. Karmic justice. The problem was the revenge smelled like swamp gas. Stringer's farts were toxic, and they hung around forever. Joe couldn't even hide out in the bathroom; he tried to compensate by keeping the windows in the bedroom wide open. Stringer said he would lose his voice if he caught a cold.

Joe bitched to Dan about Stringer's digestive upsets.

"Eat a lot of chili," Dan suggested. "It'll give you something to fight back with."

"There won't be any air left to breathe if I get as bad as him."

"Your own never smell as bad as somebody else's. Your own are sort of interesting."

Joe decided to forego the experiment. He chain-smoked instead, his own addition to air pollution. One night when they were playing on a puny little stage Angel did one of his war dances, spinning like a demented top right into Stringer-emission zone. Angel froze in mid-step. He looked like he'd run into a wall.

Joe could practically see the fumes creeping towards him, radiating outward from Stringer. He flung himself around so his back was to the audience, as if cynicism or angst had so overcome him he could no longer bear to face the crowd. Headbanging furiously, he stomped back to Dan, which was as far away as he could get, and stayed there for the rest of the night.

The music, strangely enough, was fine. Hard rock seemed to thrive on bad smells and bad blood. Or maybe it was because, whatever they thought of each other as people, they were compatible as musicians. As they all got a little more frayed, the music got better. Those last nights out, everyone sick of each other, they were taking risks they'd never have attempted before, and some of them were working. Angel, fucking with the bass line, gave Joe a whole new idea for the lead, mainly because Angel had just destroyed the one he'd been doing. Dan never faltered, and Stringer started singing around the lead, wailing up high in an eerie falsetto, probably because he was so constipated he couldn't sing from his diaphragm anymore. At the end of the song they were all grinning at each other. It was totally fucking insane. It was great.

Angel called Alice his third night out on the road. She'd asked him to call, and he didn't want to. He hated talking on the phone long distance.

He said the gigs were fine. They had good audiences. He didn't say, "But the joy's gone out of it," but that's what she heard.

"How're you doing?" he asked.

"I sleep all the time," she said.

"Not sick?"

"I just sleep. I go to work and I sleep." She wanted to complain and didn't feel like she could. "Angel?"

"I'm here."

"I miss you," she said.

She listened to static on the wire. "I miss you too," he finally said.

"I thought hearing your voice would help," she said. "It doesn't, though."

"I won't call anymore," he said. "It doesn't help for me either. I want to see you."

At least he wanted to see her.

Matt's love affair was over, he was once more in the market for the love sucks conversation. Carla had been on her own for a while now. She and Matt hit the bars and came to see Alice every few nights "to wake her up".

"I keep waiting for the axe to fall," Alice told them one night. They were all three sitting on her bed, eating popcorn and watching the late movie with the sound turned low so they could talk. "I keep waiting for him to say forget it, I can't deal."

"That would be three out of five," Carla said around popcorn.

"Three out of five what?" Matt asked.

"In the co-op. Shot down by love."

"At least you did the shooting," Matt said to Carla. "There's some satisfaction in that."

"True," Carla said. "Maybe you should break up with Angel first," she suggested.

"I don't want to break up with him at all," Alice said. She yawned. "If we can just get through this."

Matt grunted. He'd told Alice, when she told him about Angel's other women, that he'd gone to hear the band one night a couple of months ago and seen another woman with Angel, being more than friendly. Since his own honeylamb had ditched him, Matt was a complete pessimist about Alice's chances of "getting through it" with Angel.

"As long as you don't spend your whole life waiting for it to get good," Matt said sourly.

"I won't," she said. "Not my whole life."

Matt shook his head at her. She hated it when he got depressed, it was too much like her own depression. But he was her friend, it was one of the duties of friendship to let your friends wallow in cynicism when you couldn't cheer them up or argue them out of it.

"You should have stuck with Joe," Matt said.

"Not this again," Carla said. Alice didn't say anything. Since Angel had been gone she had lapsed. She didn't talk about Joe to her friends, but she let them talk about him.

"You shot down the wrong one," Matt said.

"I didn't shoot him down," Alice said. "I didn't treat him like a slut on the rampage. He shot me down."

"Oh right, the famous bathroom scene. You hurt his feelings. He was just paying you back."

Carla sighed loudly and got out of bed. "I'm getting something to drink," she said, heading for the kitchen. "Do you guys want anything?"

They didn't. Alice hoped Matt would remember what he had been about to say before Carla interrupted them. He wasn't saying anything so she looked at him inquiringly.

"I don't know," he said, as if he were giving up on the topic, "I just liked how you were together."

Alice felt a little jumping spark in her belly or her chest.

"How were we?" she asked.

He frowned, thinking about it. "You would have been easy to draw. You were always in relation to each other. The space between you made an interesting shape. How's that?"

That was wonderful. Alice would treasure it forever, in secret. She didn't have anything else from Joe to treasure, just the opposite. She wanted to hug Matt for saying it, but she couldn't. It would be disloyal to Angel. Besides, Joe had someone else to make shapes with. He was probably making a figure 8 on its side with Cynthia at every opportunity.

"That's very poetic," she said. "It made a triangle, right?"

A couple nights later, alone in bed, she had a dream. She and Angel were living in Aziz's bar, behind the counter. Only Angel wasn't there, he was off with one of his other women. Alice didn't mind, it didn't bother her at all. They weren't mad at each other anymore, and Joe was coming to live with them, he wasn't mad at her either, they were going to be Senoi. Alice was waiting for him to get there. Meanwhile she had to wait on customers. The customers were talking about her, saying what a trashy insatiable woman she was. At first she tried to explain, but they ignored her. Then she got pissed off. Why am I waiting on you? she said to them. They looked uncomfortable and stopped talking. Get out of here, she said, and they left. But Joe wasn't here yet and she was starting to wake up. And what about Cynthia? She didn't want to wake up before he got here, and she didn't want Cynthia coming with him. She tried to have a lucid dream, like a Senoi, to make it happen the way she wanted it to. She willed Joe to appear with every fiber of her being...and woke up instead.

The clinic doctor asked her if she was depressed about anything, was she taking her vitamins? She seemed a little run down.

The doctor was a woman about Alice's age. She was nice enough, but she seemed like the kind of person who had always known exactly what she was doing on this planet. "I'm worried about money," Alice said. "About finding a better job. And I haven't been drawing anything. I don't have any ideas. I just sleep."

"Sleeping's normal," the doctor said. She talked to Alice about seeing a therapist over work-related issues. It was sliding scale, and the therapist might be able to help her figure out a better job and find it. Alice wasn't interested. She had four printmaker brains at her disposal, and they were free.

In spite of what Matt said, Alice thought she and Angel had a chance. He'd been willing to try; he missed her. She could hear from his voice, even over the phone, that he wasn't lying about that. It would be okay. If he wasn't calling it wasn't because he didn't want to talk to her, it was because he didn't like talking on the phone.

She got one call, a strange one, just before he was due home. It came at three in the morning, waking her out of a sound sleep.

"Hello?"

The line went dead. A crank call. She unplugged the phone and went back to sleep.

But it had been Angel. When he got home he let her be glad to see him for about two seconds before he said, "It was me on the phone, that time." She didn't ask what time, she knew right away what was coming.

"I can't do this," he said.

Alice's arms ached from her shoulders to her wrists. The muscles in her chest felt sore. "What?" she said. Her voice sounded so pitiful she hoped he hadn't heard it. She sat down hard on one of the kitchen chairs.

"You have to listen to me," Angel said. "You have to please just listen a minute."

His face was all wrong. Don't make it worse, his face said.

"I wanted it to work out," he said. "I thought we could get back to how it was before…well, I tried."

She didn't say anything. He sat down across the table from her. They'd sat here together so many times before. Alice thought if they could just sit here awhile he would remember how he used to feel and stop doing this.

"It was like being in a straightjacket. So I fooled around with someone else." He waited for some response from her. She had a feeling that he'd been practicing this speech, that he couldn't finish it if she didn't burst into tears or yell at him. She was wrong.

"I can't be somebody else," he said.

"What if I said it's okay, do what you want?" She couldn't believe she said that. It wouldn't be okay; she could never handle that. But she might handle it until he stopped. He might stop when he realized—

"I wouldn't believe you," he said. There wasn't any malice in his voice. He was being kind. She cast about in her mind for a way to get rid of his kindness.

"It's because of Joe," she said. "You did it to hurt me, you were paying me back."

"Alice, I was fucking around before anything happened with you and Joe. I keep telling you, it's something I do." He sighed heavily, the weight of the world on his shoulders. Maybe just the weight of her. "If it makes you feel better, I'm still pissed off at Joe."

"And me," she said.

"Yeah," he admitted, "and you." But he didn't look angry. He just wanted to get it over with. This time he was saying goodbye. She wanted to fall on the floor at his feet and beg him not to leave. He must have read her impulse, he looked alarmed.

"You never wanted a baby, did you," she said.

"I don't know," he said. "I did at first," he amended. "Listen, I'm not running out on you. I'll stick around. I'll pay for the doctor, I'll be your labor coach if you want. And I'll help out…after." He meant it. As long as he was free of her, he was willing to be a father for an hour or so when he didn't have anything better to do. Because he felt guilty. He felt sorry for her.

She hated him for that. It was a relief to hate him.

"I don't want your help," she said. "I can't count on it, so I don't want it."

For a moment his face was wiped clean of expression.

"It's always like that with you," he said. "All or nothing. Your way or no way."

"Yeah I'm a control freak," she said. "Keep it simple." She got up and started picking up his clothes, which were scattered around the apartment. She dumped them into the open boxes, still on the bedroom floor. He came and stood in the doorway, watching her.

"You want me to go now?" he said. I don't want you to go at all, she thought. But he sounded relieved, even though he was trying to hide it.

"You've decided to go," she said. "Why wait around?"

He packed up the acoustic guitar. He went into the bathroom, came back with his stuff in a plastic bag. The sight of all his worldly possessions packed in cardboard boxes made her eyes fill up. At least she didn't howl. He didn't try to comfort her. He was probably afraid to. He couldn't make good on his escape if he comforted her and one thing led to another, like it usually did.

Instead he called Dan, who had just gotten home from dropping him off. From what Alice could hear, Dan needed some persuading to come back and get Angel. She felt humiliated for Angel that he had to beg for a ride.

Then the boxes were all packed, even Joe's shirt that Angel had lent to her a million years ago. She didn't want to sit around waiting for Angel to leave her forever. She stuffed some money in her pocket and put on her walking shoes. Angel was sitting at the kitchen table.

"Leave the keys in the mailbox," she said.

He looked at her as if she had done this to him and not the other way around. "You want to tell me where you're going?"

She shook her head no. She didn't know where she was going.

X.

Alice came out of her front door into bright sunlight. It hit her square in the face. She put her foot wrong on the top step and would have fallen if she hadn't jumped.

She landed on the concrete walk on one knee and both hands. Her palms were scraped, her knee hurt, but she was okay.

A block later her legs gave out and she sat on the curb. She could not take one more step in this dangerous place. Angel! she thought, as if he could save her. The thought went dark. She waited to see if she was going to cry, but she didn't. When her legs were working again she put on her sunglasses and headed for Lynn's daycare.

Lynn was outside in the sandbox. A little boy dumped buckets of sand on her legs while she leaned back against a truck tire with her eyes half-closed, smiling in the sun.

Alice felt like a cold shadow. The little kid squinched up his face at her. She took off her sunglasses so he could see what she looked like.

"Alice!" Lynn said. "What are you doing here?" But she knew already. She stood up, sand sliding down her legs, and grabbed Alice by the arms. As soon as Lynn touched her Alice's eyes started leaking tears, like she was a busted faucet. The little boy began to whimper. In one second, Alice had spoiled two people's moods.

Lynn squatted next to the little boy, talking fast, while Alice turned off the tap. Two other children had poked their heads up from inside the truck tire and were staring at her like she was something in a zoo. Alice smiled at them in a way that was supposed to be reassuring. One of the kids ducked back down, hiding; the other one kept right on staring with no change of expression.

Lynn and the whimperer sounded like they were making a deal. They closed it. Lynn stood up and said, "Kevin, this is my friend Alice. Alice, this is Kevin. Watch them, will you? I'll be back in a minute."

While Lynn went to alert another teacher, Alice and Kevin watched each other.

"Hi," Alice said.

Kevin turned his back on her. He had a perfectly round head on a thin stalk of a neck. Alice was afraid he was going to start crying again. She put her hands in her pockets and looked around the playground to give him privacy, hoping Lynn would hurry up.

Lynn came back with another teacher. "Okay," Lynn said. "We can go inside and talk for a minute."

"I want to come," Kevin said, recovering the power of speech now that Lynn was here.

Lynn got Alice and Kevin inside and poured apple juice into Kevin's cup-with-a-lid-and-a-spout. Kevin was a juice freak; he tipped his head back and guzzled. He said "Aaah," when he was done and smacked the cup down hard on the table. "More," he said. He would probably grow up to be a musician.

Lynn poured him more. "I need to talk to Alice now. Tell me if you want more juice."

Kevin watched Alice with interest—the strange world of grownups. His eyelashes were about a foot long.

"What happened?" Lynn said.

"Angel dumped me. He's waiting for Dan to pick him up at my house. I couldn't stand it. So I left."

"Oh Alice," Lynn said. She took Alice's hand and squeezed it hard. Her hand was warm and dry and strong, the best hand in the world. Alice held on, starting to cry again. Lynn's eyes filled up too.

"What did the, what did the, what did the angel drop on her?" Kevin asked in a high voice. He looked scared.

"Angel's a person," Lynn said. "It's a person's name. He didn't drop anything on her. He made Alice feel bad."

Alice wondered if all children were like this. Was she going to have to watch everything she said? How would a child react to one of her bouts of fury, when she broke things to hear the noise? Was she going to have to pretend to be calm and rational for the next twenty years?

Lynn fished a key ring out of her pocket and pried one of the keys loose. "Go to my house," she said. "I'll see you after work." Alice fled.

She took the bus. She was exhausted. At least this baby in her was making her too tired to think. She didn't want to sleep in Lynn's bed, where Lynn and Chris slept, in case her bad luck rubbed off onto the sheets. She fell asleep on the couch.

Lynn woke her up for dinner. She had already made salad and rice, and picked up a barbequed chicken on the way home. They sat outside to eat it.

Lynn looked different. Her thick brown hair was in its usual braid, she had strange stains all over her shirt from working with kids all day, what was changed? Being in love was making her more herself, Alice decided, not less.

She told Lynn that.

"Really?" Lynn looked embarrassed and pleased.

"Really," Alice said. "You still like each other, don't you?"

"We still like each other," Lynn said, smiling to herself.

Alice felt relieved, and only slightly envious. "That's great," she said. She needed to know that sometimes things worked out.

Being at Lynn's house, in the backyard with the crickets and the beech tree and Lynn heaping her plate, Alice felt detached enough to talk about what had happened without crying. Lynn made a face when Alice told her about Angel saying he'd help with the baby, how angry he'd been when she said she didn't want his help.

"Actually," Alice said, "I can see his point. But I can't deal with having him there and not there."

"Of course you can't," Lynn said. "You've got enough to deal with. You're not the kind of person who could handle a set-up like that." For awhile they just ate. Alice wasn't hungry, but the baby seemed to be.

"What about Joe?" Lynn said, when they had some food in them. She sounded like she wasn't sure she should ask. Alice dragged her fork over the plate. It screeched.

"What about him? He and Angel can be friends again, I guess." They can compare notes, she thought. She screeched the fork across the plate again. Lynn was wincing, so Alice stopped.

"He's sure not waiting around for me to give him a call," Alice said. "He's going out with their new manager, I told you that. His heart wasn't broken."

"You know I never could figure that one," Lynn said. "What was going on in your head then."

"Nothing was going on in my head, that's why."

"I don't mean like that," Lynn said. "You've always been a few stairs short of the landing when it comes to men. I mean, it was a mystery to me. You were so hung up on Angel, and then…"

Alice was hurt. She thought it was cruel of Lynn to rub it in, how she was a sensible person with a good relationship, so Alice must be an idiot because her relationships didn't work out. But why didn't they work out? Feeling depressed, she told Lynn her latest theory.

"Maybe Joe was revenge. I think I guessed, all along, about Angel and other women. Matt knew, did he tell you?"

"He didn't tell me at the time," Lynn said. "He told me after you found out."

"Well, I could have picked it up off of him. Or from Joe. I'll bet Joe knew."

"It's funny how people do pick up stuff. Especially kids. Some of them have radar. But I thought there might be more to what happened with Joe than revenge."

"Well, lust played its part."

"Was it a large part?" Lynn asked, being so wide-eyed Alice had to laugh. She loved Lynn for making her laugh. But she wasn't going to talk about Joe like he was a part.

"I never kiss and tell," Alice said. Which was a total lie.

"Yeah you do," said Lynn, "When you don't care about the guy you do. I was there, you know, on the Fateful Night." Alice gave her a warning look. Lynn ignored it. "You want to know what I think, I think you finally found somebody you could be yourself with."

Alice wished it was true, and she couldn't afford to think like that. It wasn't true anyway. Lynn had been talking to Matt, Alice was sure of it.

"Oh right," she said. "I was myself and he thinks I'm scum. He thinks I was using him. Maybe I was. Maybe the thrill came from being bad and getting away with it." But they hadn't gotten away with anything. Not one thing. That last time in the van, saying goodbye, had really been the end. Cut off from Angel, she would never see Joe again, not even to be sneered at. She wouldn't hear about him either. At least she wouldn't have to see him being in love.

Lynn was watching her. "You're blaming yourself for the whole thing, you know," she said.

"I am?"

"Yeah you are. You weren't free enough for Angel, you used Joe, you're a miserable excuse for a human being."

"Well how was it anybody else's fault?"

"Joe went after you, for one thing. Angel lied, and did it so well you weren't suspicious."

"He didn't lie. He just didn't say. I didn't ask."

"That's lying," Lynn said. "You think he didn't know how you would react?"

"He said he thought I knew all along," Alice said.

"Bullshit," Lynn said with energy. "Unless he's a complete idiot. He was keeping secrets from you because he didn't want to deal with what would happen if he told you the truth."

Alice was starting to feel better. "That dirtbag," she said. "Do you have any cake?"

"As it happens, I do."

"I'll get it, I need to move," Alice said. She brought the cake back out, and said, "Now do Joe. Tell me what a shit he was."

Lynn ate cake and thought about it. "Okay," she said, and then spoke like she was reciting a lesson. "Joe knew what he was getting into. And he still did it. You can't tell me you seduced him."

"No," Alice said. She wished she had seduced him and cast him aside. It would serve him right.

"He betrayed Angel too. It's not like you're the only one who's been careless of other people's feelings. Nobody was being kind, Alice. If he's with someone else already—"

"Don't talk about that," Alice said. "I don't want to think about that." At least she'd never met Cynthia.

Lynn studied her. "Some revenge," she said.

"You'd think," Alice said, trying to make a joke, "I'd feel bad about just one or the other." She felt bad about both of them. There was no point in that. Joe had already forgotten her and Angel was prepared to do the same. It was time to do something else.

Alice started by unplugging the phone. That way she wouldn't be waiting for it to ring. She kept imagining Angel calling, telling her he wanted to try again. She knew he wasn't going to. She told herself he hadn't really cared so much about her anyway, if their first problem was their last. It wouldn't have worked even if they had tried. It would have been worse. She would have been wondering, every time he didn't come home, if it was because of another woman. She would have had to let go of him in the end.

None of this thinking helped. No matter how she sliced it, it was still plain old pain cake. When it got too bad she broke the remaining glasses in the kitchen and then had the task of sweeping up the shards. She had thrown them so hard she dented the kitchen floor. She cut her foot on a piece of glass on the bedroom rug.

Some days she didn't want to get out of bed at all. Something about being so down brought out the worst in people, or the worst people, as if they smelled her despair. One day started with a woman pushing in front of Alice in the checkout line of the grocery store while Alice's attention was on a magazine. The woman showed Alice her profile, daring her to speak. She knew she could do it, that Alice was in no shape to fight back, that was the point. Then the bus driver, seeing Alice run for the bus, shut the doors and pulled away just as she got there, looking right at her.

Her tips were abysmal that night. She walked home because she didn't want to deal with any more bus drivers, and a man crossed the street to follow her, making sucking noises and saying, "Hey chicky, chicky, you know you want it."

That did it. If she had just been herself she might have tried to ignore him, but she was something more now, she had a child to protect from the random malice of the universe. Alice turned around and faced him, her hand in her shoulderbag, feeling around for her steel etching needle. She would have preferred a large blunt instrument, but she had to use what came to hand. It was in her hand, then. He saw it.

She didn't say anything. Go ahead and try it, she thought at him. What should she go for? Face? Stomach? Chest? If she killed him she would end up in jail, and they'd take the baby away from her. So go for the stomach. Give him indigestion for life.

He raised his hands. "Whoa," he said. He wiggled his hands, pantomiming fright, making fun of her. "You scare me," he said. "Scare-y."

Fuck you, she thought at him. Fuck you, asshole.

He peered at her, making a face. "Hey," he said. "You're one ugly woman, you know that?"

And you're a piece of dogshit, she thought. She didn't say it out loud. She didn't want him following her, trying to make himself look good. A car drove by, and that was enough for him. It gave him an exit cue. "Fucking cunt," he said, and then he left. She flagged the next cab she saw and made it home okay. She wasn't even shaking.

At least she didn't have insomnia. She had hit that point in her pregnancy where she needed to sleep more than she needed anything else. She had read somewhere that cats could sleep twenty-two hours out of twenty-four. She could do that. But she had nightmares.

After a couple of weeks, Alice plugged the phone back in and cleaned the house. She got rid of everything that reminded her of Angel, the pictures she'd drawn, the photograph she had. She put it all in an envelope and gave it to Lynn, who would keep it for later, for the baby, in case s/he wanted to see what the old man looked like.

Alice was no longer sure that the baby was a girl. She didn't want to start having illusions before her child was even born.

When the house was clean, she called Matt and invited him over. He worked as a waiter in a fancy restaurant, and while she didn't think she could manage that, she thought she might find work there in the kitchen, learn how to cook, get a paying skill she could use in the daytime.

"You hate to cook," Matt said.

"If I was paid to do it, I could manage."

"They're not hiring. They're overstaffed already. Everyone wants a job there. I don't know why," he said. "It sucks."

He had lost weight. He never smiled anymore.

"I think you should stop doing the bar scene for awhile," Alice said. "It's making you worse. Your heart is broken this time."

"Oh I know," he said. He rubbed his chest, where his heart was. "It's actually sore, you know that? Like a bad song. Is yours sore?"

Alice rubbed her heart. "Yeah," she said. "And my breasts are killing me."

That got half a smile.

"And my back, god, my back is a wreck."

"My eyes hurt," he said, "from looking too long at the sad old world."

"That sounds like a song," Alice said. "We should write it down and make some money out of all this pain. It'll be a hit."

They wrote the most maudlin song they could. Matt did the music, since he'd been a musician and still had a guitar. He did all the clichéd licks he could think of. They used a lot of rain metaphors. It started out: “My eyes are raining, from looking too long on this sad old world, and my breasts are killing me.”

They called it “Misery Loves Rain”.

Matt started coming over to Alice’s a few nights a week instead of hitting the bars. Sometimes Carla came too. If Alice was too tired to get up they got into bed with her and went to sleep and saw each other in the morning. Alice and Matt had slept together for comfort before; species didn’t seem to matter when you were friends, when there was no sex involved. Matt started calling Alice’s house the veterans’ ward, because they were recuperating from the wars. Carla said it was better than waking up with a stranger, even though Matt talked in his sleep and Alice hogged the blankets.

The man downstairs called the building owners and told them Alice was soliciting. That was how the building manager phrased it to Alice. “Whore,” was what the man downstairs said, whenever he saw her. Alice noticed that the man had never said anything about Angel or Joe; it was Matt who got his back up. He wasn’t just a grumpy old man, he was a racist shithead.

Alice wanted to move anyway, and the building manager said the owners didn’t believe the man downstairs, just try to keep the noise down. But the feeling of living here was definitely not good. When the man downstairs called Carla a whore, she looked him in the eye and said, “I don’t think so. I wouldn’t fuck you for a million dollars.” Alice thought he would have apoplexy on the spot. Once she would have felt sorry for him; she didn’t now. She was too busy trying to find another place to live.

Matt gave her a housefinding party, for singles only—Lynn had to come alone, Chuck couldn’t bring Baby. They put Alice’s housing problem on the table. They fantasized what her house would look like so well Alice could see it. It should be within sight of water, with a yard and plenty of sun for a garden. Alice wanted a big tree, too.

"It sounds like my house," Lynn said.

"I think it is," Alice said, stunned. "Are your upstairs neighbors moving?"

"We could have a bunch of wild parties at Lynn's," Chuck said, "and force them to move."

"Bad idea," Carla said. "You'll get Lynn thrown out too."

"I'll ask around the neighborhood," Lynn said. "See if anyone's leaving."

After the party Alice was sure she was going to find a place immediately, move away from here, and have a wonderful life. She would have a garden and grow all the food for herself and the baby. Her prints would become powerful and focused because she was so grounded. They would sell for tons of money and she could quit doing shit jobs. She would never think about Angel anymore, not even to think of him as a liar and a cheat. In her spare time she would take aikido. She would be really good, a natural. She would be so good they would put her in a match against men, where she would come up against Joe and calmly throw him across the room. Would she break his bones? No, she wouldn't have to—he would be totally humiliated. He would be so humiliated at being bested by Alice that it would make him impotent for months, maybe forever.

Nothing happened. Then the bathroom graffiti in the printmaker's co-op changed. The Lin Yutang quote, about the fool persisting in his folly and becoming wise, had appeared on the wall months ago, after a rent-raising party. When Alice first saw the words scrawled across the political arguments and pomposities about art that adorned the wall, it had given her a shock of pleasure. It was like opening a fortune cookie and finding a Zen koan instead of the usual Confucian bombast. But now Lin Yutang's name had been scratched out; over that someone had written in thick block letters "William Blake". It was Matt's handwriting. Alice asked him about the quote.

"It's from *The Marriage of Heaven and Hell*," Matt said. "It's one of the proverbs of hell."

Alice's quote-to-live-by was no longer a pearl of Oriental wisdom, it was a proverb from hell. "You mean it's supposed to be ambiguous?"

"Yeah," Matt said. "I think the wording's off, too. It's been driving me nuts."

Alice got so depressed she nearly called Angel. Using her last ounce of self-preservation, she called Matt instead.

"What are you going to say to him?" Matt wondered.

"I'm thinking I'll tell him I'll take a number and stand in line with the rest of them, if he just lets me back in line."

"You're raving."

"If I really love him, I can deal."

"Why don't you just ask him to put his foot on your neck and grind you into the ground?" Matt asked.

Well, why not? It would come to the same thing in the end. So tell me how well I'm doing on my own, Alice thought at Matt. Make me believe you. Give me some concrete examples.

"I don't know why you don't call Joe," Matt said. "If you're going to call anybody."

"Matthew, he's with someone else." She spoke slowly and distinctly, so he would understand. "Someone who's beautiful, smart, and is going to make them rich and famous. Besides, I hate him."

"He's on the rebound."

"What, all that isn't enough?"

"If that's what he wanted, what was he doing with you?"

"Jesus! *Flatter* me why don't you."

"I'm not insulting you. What do you need with that? You're a printmaker. You have a 'wildly original countenance' and a beautiful soul."

"Maybe he likes variety. Maybe she has a beautiful soul. How the fuck should I know? I don't know what he likes. I don't know anything about him." Except that he's afraid of dying before he gets it right, she thought. But that could mean anything.

"You keep saying that. You're protesting too much."

"I'm trying to get a grip on reality," she said. "I'm trying to use my head." This was the problem with Matt. He was obstinate. He got these ideas in his head. At least he'd distracted her from thinking about Angel. "I need to make it on my own anyway," she said. "That's really what I need now, to stand on my own two feet and legs."

The next day Matt brought her a tape he'd made. He thought it would help her stand on her own two feet and legs. "Every time you think about getting in line for Angel, play this tape," he said. The tape was a compilation of songs about people who had been screwed over by lovers, but no one was whining or nostalgic. They had had it and were going on to something else. Alice's favorite was a song by X. It sounded like musicians, more than one, had given Exene a bad time. Alice could relate to that.

Exene sang it pissed off. She sang it like she'd learned her lesson and didn't need any of these stupid fuckers anymore. Singing along with her, Alice felt hard as nails, smart and mean.

Alice told Aziz she was pregnant. He knew she wasn't married. She was pretty sure he would fire her, but she told him as if she expected him to give her a job in the kitchen because the smoke in the bar wasn't good for the baby.

Aziz narrowed his eyes to slits, something he did frequently. Alice had never been able to tell if it was because he wanted to look like he was thinking, like he was sharp and nothing could be put over on him, or if it was because he really was thinking.

He shook his head no. "Yes," he said.

She waited to see which one he meant. "The smoke—not good when you're pregnant," he said. "What can you cook?"

"Lasagna," she said. "Eggs. Chicken soup." She was too surprised to think of something to say that would persuade him to give her a job in the kitchen.

"That is it?" Aziz asked. "That is *nothing*!" He seemed personally offended by her lack of culinary expertise. "How will you feed a child, if you don't know how to cook? Go. Right now. Tell them I said so."

Freddie shook Alice's shoulder after Aziz left. "You heard him," Freddie said, "shut your mouth and go into the kitchen before he changes his mind."

"He didn't say anything about my dirty hands or my godless ways," Alice said.

"No one cares about that in the kitchen," Freddie said.

Aziz even raised her salary since she wouldn't be making tips. Maybe Aziz figured that, bad as it was to be pregnant and unmarried, it was better than getting an abortion and taking yourself out of the hands of fate, who he called god.

The new job gave her earlier nights, since the kitchen closed before the bar. No one let her lift anything heavy. The cook sneaked food to Alice to take home, trying to fatten her up.

"Isn't it strange?" she said to Matt. "I loved Angel and he freaked out completely. And Aziz, who I'm not even sure I like, is being an actual help."

Matt grunted. "Love," he said, disgusted.

The printmakers had hired a model to sit for them twice a week. Alice couldn't use the acid anymore, but she could still make drypoints and draw.

Carla gave her an old pair of jeans when Alice's didn't fit anymore; Matt lent her his car once a week for errands and to go to the beach. The people at work were giving her advice about pregnancy and Aziz's wife made Alice a whole tray of baklava to take home. This baby didn't have any father, but she already had a lot of godparents.

Six weeks after Angel had left her, Alice had her uncontrollable crying down to once a week and she was only sleeping twelve hours a night. She figured she was doing good.

One day she walked in on Lynn and Carla talking in the studio.

"But I don't know how to tell her," Lynn was saying. Carla saw Alice and shut her mouth on whatever she'd been about to say.

"Tell who what?" Alice said.

Lynn turned around and saw Alice. She didn't look happy to see her.

"What?" Alice said.

Lynn had a battered brown envelope in her hand. It was puffy.

"Angel's been keeping tabs on you," Carla said.

Alice felt such a rush of joy she had to sit down. She sat in the armchair the model used.

"He has?" she said.

"He's got a girlfriend," Carla said, cutting off the joy with one good clean thwack.

"It was bound to happen," Alice said, taking it. Lynn and Carla were watching her. They looked relieved that she was being so calm. "How's he been keeping tabs on me?"

"Me," Lynn said, looking guilty as hell.

"You're Angel's new girlfriend?" Alice said.

"Me? Are you crazy?" No, thought Alice, I'm in country-western hell. "I don't know who she is," Lynn said. "He's been calling me to see how you are. He came by last night and brought me this. He asked me to give it to you." She handed Alice the envelope.

Alice opened it. It was full of money.

"What's this?" she said, pulling it out.

"The band's getting a lot of work," Carla said. "It's legal."

There was a piece of folded paper in with the money. Alice unfolded it. It was in Angel's spiky handwriting that Alice used to think was artistic. It said: "Please take this for the baby." There was no signature. Alice guessed he didn't want to implicate himself.

"What's that?" Lynn asked, like it might be Cleopatra's asp. "I didn't know about that."

Alice handed the note to Lynn and looked at the money scattered over her lap. It might be enough to buy another car. If she did she would be in an accident, she knew it.

"He can take it back," Alice said. "He can take it and shove it up his asp." Nobody got the joke. They probably thought she was so upset she couldn't make words anymore.

Alice stuffed the money back in the envelope. She wanted to burn it, or tear it up. Some of it fell on the floor and she kicked it. Uncontrollable crying seemed to have started for the week.

"How's Joe and whatsername? Like lovebirds, right?"

"I don't know. I never see him," Lynn said.

Alice covered her face.

"Oh Alice," Lynn said. She was crying too. She put her hands on Alice's head and pressed it into her own belly. They sobbed noisily. After awhile, hearing how they sounded, they laughed a little. Alice wiped her nose on her sleeve.

"What happened to Carla?"

"I'm right here." Carla had a couple of glasses of water and some wet paper towels. She passed them around. "I think you should keep the money. It's for the baby. He should pay something."

"He wants to help you out," Lynn said.

"He only wants to help because it's easy and he doesn't care about me," Alice said. She hiccuped, drank more water. "He's trying to buy me off."

"You could put it in a savings account," Carla said. "That way you don't have to think about it, but if you need it, it's there."

"You can use some of it to pay the midwife," Lynn said. "Or for daycare, later."

"You'll be doing all the real work," Carla said. "Why shouldn't he pay for the midwife?"

"Because if I use his money for a midwife I'll die in labor," Alice said. "He made fun of me for not being able to make money. I'd like to throw it in his face. Where are they playing? Are they in town? I'll do it tonight." She didn't have to take this from him. She didn't have to let him grind her into the ground.

"I'll give it back to him," Lynn said quickly.

"You think that's a bad idea," Alice said. They were both looking at her like she had completely lost it. It still seemed like a good idea to her, but she wasn't going to get any help with this one, she could tell.

"Okay," she said. "I won't." She took the note back from Lynn and examined it intently. She could always write "fuck you" on the back of the note and send it to him that way, but Lynn wouldn't want to give it to Angel like that. It wasn't Lynn's problem anyway, it was Alice's.

They were both watching her, waiting. Well, the best defense was a good offense.

"I can't believe you've been talking to him all this time and didn't tell me," Alice said.

"I didn't know what to say," Lynn said. "He was worried."

"He's not that worried," Alice said. "He didn't call me, did he?"

"But he—," Lynn began.

"Don't tell me. I don't want to hear about it. You can tell him you gave it to me. But don't tell him anything else about me *ever.* I mean it. Not one thing."

Lynn and Carla didn't look at each other; they looked at Alice. Carla's look meant get a grip. Lynn's was just stricken.

Alice relented. "You can tell him I made you swear an Oath of Silence," she said.

"What are you going to do with it?" Carla asked. "Burn it?" That was perceptive.

"No," Alice said truthfully. "I'm going to sleep on it."

After that, Alice decided it was time to be a printmaker again. Hadn't she told Joe that everything was okay as long as she was working? She hadn't done any real work in too long. If pain was overmastering her, well, fuck it, she'd draw pain.

She couldn't draw pain in soft charcoal as a live naked model, someone she didn't even know, reclining in an armchair and getting a sore neck. She needed a metal plate, a tool with a sharp point, and acid. She started with drypoint, but she was losing the image just as she was getting somewhere. She added aquatint and hard ground. Chuck put her plates in the acid for her, like he'd done before. Alice walked Baby.

Chuck didn't understand about love, he told Alice. He meant all the shit she and Matt were going through. Alice thought Chuck probably understood about a different kind of love. He knew she was feeling badly and treated it simply. He put her plates in the acid for her.

Alice drew her nightmare. It didn't make it go away, but at least it gave her a way to trap it. It still won when she slept, but in the studio she drew it the way she wanted it to come out. In the early stages it was simply a blur of shadowy shapes. As the plate progressed a figure appeared in the shadows. It came up clear and hard like rock or bone, reaching out at the viewer. By the final stage the figure had faded into the background again, re-absorbed, dissolved, a shadow without weight.

Alice didn't show the prints to anyone but Chuck. He didn't comment, except to say "Yow" or "Creepy". Alice pretty much agreed. But they weren't for anybody to like. They were for her.

She started drawing herself. It didn't look like her, she didn't want it to, a woman sitting at the base of a tree. A man with dark wings flew out of the tree. The winged man didn't look like Angel either. The background was water and sky; she thought about how to put Joe in the water but didn't do it. "Cool," Chuck said about that one, surprising her. She was pleased. She might show the prints to Lynn and Matt and Carla someday, not right away, but soon.

She bought a bike for getting around, and now when she felt trapped she took a ride somewhere, breathing deep, feeling her legs get strong. The baby was talking to her; she could hear. That star she'd seen from the playground was getting reeled in again, slow but sure, hitches and snags on the way, but still coming along. She thought of the tree woman getting stronger, rounder, more rooted and more transparent at the same time, showing the night sky in her belly, a spiral nebula of stars. Then the winged man could turn into a bird. He could become just another feature of the landscape, no longer the focal point.

Joe thought he would be glad to get home after the tour. He was looking forward to the peace and quiet. A couple nights of it changed his mind. It was too quiet. He did his laundry, called Cynthia and work to let them know he was going, threw his bedding and a guitar into the van, and headed for the peninsula.

It was quiet there, too, misty rain for most of the week, hardly any campers. But it was a good quiet. He sat up with the ranger one night, talking about the clear-cutting. Not too far away there was a guy living in a big tree so the loggers couldn't cut the tree down. He'd rigged up a platform so he could sleep there. Joe thought about that like it was something he might do. The ranger could bring him food, he could piss anywhere, he could probably even shit in a bucket, but giving up smoking would be tough.

He drove home when the week was out. He wrote a song about the man in the tree and smoked like a fiend while he still could. He started a song about Angel and worked nights at the warehouse.

Then the band started rehearsing again. Angel was writing songs too—one about love and one about betrayal. Joe figured the love song was for Alice, and the betrayal song was for him. Angel was purging his past. It was good someone was; it gave them something to work on. The songs Joe was writing he wouldn't play for anyone.

He worked on Angel's songs instead. He thought the love song was too saccharine. He turned it on its head with a lead like burnt sugar, bitter as carbon in the back of your mouth. When he had fixed the love song, he went to work on the betrayal song. It dragged, it was whiny. Joe perked it up with a spitting-in-the-eye-of-fate riff. Angel looked at him like he thought it was a spitting-in-the-eye-of-whoever-had-betrayed-you riff. Angel could take it how he wanted. Joe didn't know how Angel took it, but he used Joe's ideas. He had to. They made the songs better.

This was how Angel and Joe talked now. Joe didn't think Dan or Stringer even noticed the undercurrents. They were getting used to the changed status, as if Angel and Joe had never been friends.

After a month Cynthia had found them so much work that Joe was seriously thinking about taking a leave of absence from his warehouse job. It was either that or quit, and he wasn't about to give up his day gig. He took some time off to go listen to music at night, when he was in town. He ran into Jeannie at a club and she caught him up on all the musicians' gossip. He went to hear her play a couple of times, thought about asking her out. He might. They got along. He would have to find out if she was in a woman phase or a man phase, since she was bi, but the sex didn't really matter. He just felt like he could use some female company.

He went to the library to get more science fiction and came home with books on pregnancy instead. The librarian who worked afternoons was talkative. She had three kids of her own. When she saw the books he had she started telling him what was wrong with the books, what the doctors didn't know. It sounded like everything. She picked out some different books for him. She talked about her pregnancies. She talked to him like he was going to be a father.

That night Joe dreamed that Alice was in bed with him. She kept disappearing. She turned into his pillow, and then his parents were standing in the doorway, telling him that pillow-fucking would never make a baby. Joe told his parents to go away, there was already a baby, they were wrong. The dream changed, turned a corner into something else, something about the answering machine not working. It turned the corner again and Alice was there, she was naked and he was inside of her and everything was all right. She was Alice, and she was Angel, too. He hadn't lost Angel after all, hadn't betrayed him. He hadn't lost either one of them. Joy filled him, so intense he woke. For one moment, he thought the dream was true.

Michelle was giving Joe's brother a birthday party. Joe bought Frank a bottle of champagne and a bouquet of exotic flowers, the kind Michelle couldn't grow in her garden. Frank and Michelle liked flowers.

Michelle had wanted to have an outdoor barbeque for Frank,

but it was raining. Joe and Frank stood in the rain, drinking champagne, turning chicken on the grill. Michelle was pregnant again. Jeremy, their three-year old, ran around being as crazy as Angel when he was crazy-drunk.

"I heard the band's doing really well," Frank said. Frank was a chiropracter. He believed in what he was doing. Michelle used to work as a secretary to make ends meet, so Frank could heal people with no money through their spinal columns. She had finally taken over the job of getting money out of Frank's patients. She had put Frank's business in the black.

"Yeah," Joe said.

"Mom told me you're on the road all the time. She said you're finally making some money."

Joe nodded, sipping champagne. He couldn't see the point of champagne himself. It fizzed in his nose. He sneezed.

"How's the sick people?" Joe asked.

"Good," Frank said, and told Joe about this woman with asthma he was treating. The asthma was going away. Frank went on about it for awhile. Joe was glad for him, or tried to be. He turned over a piece of chicken. It wasn't done, so he turned it back.

"You don't seem very excited about the band," Frank said. "You didn't even knock on wood."

Joe wanted to tell Frank about what had happened with Alice and Angel. Frank knew all about Angel; Angel and Joe had lived with them for awhile after Angel came out of rehab, before Joe had found them a place to live. Frank had worked on Angel's back. Michelle had left them babysitting Jeremy while she ran errands or just got out of the house.

Standing in the backyard, looking at a garden, a fence, all the family and friends inside, Joe couldn't say anything. He should have invited Frank to go see the trees.

"I am sometimes," he said.

"How's Angel?" Frank asked.

"He's doing fine," Joe said. Everybody in his family asked him about Angel, like they were asking about his wife.

Joe had to leave early. He had to play tonight. It wasn't an excuse, even though it felt like one.

"But you'll miss the cake," Michelle said, like that was the end of the world.

"It's okay. I'll be here in spirit," he said, although he wouldn't. He kissed Michelle on the cheek. Joe liked Michelle. She had visited Joe's apartment once, with Frank. She had pushed dirty clothes off the chair onto the floor to make a place to sit. She hadn't tried to clean anything or looked at them with pitying feminine contempt. She had talked with Joe and Angel about the band, offering suggestions and asking questions. She taught them how to play gin rummy, for when they got famous and were on the road all the time and bored.

"You should come around more often," she said now. "You make Frank laugh."

Joe hadn't noticed that, but he appreciated Michelle saying it. If it had just been Michelle and Frank, everyone else gone, he would have told them what had happened. It had been nearly three months now; he needed to tell someone and get over it. He kept remembering how Angel used to be, and how he was now. He remembered how Alice had pressed her belly against the tree that day, when Joe was spying on her. He knew why she'd done it now. He wanted to know if she kept crackers by her bed for morning sickness. He wondered if she was getting enough calcium.

"I will," he said.

XI.

The band didn't play in town again until a rainy Saturday night in early June. Nearly three months pregnant, Alice was bursting with energy. Lynn's upstairs neighbors were actually leaving and Lynn was moving into their apartment. Chris was going to live with her and they needed the extra space. Alice had already put down a deposit on Lynn's old apartment. She could spend the evening sorting through her books, getting ready to make tracks out of here. Or she could finish old business.

She took the envelope full of Angel's money out from under her pillow. She had sealed the flap with tape to keep herself from spending the money. After being slept on, the tape was coming undone and the envelope was weak at the seams. Alice took out enough cash to get her into the club. Then she swaddled the envelope in packing tape, making a nice solid bundle of it.

The band was playing at one of the big clubs, and the club was packed to the gills. Alice wondered if Angel's new girlfriend was here, if she would recognize Angel's new girlfriend if she saw her. She wondered if Cynthia was here. It seemed like the place was crawling with perfect-looking women with blonde hair, so Alice gave up on that. She wasn't competing with them anyway. They weren't the enemy.

She had dressed for battle. She was wearing Carla's jeans, her own black boots, and the Mage t-shirt she had conned Matt into giving her. The lightning bolt on it pointed to her belly, where the baby was starting to push out. Over that Alice wore a black suede jacket so old it had a sheen like a graphite stick. It was a little warm for the weather, but it was good printmaker armor. She put on warpaint, outlining her eyes in black. She had washed her hair, too. If she had known how to do it she would have anointed her head with oil, or whatever it was they did back in the eye-for-an-eye days.

Standing squeezed into the crowd, Alice could hardly see the stage. She was too short. The band sounded like a four-headed hydra, like one thing all together. They sounded good. The crowd-surfers were out in force, the mosh pit was from hell. Alice got kicked in the head twice trying to get closer and then gave up.

She retreated and considered her position. She had thought it would be easy, giving Angel his money back. She would wait until the band was through playing and walk up and hand it to him. Or toss it into his lap. Or smack him on the side of the head with it.

But it was not that kind of gig; Angel wasn't going to be that accessible. They were headlining, moving up in the world. She could try getting backstage but she didn't even know where backstage was, and she had a feeling that there would be someone she had to get past. She would have to ask them to get Angel to let her in. He might say no. Even if he said yes, how satisfying would it be to just hand over his money, especially after he'd done her the favor of letting her backstage? It would feel better to throw it at him. That would be a heroic gesture.

She was going to have to get through the mosh pit. Crowd-surfing was a possibility. The samurai women, pregnant or not, would have donned their lacquered armor and unsheathed their swords and gone straight into battle. But Alice wasn't a samurai. Besides, she didn't have the outfit.

If only she was a huge guy the mosh pit would have been a piece of cake. A huge guy in heavy boots with a heart of stone.

The band was leaving the stage. Oh no, no, no, Alice thought. You can't go yet. The crowd agreed. They were applauding wildly, yelling and whistling. They hadn't had enough.

Then she saw him. The huge guy she needed. He wasn't just huge, he was mammoth. He was a Hulk. She couldn't tell if he had a heart of stone, but he had heavy boots on. He had an open face. He looked like someone you'd ask for directions if you were lost. And he was alone.

Alice made a beeline for him. At first he thought she was trying to pick him up. When she told him what she wanted he was suspicious. What was in that envelope? Alice told him, shouting over the sounds of feet stomping. She let him feel the envelope so he would know it wasn't dogshit or a bomb. He was still suspicious. His open face must have gotten him into trouble before. So she said she was doing it for someone who loved this band and wanted to give them something.

"He's tired of giving money to charity," she improvised. "He wants to give it to starving artists, and these are the ones he's chosen."

"Why doesn't he do it, then?" the Hulk asked.

"He doesn't live here," Alice said. "He's from Minneapolis and had to go home to clinch a big business deal or he would have. He's a little weird," she confided. "He doesn't want anyone to know he's into hard rock. And he doesn't trust the mail. With cash. You know." She rolled her eyes. "Rich people."

The Hulk looked at the envelope dubiously.

"Why'd he give it to you?"

Alice was affronted. "He's a friend of mine."

Now The Hulk eyed her dubiously, like why would a rich person be friends with her. Alice eyed him back. She was telling lies to be proud of and he wasn't believing her. Chivalry was dead.

"Never mind," she said. "I'll do it myself." She should have brought Chuck with her. He would have done it without asking questions.

The band came back on. They were trying to act casual while the crowd noise swelled to a roar. They tuned their guitars.

"I'll do it," the Hulk said, surprising her. "Climb aboard."

The Hulk moved through the mosh pit like a swimmer in deep water. The water was rough, but he made steady progress. Riding high on his shoulders, Alice felt like letting loose a war cry but she restrained herself. It would upset the Hulk, and the envelope was clenched between her teeth and she didn't want to drop it. As they waded deeper into the crowd she had to shift a couple of times on the Hulk's shoulders to dodge crowd-surfers; he grabbed onto her knees, holding her steady, and she tried not to pull the hair out of his head. They were almost there. She could see Angel bent over his bass. Her heart or someplace near it stung like lemon juice in a paper cut.

Angel looked up and saw her. He took her in, her face, the envelope clenched between her teeth like a rose or a knife. A crowd-surfer passed between them, legs flailing.

Angel had stopped playing. He opened his palms towards her, Ward Cleaver after a hard day at the office and now June couldn't handle the Beaver. What? Angel was saying. What now?

Alice took the envelope out of her mouth and hurled it at the stage.

At the moment she threw it someone crashed into the Hulk and spoiled her aim. The envelope hit Stringer in the head. Stringer swatted at it before he saw what it was. When he did see, he swiped at it with his toe. The envelope skittered across the stage.

Angel had shrugged out of his bass. He dove for the envelope, his hair flying, the Indian warrior leaping on his enemy. The envelope shot into the crowd. Angel was right behind it, skidding on his elbows. The front of the crowd began to surge, and then to spin, like a whirlpool.

Alice leaned forward as if the Hulk were a horse, as if she could make him go where she wanted him to go. But he wasn't interested in getting into a brawl. He was turning around, getting the hell out of there. She had chosen well. This guy had brains. It was no time for heroic gestures.

Partway through the encore Angel stopped playing. Joe looked over at him, what was he pulling now? But Angel was staring into the crowd, his hands out. Then something like a lopsided frisbee came hurtling through the air. It hit Stringer. What the fuck? But Angel was already out of his bass and moving. Angel knew what it was.

Dan yelled something at Joe and Joe realized he'd stopped playing too. "I don't know," he yelled back, which covered everything. Then Angel went flying into the crowd, and the crowd turned rambunctious. Angel must have landed hard on somebody. He must have pissed somebody off. He'd started a brawl.

It was like old times. Joe slid his guitar strap over his head, ran to the edge of the stage, and dove in.

Angel was a good fighter. He was fast and mean. By the time Joe got to him he had cleared a space around himself. With Joe to stand guard, fending off one guy who was too drunk to quit, Angel had the breathing space to crouch down and grab something off the floor. Then Angel stuck his head between Joe's legs and stood, lifting Joe on his shoulders. Joe reached down and Angel put a bulky, funky-looking, 8 x 10 brown envelope into his hand.

Dan was standing at the edge of the stage. Wobbling on Angel's shoulders, holding himself steady with one hand on Angel's head, Joe threw the envelope to Dan.

The envelope had had a long journey. It had been through a lot. First Lynn's hands, fretful with indecision, then Alice's head, sleeping on it while she dreamt unquiet dreams, and now Angel's booted foot, holding it while he fought, had torn one untaped corner. On its flight to Dan it sprung a leak. A few bills rained gently onto the people in front, like manna from heaven.

Alice dismounted from the Hulk at the edge of the crowd. She tried to thank him but all he said was, "I had a bad feeling about this," and disappeared as fast as he could.

Alice climbed up and stood on an abandoned barstool to watch. If this was a story she was going to tell her grandchildren she needed to see the outcome.

She saw Joe rising above the crowd. His head was down, then he raised it and looked towards the stage. He drew back his arm and threw the envelope. The gesture was so fluid and controlled that Alice felt a pang of admiration and envy. The envelope sailed through the air and landed in Dan's waiting hands.

Stringer was saying something into the microphone, trying to get people to calm down. In front of Alice people were standing on tiptoe to see what was going on, moving aside for the people who were trying to get away from what was going on. Then Alice saw Joe hoist himself onto the stage. All the ropy muscles in his arms stood out. He turned and reached down a hand for Angel. Angel had blood on his face, but he was grinning.

Her mission was accomplished. Not by her, Joe and Angel had finished it. She could go.

There was no way they were going to finish the encore. They weren't even going to try. Stringer, finding the other three backstage drinking beer, had a fit over that until Joe told him relax, they'd started a riot, they'd be famous tomorrow. Angel laughed from behind the wet paper towels he was holding pressed to his mouth. Blood spotted the front of his shirt.

Dan picked at the busted-out corner of the envelope. "Who's throwing money at us?" he asked Angel.

Angel leaned over and plucked the envelope out of Dan's hands. "It's my money," he said. "I can't give it away."

"But what happened?" Stringer wanted to know. "I was just standing there and all at once, out of nowhere—"

"Alice threw it at me," Angel said. "She missed."

There was a silence. Alice? Joe was thinking. Alice was in that mess out front?

Dan lit a cigarette, leaning back in his chair. "I told you not to give it to her," he said to Angel. "That one's not just poison, she's a double dose."

Joe looked at Angel to see how he would take this. Angel wiped his upper lip with the paper towel. He didn't look insulted, not for himself or for Alice. Joe lit a cigarette for something to do. When he looked up Angel grinned at him like they were sharing a joke. Joe had missed the punch line.

Stringer, totally unconcerned with trivia, wondered out loud what to say to the press.

"Calm down," Dan said to Stringer. "Drink a beer. Be a rock musician, for chrissakes."

Stringer stared at him, and then he popped himself a beer. He got a goofy grin on his face, like Dan had just told him he'd won a million dollars. He cracked them all up. He even laughed himself.

"But what if somebody asks us?" Dan asked, now that Stringer wasn't worrying. "What are we going to say?"

"No comment," Angel said. "We can always say that." He was still watching Joe, like he wanted him to understand something but he wasn't going to tell him what it was.

"That's what politicians say," Dan said. "You should say you ditched some girl you knocked up, sent her a thousand bucks, and she threw it at you. You'd be a rock legend."

"Rock legends don't give women money," Joe said. "They wait to be sued." They thought that was funny. They were giddy. He was too. His thoughts were whirling around one still point.

"My girlfriend wouldn't like it," Angel said. "Anybody got a cigarette?"

Joe shook out a cigarette and handed it to Angel. Stringer started wondering out loud whether Alice would sue Angel later, after they had made their millions. Angel was watching Joe like a cat at a mousehole.

"You ditched her?" Joe said. If Angel had had a tail, it would have twitched.

"Two months ago."

Joe took a last, long drag on his cigarette. It fired up his lungs and his brain synapses. Then he put out the cigarette and stood. "Give me your car keys," he said to Dan, breaking in on Dan's argument with Stringer about the promotional value of a hypothetical paternity suit.

Dan gave Joe his car keys. Joe pried the van key off his key ring and handed it to him.

"What's this for?" Dan asked.

"You'll need the van to get the equipment back. There's a housekey under the front step. Use that to get in."

"What about you?" Stringer asked. He looked confused.

"I got something to do," Joe said.

"Like what?" Dan asked, a terrible suspicion dawning on his face.

Angel made a fist around an imaginary knife and stabbed himself in the heart. Joe was the only one who got it. It was part of the sign language he and Angel had made up years ago. It meant lovesick.

"What's that for?" Stringer asked. Joe already had his jacket, his cigarettes, wallet, and keys. He was on his way out the door when Angel spoke.

"Alice," Angel said.

Joe heard Dan groan. "I thought you had some sense," Dan yelled at his back.

Alice left the club feeling chastened. She hadn't thought to take any money out of the envelope for cab fare. She took a cab for a four-dollar ride, watching the meter and getting out when her money was up. She gave the cabbie a dollar tip and went the rest of the way on foot.

Watching the cab drive away, the taillights reflected in wet pavement, Alice was overwhelmed by a sense of failure. She had botched her warrior's gesture. Instead of feeling strong and free, she felt let down. At least Angel had his money back, she'd made things safer for herself and the baby, got rid of some karma that came with Angel's money.

And Angel was okay. Angel and Joe were okay. She could tell from the way they'd looked, Angel's back as he pushed Joe onstage, the stretch of Joe's long arms reaching down to haul Angel up. They were friends again, Alice didn't have to feel guilty anymore. She had shed two burdens. So why didn't she feel lighter?

She got used to burdens, that's why. She used them to ground herself. They made her feel Significant. It would probably take her a day or so to feel really good again. Making up her own life as she went, and then living it, that was another kind of grounding, harder to manage, slower, but it worked. No more cheap thrills. She'd be a warrior for real, this time.

She was lighter in one way. She was out on the streets, alone, and totally penniless. Thinking that, she cheered up. She moved easier. She was having an adventure. She was on her warrior's path, and who knew, sometime in the future there might be something better than cheap thrills on it. So her heart was broken, so what. So her heartbreakers had forgotten her already with other women and each other, she was damned if she was going to be sad about that forever. She was herself again. And she wasn't alone anymore. She had a passenger, a companion on her journey.

When she got home she'd start right away. She'd pack her books.

Alice opened all the windows wide so she could smell the rain. She took off her boots to let her feet air out and turned the radio on low. She made herself a cup of herbal tea and started pulling books off the shelves. Keep, sell, give away...she sang along with the radio.

When the doorbell rang she froze. It was probably Carla and Matt. Matt was feeling enough himself again to squire Carla around while she checked out the territory. He wasn't ready for it himself, he just went along to take notes on technique and fend off the rough stuff. Now that Alice was awake at night they came by to tell her the horror stories about the guys they met in clubs. It was probably them.

The doorbell rang again. It couldn't be Angel. Could it?

She buzzed the downstairs door open. Her heart was thudding in her chest. She pressed her ear against the door to listen to the footsteps coming up the stairs. It sounded like one person's footsteps, not two people's. It reminded her of ghost stories when she was a kid—he's on the first step, he's on the second step...

The knock on her door sounded loud. Maybe it was a serial killer. Maybe it was Matt. She couldn't take the suspense, so she opened the door.

Joe was standing in the hall.

The book in Alice's hand chose that moment to make a leap for freedom. It landed on her foot. She knelt and picked it up and Joe was still there. Her nemesis had come calling.

"Are you alone?" he asked.

Alice looked around for someone else to be there, Matt or Carla. No one was. "Yes," she said.

"I can't believe you did that," he said. "You buzzed me in and didn't even check to see who it was. It could have been anybody." Up close he didn't look like she remembered him but she couldn't figure out what was different.

"Well, it was you," she said. Unless it was his evil twin. Maybe that's why he looked different. But Joe would have to be the evil twin, if there was one. So it was probably really him.

He came in and shut the door. He stared at the book boxes. He picked up her mug of tea and sniffed it. "What's this?" he said, like it was eye of newt.

"Raspberry leaf tea," she said.

"Calcium," he said, and set it down.

"What?"

"It's full of calcium."

"The gypsies use it," she said. "For easy labor."

"That's the calcium."

"You want some?"

"No. It smells awful." He turned around and looked at her. "Who were you expecting?" he asked, like she would tell him if he took her by surprise. The nerve. She hadn't even invited him in.

"What are you doing here?" she asked back.

She stood in her kitchen, packing up, going away, barefoot and pregnant. When she first saw him standing in her doorway she had gone so white he'd been afraid she was going to pass out. Now she was looking at him like he was something she might need a box for, and she didn't think she had a box that size.

He couldn't tell if she was showing yet, her t-shirt was too big. He wondered whose shirt it was.

"I thought you were with Angel," he said.

"When?"

"When what?"

"Start over," she said. She dropped the book into a box.

"I thought you were with Angel all this time."

"I'm not," she said. "I haven't been. He left."

"Yeah, well," he said. "So I heard."

"You came over because I'm not with Angel."

"Right," he said. Why was this so hard? Didn't she understand? Maybe she did understand and didn't want to hear it. Who had she been expecting, and why was she packing her books? Where was she going?

"So," she said, "now that Angel's gone, it's open season?"

He wasn't prepared for anger. She looked like she wanted to eat his balls for breakfast. At least her color was coming back.

"You can tell me what a bitch I am face to face," she said. "You don't even have to lock me in a bathroom. Does your girlfriend know you're here?"

"What girlfriend?" Had the pregnancy affected her mind?

"Cynthia," she said, sour. "That girlfriend."

"Cynthia!" He tried not to laugh and succeeded. "Cynthia's got a husband with ulcers. And even if she didn't...Who told you I had a girlfriend?" He saw the answer in her face. "Angel," he said.

She didn't say yes or no. She didn't have to. She made a motion like she was going to put her hands in her pockets, but she didn't have any pockets.

"So what did you come over for?" she asked, as if Cynthia was totally beside the point.

Because I wanted to, Joe thought. Because I miss you. Because you don't know enough yet to call me when you're missing me. And she was missing him, she wouldn't be so mad at him if she wasn't.

But she wasn't ready to hear that. He hadn't answered; she watched him thinking it out.

"Did you ever get your car out of the shop?"

"I junked it," she said. "It was a piece of shit." She said it like she was describing him.

He nodded a couple times, like this was interesting information and he was digesting it. "Do you want to go see the trees?" he asked.

"You came over *now* to ask me if I wanted to go see the *trees*?"

"Yeah. I came over now to ask you if you wanted to go see the trees." She was giving him a look. He could outstare anybody when he wanted to; it went with being a good liar. "Is it okay if I smoke?"

She pointed to the chair nearest the window. "Over there," she said. She wasn't throwing him out.

"Do you have anything to drink?"

"Water," she said. "Raspberry leaf tea."

"Water's fine."

"You'll have to drink it out of a mug. The glasses got broken."

Joe sat down at the table. She filled a mug with water from the tap and set it down in front of him. She leaned against the counter and watched him smoke. Her mouth moved on hidden words, or maybe she was wishing she could smoke too.

He could feel a smile starting, and he didn't want to smile. It was too soon to smile.

"You can drink your water and then you can go," Alice said. So she'd seen the smile. He drank the water in small sips. She folded her arms across her belly. She stared out the window like she was staring out to sea, like a fisherman's widow. He didn't believe it.

"Can you go tomorrow?" he asked.

"No."

"Why not?"

"Because," she said, biting off the words, "I finally got it together on my own. I don't need any *rides* from you."

"That was...I was pissed off when I said that."

"That's right," she said. "You were."

"Listen, Alice. I didn't come over here to mess with your head. I thought...we could try to be friends."

"Friends," she said.

"Yeah. Friends."

"What for? You didn't want to be friends before."

"I like you," he said.

Alice sat down at the table. Her face was so funny he almost laughed.

"If you were me," she said, "would you believe you?"

"I'm not you."

"Come on."

"Yeah, I would." He was lying. Of course he wouldn't believe him. Nobody would. Not even Alice.

Now he could see the smile starting on her face. She squashed it too, like he had.

"I've got a couple days off. We can stay overnight. I'll borrow sleeping bags and a tent. I'll sleep in the tent and you can have the van." When she didn't say anything he added, "Or you can have the tent." One of her eyebrows was being sceptical, but she wasn't saying no.

He finished the water, ground out the cigarette. "I'll pick you up at eleven," he said. He stood up. He had to leave. He needed to shout.

"I haven't said I was going."

"You can think about it," he said. "You can tell me tomorrow." You're mine, he was thinking. You're mine, Alice.

"Eleven's too early," she said. "I can't decide by eleven. I won't even be awake."

"When?"

Her mouth moved a little, chewing it over. "One," she said.

Joe drove home paying no attention to lights and slept like a log. He woke early, took a shower and drove to Dan's, woke him up and didn't listen to him at all. He got the van and drove out to Frank and Michelle's to borrow sleeping bags and a tent. He must have been acting strange, they looked at him like he was.

"What's up?" Frank finally said.

"I'm going camping for a couple days," Joe said.

"Oh yeah? With who?" asked Michelle.

"Someone," Joe said. "I'll tell you later."

"He's going to knock on wood," said Michelle, who made fun of Frank and Joe for doing just that. "Should we say 'break a leg'?"

"Yeah. Pray for me to break a leg."

Alice woke up with plenty of time to think about whether or not she should go with Joe. She had time to call Lynn or Matt and get some sensible advice. She called work instead. She said she had to take an extra day off, a mental health day. She already had today off.

Then she drank some tea and packed a knapsack. She thought about how much better she was doing with just the baby and herself, no men to drive her nuts. To keep that thought firmly in place she put on the X song. Like all fuck-you songs, it was high energy. It had Alice dancing.

Joe was there at one. He rang and Alice came down the stairs without buzzing him in. Seeing him standing on her doorstep she was suddenly nervous, like this was a blind date.

"You ready?" he asked.

For what? she almost said. "I'm packed," she answered, "if that's what you mean."

"Oh," he said, looking at her knapsack like he'd just noticed it. She guessed he was in his usual early-in-the-day mode, half-asleep.

On the ferry they got watery coffee and rolls. Alice ignored the coffee and wolfed her roll. Joe gave her most of his roll, pouring his coffee over the rail. The wind whipped his hair back.

"Where's your sunglasses?" she asked, thinking that was what made him look so different.

He felt in his pockets, found his sunglasses, and put them on. Then he took her hand. Now that she wasn't with Angel, she didn't feel anything about Joe holding her hand.

"I thought you just wanted to be friends," she said.

"Okay," he said, turning his head to look at something or hide his face. Okay? That sounded ambiguous.

"It's all I want," she said, making it clear right from the start.

"I said okay."

"You think you'll talk me out of it."

He looked at her. "If you're not going to believe anything I say," he said, "what's the point of saying anything?"

The wind blew his hair all over his face and shoulders. It flattened his t-shirt against his chest.

"No point," Alice said, squinting into the light. She let him hold her hand.

Back in the van she didn't talk about friendship. She didn't talk about anything. Joe didn't either. It was a little like the first time they'd driven out here, except she hadn't been full of burning questions then. They stopped to eat after a couple of hours because she was hungry again. They got sandwiches and ate in the van.

"When did you find out Angel left me?" Alice asked, her first burning question.

"Last night," he said, looking surprised.

Last night? That gave her a thrill. She ignored it. "How come you didn't know before?"

"Angel hasn't been talking to me much," Joe said.

"But he told you that?"

Joe swallowed sandwich. "Yeah." He didn't want to talk about Angel. She did.

"He was fucking other women the whole time," Alice said. "Did you know that?"

Joe wadded up the paper his sandwich had come in. "I knew."

"You never said anything."

He busied himself putting the waxed paper into a paper bag instead of just dropping it on the floor. He was probably deciding what to say. "I thought you might know," he said. "It didn't mean that much to him. I thought it might not mean that much to you."

"Well it would have," she said. "It did." She stared out the window and let herself feel what she felt about Angel.

"So you and Angel aren't friends anymore?" she asked after awhile.

"He hasn't been talking to me. I wouldn't call that friends."

"Are you enemies?"

"I don't know what we are. We can still work together." He looked at the sandwich in her lap. "Are you gonna finish that?"

"I'm not hungry. I get this ravenous hunger and as soon as it's satisfied I'm not hungry at all. It's like an on-off switch. You want it?"

"You ate my breakfast," he said. "I want it."

She passed it to him.

"I think Angel blamed both of us," Joe said, wiping his mouth with the back of his hand. "Not just you, not just me."

He finished the sandwich, started the van, and punched in the lighter. "Will smoke bother you?"

Alice shook her head and rolled the window down farther. "Did you know about the money he sent me?"

"Not until last night. I didn't even see you." All at once he laughed. "You started a riot, did you know that?"

"I was in it," she said. And then, "He gets a girlfriend and pays me off. He didn't even give it to me himself, he gave it to Lynn. Keeping his hands clean."

Joe didn't say anything.

"Aren't you going to stick up for him?" she asked. "Tell me he was just trying to watch out for me? That's what everybody else says."

"He was trying to watch out for you," Joe said. "And keep his hands clean at the same time."

"What would you have done?" she asked. He looked startled. "If you were me, I mean."

He thought about it. "Kept the money," he said. "Tried to start a riot."

"I didn't mean for that to happen. I didn't mean for people to get hurt."

"It wasn't that bad. Pretty small-scale, actually. Angel got a split lip, nothing he's going to die from. When I left last night Stringer was wondering what to tell the press."

"You really didn't know about the money? Or anything?"

"No. I still don't know how you got that close to the stage without me seeing you."

"I came in on the left," she said. "Where Angel was." Then she told him about the Hulk, all the lies she'd had to tell to get him to help her. Joe laughed so hard she forgot who she was talking to and mentioned that her imaginary philanthropist came from Minneapolis. Joe split a gut over that, so she guessed he knew that all her made-up people came from Minneapolis lately.

Hearing him laugh, she realized she hadn't botched her warrior's gesture after all. She hadn't made a warrior's gesture. She'd made a fool's gesture, but whether or not it had been successful was a mystery. You knew when a warrior's gesture had been successful—even if you lost the battle you had a sense of moral superiority. A fool's gesture needed hindsight. You had to wait until things worked themselves out to see if your gesture had been fraught with uncanny significance, totally meaningless but funny, or just plain dumb. Which reminded her.

"Remember that quote about the fool persisting in her folly and becoming wise?" she asked.

"Yeah," he said. "What about it?"

"It wasn't Lin Yutang who said that. It was William Blake. It's from the *Proverbs of Hell.*"

She explained about William Blake, that he was a poet, a printmaker, and a mystic. "He saw angels," she said. "He was religious, but not like most people are. He didn't think reason was better than passion." Then she heard the word "passion" hanging in the air between them. It echoed like she'd shouted it down a well.

She took a deep breath. "Anyway," she said, "he didn't think it was simple, to live right. The *Proverbs of Hell* aren't supposed to be simple. They're supposed to wake you up, to make you wonder. They're from hell, so you can't just swallow them whole even when they sound right. They're supposed to make you think. Or feel. Maybe both." She was getting bogged down, trying to make it clear. "They're not *rules*," she said. "You know what I mean?"

"You mean you fucked up the quote?"

"Yeah," she said. "I sort of did."

"Did you find another quote yet?"

"Well, no."

"Is that why you're getting rid of your books?"

She thought of him standing by the boxes of books on her kitchen floor, frowning at them. "I'm moving," she said.

He shook out another cigarette and lit it. He blew smoke out the window and stretched one leg, rearranging himself in the driver's seat. Then he said, "Moving where?"

She should tell him she was moving to Minneapolis. If she could do it deadpan he might even believe her. Just thinking about it she couldn't keep a straight face.

"What," he said.

Act like an adult, she told herself. "I'm moving into Lynn's old apartment. She's moving into the apartment upstairs with her boyfriend. So I'll finally have decent neighbors." She went on and told him about the man downstairs getting nastier after Carla and Matt started keeping her company at night. She wanted Joe to know that things hadn't been easy, but she hadn't been alone and friendless just because he and Angel weren't around. She also wanted him to know exactly who she hadn't been alone with, that she didn't need a boyfriend to keep her from being friendless.

Joe told her about a man living in a tree to keep it from being cut down; he said he'd written a song about it. She was pretty sure he was saying something else too, but she couldn't tell what. She wanted to hear the song but he wouldn't sing it. He said he didn't feel like it. "Maybe later," he said.

She told him about a book she was reading about the earth being alive and he was interested in that. It was like the nights they used to spend at the warehouse, they talked about everything.

They got to the campground before the sun set. It was nearly full, but they found a space. Joe pitched the tent to mark their territory and they went looking for food. Alice was hungry again; they got dinner and ate everything except the bread, which she put in her shoulderbag.

"For breakfast," she said. "In case I wake up starving. Sometimes I don't."

"No morning sickness?"

"Nope. I never got that," she said. "I get other stuff."

After dinner they walked around the campground, checking out the other campers. Families, couples, student types, and a lone biker were sitting around their campfires. The firelight on their faces made them seem like people in a dream. Some of them looked up and saw Joe and Alice, nodded or said hello.

When they got back to their own campsite they built a fire and watched it burn. They still had things to say but they weren't saying them. They were resting their jaws, listening to the fire eat wood.

Alice yawned. "I have to go to bed," she said. While she walked down the road to the bathrooms Joe moved his stuff into the tent. She came back and said goodnight. All at once she was staggering with tiredness, she was asleep on her feet.

Joe sat up awhile. He smoked and watched the fire burn down, thinking of a song, hearing a riff that went with the trees standing all around him, the night stretched over his head. He jotted down some notes in the notebook he kept in his pocket. No words yet. And then he was tired, too. He could tell by looking at the van that Alice was asleep. He kicked dirt over the fire, making sure it was out. Then he went to the bathroom, came back and crawled into the tent. He fell asleep as soon as he lay down.

He woke in the middle of the night. He lay still, smelling the tent, the sleeping bag, the trees. He thought he'd heard something, like an animal crying out. Maybe a bird. He waited for it to come again. It didn't.

He was sinking back into sleep when he heard the van door creak. It shut softly. Someone was walking around, stumbling over something. Then silence. He pulled on his jeans and stuck his head out of the tent. He had left the flashlight with Alice.

There was a darker shadow by the dead fire. The shadow changed shape. It could have been Alice turning to see him. If it was she didn't say anything.

He came on out. The grass was wet on his bare feet, the dust by the fire was soft. He touched the shadow, felt Alice's hair under his hand.

"It's me," she said.

He felt around for the log she was sitting on, and sat down next to her. They kept their voices low. "What's up?"

"Nothing. A nightmare. I can't sleep."

"You can't get back to sleep?"

"I'm afraid to go back to sleep. I have to wait awhile. You can go back to bed. I'll be all right."

"What was the dream about?"

She shifted on the log. "My mother."

"Your real mother or your foster mother?"

"My biological mother," she said. "Only...it's like she's a witch. She has black lipstick on. She grabs me. She's got a grip like iron. As soon as she touches me I wake up because I'm so scared. If I fall asleep too soon she's waiting for me. I can only fight her when I'm awake."

"You've had this dream before?"

"The first time right after Angel got back. A lot since he left."

"I remember you telling me, the Senoi ask their dream enemies what they want."

"I already know what she wants. She wants me, or she wants the baby. She can't have either one of us." Alice hissed the last words, then was quiet. A mist was coming in from the ocean. Joe was cold; he could feel her shivering next to him. She touched his arm and said, "You're freezing. Go back to bed."

"Come with me." She pulled her hand back. "I don't mean like that," he said. "There's two sleeping bags. We can talk. It'll keep you awake."

"I have to go to the bathroom first," she said. The baby pressing on her bladder, he thought.

In the van, tucked inside their sleeping bags on the mattress, Joe asked Alice about her mother. "Did she scare you when you were a kid?"

"I don't remember that. Sometimes I think now I was afraid she was going to leave, but I'm probably rearranging my memory because of what happened."

"What was she like?"

"She was fun," Alice said, slow, thinking out loud. "She made everything fun. Just being around her...I remember this one time, my father was out of town. Instead of eating a regular dinner, we had raisins and chocolate and peanuts and juice. We pretended like we were stranded on an island and that was the food we'd gathered. We turned off all the lights and had candles for our fire...

"She talked to everybody, people in the street, in the checkout line at the grocery store...she was always making jokes, making people laugh. She even made my father laugh."

Alice was quiet for awhile. Then she sighed hard. "You know something? It's been fifteen years. I don't know why she's got to come back now."

Joe stared at the changing shadows on the ceiling of the van, tree branches caught by the lights around the bathrooms. He could sense Alice next to him, some feeling that emanated from her. Then he thought about what she was saying about her mother, how her voice sounded. "Was she anything like Angel?" he asked.

Alice didn't answer.

"Alice?"

"Yeah," she said. "She was like Angel." He heard her move inside her sleeping bag to face him. "I think that's what it is," she said. "And I've lost her forever, so she's haunting me. Being pregnant is like…it slows you down. You have to face your losses."

"You haven't lost her forever," Joe said. "You've got part of her in you."

"Being unfaithful, you mean."

"I wasn't thinking that. She liked people, right? She knew how to play?"

"But she didn't know how to mean it. She didn't stick to anybody or anything. I don't want to be like that."

"Well you're not. You got sticking to things on your own."

"I don't stick to things," she said.

"Christ, Alice, you don't know how to unstick."

"What do you mean? You mean Angel."

I mean me, he thought. "There's your friends," he said. "And printmaking. You stick to that."

"But I don't always know where I'm going with it."

"So what? Why do you have to know? And the baby. You decided to have the baby and that was it. No money, no help, you're still doing it."

"But I have bad dreams. I'm scared. I might be a terrible mother. I don't know how to do it."

"You'll learn how to do it."

"I don't know if I will. Kids are great to watch, but dealing with them is a whole nother thing. Lynn's so patient and reasonable when they're being a pain in the ass. I'm afraid I'll just lose it and warp the child for life. And the babies...I can change a diaper now but that's about it. Well, and I know what projectile vomiting looks like and that it's no big deal. But I'm still afraid I'll do something stupid and they'll die."

"Angel and I used to babysit my brother's kid when he was a baby. He's three now, and he seems okay."

"You and Angel took care of a baby?" Alice said. "Did you have any experience?"

"None. We got used to him by deciding he was totally stoned all the time. He liked to stare at light."

"Then there's the whole labor thing," Alice went on. "What if I don't do that right? What if I've done something wrong already, while she's still a little fish? That's life and death, you know? If I mess up there, no second chance..." Her voice trailed off. She was scaring herself. She was starting to scare him.

"In this book I read," he said, "they did a study of expectant mothers. The ones who had nightmares when they were pregnant had the shortest labors. Because they had dealt with all the fear when they were pregnant. So when they went into labor they could just do it, they were okay. I think you're supposed to be scared now."

Alice didn't say anything.

"I'm not making it up."

"When did you read this book?" she asked.

He was glad she couldn't see him. He could say it was a book of Michelle's. It made him look like a total wimp, him thinking she was with Angel and then reading up on pregnancy. It made him look like a lovesick dog.

"A couple weeks ago," he said. "I got it out of the library."

Alice didn't say anything for so long he thought she'd fallen asleep. Then he heard her unzipping her sleeping bag. It sounded loud. She reached out and unzipped his sleeping bag. It got stuck and she worked it loose and finished the job. Her nose bumped his in the darkness.

"Ow," he said.

Alice kissed his nose. Then she kissed beside his nose. Then she kissed his mouth. With one hand on his shoulder she pressed him down into the mattress. She was half out of her sleeping bag; he felt goosebumps on her hip from the cold air seeping in. He pulled her into his sleeping bag. She was all knees and elbows and the sleeping bag was too small. That was all right. They could manage.

Acknowledgments

I would like to thank everyone who shared their stories and their expertise:

Melissa Klein, Ned Hinkle; Joe Diaz, John Sands, Mary Schenklin, Brian Wright; Matthew P. Dumont, M.D., Topher Carnes; Todd Jesdale, Lee B. Vickery, Betsy Kelly Shea; Maris Boyd Gillette, Fuji Lozada, Rebecca Ruhlen; Lisa Carter, Natasha Hanna, Sam Turano; the Summa tribe (plus in-laws), the Conger/Aga family (ditto); Daphne Steele; Ursula Le Guin and everyone in the September 1992 short fiction workshop at the Flight of the Mind.

And Mission Control on this one: Cath Amory and Nancy Josephson; the students, staff, and faculty at the Department of Anthropology, Harvard University; and for the last bit, Eli Dan and Susan Kippen.

And the space crew: Jessie Summa-Kusiak, Emily Arkin, Hsuan Tsen, Jef Czekaj, and Simone Alpen.

About the Author

Pam Summa received a BFA in printmaking from Massachusetts College of Art in 1981. She has been a housepainter, a muralist, a waitress, a gardener, and a welfare mother, among other things. For the past 18 years she has been an academic editor specializing in anthropology and a fiction writer; for the past ten, she also has been a writing and creativity coach. She lives in Somerville, MA, where she is working on her fourth novel.

Turn the page for an excerpted preview of
The Night Trippers.

Coming soon from Mystic River Ink.

In the middle of the night Joe asked her, did you miss me?

The words rolled off his tongue just as if he'd meant to say them. It must have been more of a strain than he'd thought, pretending he didn't want to jump her.

"Did you, Al?" he repeated, not believing himself. But he may as well be hung for a sheep. Or was it a goat?

"Yes," she said. "I missed you bad." She wasn't making a point or being swept away by the romance. It sounded like the simple truth and he believed her.

He went back to what he had been doing, stroking her back like she was a cat. He used to have a cat who curled up on his shoulder and sucked his earlobe when he slept. He could sleep now. After the first round they had zipped the two sleeping bags together, so he was nice and warm, all his muscles loose and sort of humming. Even his bones were humming.

"Why were you like that when you saw me again?" she said. "When you shoved me into the bathroom and…god, the way you looked at me, the things you said…"

He thought it was interesting that now they had finally gotten naked and close, they had to ask questions. Just as if they both wanted the other one to get more naked.

"You acted like I was the evil woman," she said.

"That wasn't it."

"Then what?"

"When I saw you sitting there after the gig, going to sleep and sort of disappearing inside Angel's jacket, I had this impulse to pick you up and carry you out to the van and just drive away. But I couldn't. I got mad instead."

She wriggled down next to him and put her arm around him with a little sigh. Her body was different. Her belly stuck out some with three months of baby in there. Her breasts were softer. "And bigger," she had said just before round three, as if that mattered. He could count her ribs with his fingers and her nose was cold.

"I went looking for you once," she said. "Before you yelled at me. Chuck drove me to the warehouse one night after work. I was going to wait inside the van for you. I felt like I had to talk to you or go crazy."

"What were you gonna say?"

"I never figured out that part."

"Is that why you didn't do it?"

"We couldn't find the van. Maybe you weren't working that night. We looked everywhere."

With one part of his brain, that was flickering like a candle in a high wind, he wondered what to call his new song. Strip Tease? Truth Serum? Then she put her leg up around his hip like she was climbing a tree. Love Monkey, he thought, and let the candle blow out.

There was some guy waiting on his front step when Joe got home. The guy said his name was Josh, Cynthia had hired him to be their new roadie. Joe had forgotten all about the new roadie. At least none of the other guys were here yet; he didn't have an audience. Joe grabbed the tent, Josh brought the sleeping bags, and they dumped everything in the bedroom. Then Joe shut the bedroom door. Hiding the evidence.

"I need to take a quick shower," he told Josh, and showed him what stuff he could load if he wanted to get started.

Josh nodded. He didn't have a word to say. He was medium height, with pale skin, black hair, and the kind of body that looked like it belonged behind a desk. But some people looked soft and were all muscle underneath. And Cynthia had hired him, he must be a real roadie.

Joe showered fast, washing away the combined aromas of Alice and woodsmoke and sleeping bag sex. As he got dressed he heard voices in the other room—Angel and Dan.

Joe took a deep breath and let it out slow. He had nothing to feel guilty about this time. Right? He came out of the bathroom and sat down in a kitchen chair to put on his sneakers. Dan came in from the living room.

"We're almost finished," Dan said. "What's taking you so long?"

"I just got home," Joe said. "I took ten minutes." Then his sneakers were laced and he looked up. Dan was staring at him. Joe stared back.

"Well take another minute and do something about your face," Dan said. "You can't go on like that."

Joe hadn't shaved today, but so what? He wasn't a banker. "What's the matter with my face?"

"You look like a fucking bride," Dan said. Then he laughed. He could never keep from laughing at his own jokes.

Angel was in the front room. He was winding a cord around his bent arm, under the elbow and over the palm. Under and over. He had a cigarette in his mouth. He was wearing a t-shirt with the arms cut out to show off his shoulders, his upper arm definition, his lightning tattoos. His thick black hair was pulled back in a ponytail and he squinted against the cigarette smoke, being inscrutable.

"How's Alice?" Angel said.

Joe could feel Dan freezing into attention behind him. Joe went over and opened his guitar case, checked to make sure he had extra strings, and closed the lid. He clicked the fasteners shut, one, two, three, four.

"Fine," he said. He hefted the case and faced Angel like he had nothing to hide.

"She still pregnant?" Angel asked.

"Yeah," Joe said. He sounded pissed off. He was. Not for the reason Angel thought. "What did you think?" She miscarried out of grief?

Angel smiled. He let Joe see how pleased he was that he could push Joe's buttons. It's so easy, he seemed to be saying. And I'll do it whenever I feel like it. Just for the hell of it. You can't stop me.

Maybe I can't, Joe thought. But I can beat the living crap out of you. Say one more thing, and I'll let it rip.

Angel's smile got wider. He didn't say the one more thing. He let Joe see that he wasn't scared of him, he was biding his time. For once Angel had the moral high ground, and he was enjoying the view. Maybe he would settle here, plant crops and sit on the porch.

Josh walked in. He looked around at everyone playing statues. The air was so thick you could cut it with a knife.

"Let's get going," Dan said. "We're wasting time." Like he couldn't believe they were acting so petty. He headed across the room, right between Joe and Angel, directly in the line of fire.

"Yeah," Angel said. "Don't want to be late. Can't have that." Because Joe used to give him shit for being late.

But Joe's righteous fury had passed. Without it he felt like a kettle moved off the fire before it boiled.

Josh rode in the van with Joe. He didn't say boo. He was probably wondering what he'd gotten himself into.

Some of the kitchen staff were speaking in Arabic; Alice had the feeling they were talking about her. She chopped parsley diligently, watching the knife, trying to concentrate. She ached all over, like she had a fever.

They had spent most of their camping trip walking in the woods, even going out once in the dead of night with the flashlight, and then Joe had turned off the light so they could feel the trees all around them. In a darkness so thick she couldn't tell which way was up, Alice had put her hands on Joe's waist to keep from falling into the void, and he had set his hands on her shoulders...and she had gone into an altered state. She had felt Joe's living, breathing self as if it were her own. She had heard the song in his blood—well, he had been humming it all day, off and on—and then she had grown impossibly tall and vast, as if she had to be huge to contain this feeling, which was of near weightlessness, but rooted in the earth...It was the trees. It was their reaching up toward sky and down into earth, and it felt like flying. While the feeling lasted she had not been dizzy or afraid of the dark—she had danced with the trees, with the whole universe.

"A-lise. Wake up, A-lise." Bilel waved his hand in front of her nose. "Aziz is here," he hissed.

"Shit," Alice said.

Kitchen gossip had it that Aziz was fit to be tied because Alice had taken a day off with no warning and called it a mental health day. She took a deep breath and wiped her hands on her apron, getting ready to be raked over the coals.

"Are you well?" Aziz said. It was an ominous beginning.

"Fine thanks," she said.

"If you're sick in the head," he said, "I should get somebody else to cook."

"All cooks are crazy," she argued. "Everybody knows that."

Bilel was standing right there. He tried a scowl, but he only looked hurt. "Me?" he said. "I am not crazy."

"You're a mad genius. Your creative fire is an inspiration to us all."

Bilel folded his hands over his stomach. "I think that is true," he admitted.

"But *you* are not a cook yet," Aziz said to Alice. "No more crazy days, or you don't work in my kitchen anymore. You go."

She waited but Aziz seemed to be finished. He hadn't fired her yet. He hadn't fired her in weeks, come to think of it. Not since she had told him she was pregnant. And now he was restraining his innate urge to yell. He must think she would miscarry if he yelled at her. His face was turning purple but his lips were sealed.

Or was he just being nice? Nice to her, for her own self and not for her role as expectant mother?

"*Why are you looking at me?*" he screamed, not at her, but at all of them. The kitchen staff had stopped work to watch. "I don't pay you to look at me! Get to work!"

They went back to work with alacrity—the kitchen rang with it. Thank god. She had thought for a minute she was going to have to tell everybody Aziz wasn't so bad after all. He looked around at the frenzy he had created, and then left, satisfied. From all over the kitchen came sighs of relief, except from Mohammed, who had been choking on mirth, and now allowed himself to guffaw. "You speak of the fire last week?" he said across the kitchen to Alice. Bilel had started a fire in the grill with an olive oil-spill, ruining six kebobs and inspiring a spate of jokes at his expense. Aziz didn't know about the fire. Mohammed's comment had the rest of them laughing with wide open mouths, all their teeth showing, all their fingers pointing. Bilel ignored them. He was a mad genius. What were a few fires between him and his Muse?

Later that night Alice got called to the phone. No one ever called her at work, but Mohammed insisted the call was for her, an emergency.

"Hi," Joe said.

"What's wrong? What happened?"

"Nothing. They wouldn't get you unless it was an emergency, so I told them it was. Is anyone watching you?"

"Only the entire kitchen," she said, turning her back on them. "Everybody's talking in Arabic tonight. I think they're talking about me. I must be acting strange. They won't let me near the blender or the fryer."

Joe laughed. "How are you doing?" she asked.

"I knocked over a mike stand onstage. Walked right into it. I kicked it so it would look purposeful."

She could see him doing that; it made her laugh. She glanced over her shoulder. Bilel was making faces at her. "I should go. Why did you call?"

"No reason."

Alice smiled into the phone—a sappy smile. No one could see her except Joe. She was sure he could.

"You got us in the papers," he said.

"What?"

"The other night. They think we started a fight with the crowd for the hell of it and then started throwing money at them. Nobody saw you though."

"Good. I don't want to use up my fifteen minutes of fame on that. Drive carefully, okay?"

"That's how I drive."

Joe hung up the phone. He stuck his cigarette in a corner of his mouth and scooped up the leftover change. He could feel someone looming; Dan was standing at his elbow with a beer in each hand.

"You're calling her?" Dan said. "You just saw her."

"Don't start. I mean it. Don't fucking start with me."

Dan pushed a beer at him. "Here," he said. "I got this for you." The draft beer was free at this club, all you could drink. That was supposed to make up for no electrical outlets and a sound board that should have been junked years ago. The beer tasted foul.

Joe didn't say thanks. He sipped the beer, trying to strain it through his teeth. He looked around at the club, the sweating, milling bodies, the inversion layer of smoke. Angel was sitting on the edge of the stage, talking to admirers of both sexes. He was chatty and smile-y, acting the part of the genius laid-back musician. Only another musician would have figured out what kind of crap he'd been pulling tonight.

The other night had been the first sign of a thaw. For a short while Angel seemed to have forgotten that he was supposed to hate Joe. So tonight Angel was making up for his lapse. He was jacking off on his bass with half the songs in the set. He was grandstanding, fucking with the rhythm, throwing Joe off.

Dan noticed where Joe was looking. "Hey," Dan said.

"Hey, what."

"Don't let him get to you." Dan sounded like he wasn't sure of his own advice.

"What the fuck did he expect?" Joe said. "Did he think I was gonna leave her alone?" Dan's brow furrowed. He had no answer to this. "He's got another girlfriend, right? Am I right?"

"You're right," Dan said reluctantly.

"Okay, then," Joe said. So he'd gone after Alice when she was Angel's girlfriend, so what. Okay, he shouldn't have. It was a bad thing to do. But Joe cared about her—Angel didn't. Angel acted like Joe should give her up just to keep in good with him.

Joe watched Angel charming the populace. "He doesn't want friends," Joe said. "He wants disciples."

Dan sighed heavily. He shook his head at Joe, that's not it. "He can't help himself," Dan said. He sipped beer and made a face. "You want me to talk to him?"

"Fuck no. Don't tell him anything."

Alice was home by midnight. If Matt was home he would be awake. He would say I told you so, and she didn't even care. But she got his answering machine.

"Well listen," she told the machine. "Something's happened. It's not an emergency or anything. I mean, it's not something bad. At least I don't think it's bad. You'll probably think it's good. Anyway, give me a call when—"

"What?" Matt's actual voice said.

"You're there."

"Having a bath," he said. "Standing in a puddle. Two puddles. One for each foot. Hold on. I want a towel."

When he returned Alice said, "Do you want to finish your bath and call back?"

"No. I'm having morbid thoughts. Tell me your news."

Matt laughed at the mosh pit part of her story, but he didn't respond to the rest with as much enthusiasm as she had expected.

"What?" she said.

"What what?"

"You're not saying anything."

"I was just wondering," he said. "Did you steal him away from his perfect new girlfriend, or are you sharing him?"

She explained that Joe's perfect new girlfriend was nothing more than a figment of Angel's disordered brain—a bare-faced lie. Angel had *lied* to her. Did Matt believe it?

Matt had no trouble believing it. "Oh I was right," he carolled. "I was so right." He sounded more chipper. "So go ahead," he said. "Tell all."

Alice did. After all, this was what she had been waiting for—the luxury of telling all to the one person as wildly, foolishly romantic as herself.

Joe got back a little after two. He had missed dinner and he was hungry. Alice heated up something she and Bilel had made at work and Joe started eating out of the pan while the food was still cold. He didn't speak, he shoveled in food.

"You really are hungry," she said.

She'd never seen him eat like this. He usually chewed.

She went in and changed the sheets on the bed so he wouldn't feel like an animal in the zoo at feeding time. She wanted to start with clean sheets anyway. Not the sheets she'd slept on last week, when Angel's money was still stashed in her bookcase.

Joe came in as she was finishing up. "It was good," he said.

"It has a secret ingredient." She wanted to kiss him hello but she didn't know how. Wrong mood or something.

He looked around the room, not interested in secret ingredients. "Is it okay for me to smoke in here?"

She got him an ashtray. She set up the fan in the window to pull air out, so the smoke would go away from the baby. Joe sat on the floor and lit up. He inhaled, savoring the nicotine. He turned his head to exhale out the window.

"I want to ask you something," he said.

"Okay." She sat down on the bed.

"How do you feel about Angel?"

No wonder she couldn't kiss him. She'd been waiting for something like this ever since they crossed the platonic line. She had thought he would be sneakier about it. His between-the-eyes bluntness made it easy to answer him straight.

"Mad," she said. "Mad at him."

Joe didn't like that much, she could tell. Nine guys out of ten would have been pleased. They would have enjoyed hearing her badmouth an ex-lover. They would have preened themselves, thinking how bright and fine they looked in comparison.

Joe was too smart. He wanted to be adored for himself, and not because he wasn't Angel. He wanted to stand alone.

"You miss him?" he asked.

"Not recently," she said. "I don't mean...it's not because...not for a while." Since she was being honest she decided to go the whole way. "Except when I saw him again. The other night. That was hard."

He was still waiting.

"Off and on," she said. "At first I missed him more, now I hate him more."

Joe smoked. His expression was getting blanker by the second, like someone was erasing his face. "He asked how you were."

She felt the hairs move on the nape of her neck. It hadn't occurred to her that Angel had a thought to spare for her. He wasn't in love with her, why should he care? He must think she was his hired womb. Even though she'd made it pretty fucking clear—

Joe had achieved total control of his face; it didn't even resemble skin. "He asked how you were coming along," Joe said.

Was Joe upset because it was Angel's baby? She put her hands on her belly. It's okay honey, she thought at her child. I won't wimp out on you. I'll do whatever I have to do.

"You don't have to look like that," Joe said. "I don't care about that."

His eyes were blue-green, but without the stingy pupils of a lot of light-eyed people. He had nice large pupils. The better to see her with. She sat there and let him look.

"I'm ready to tell people about you and me," he said. "I don't want to hide this time."

"Who's hiding? I already told Lynn and Matt."

He took a last drag and rubbed out the cigarette. Then he came over and sat down on the bed next to her. His face had eased; now he just looked tired.

"What did they have to say?" He asked like it might not be good.

"'I told you so.' That was the jist. They always liked you. Matt's been giving me shit about you for months. He used to say, 'you found somebody to read to.' He was always after me to steal you away from Cynthia."

"You told Matt you read to me?"

"Yeah," she said. "And Lynn. It cracked them up."

"What's so funny about it?"

"Because," she said, realizing he didn't know this about her, "I used to try reading aloud to them. Everyone in the co-op got sick of me trying to read to them. They thought it was funny that I finally found someone who—"

"Did you tell them why?"

"Well yeah. You know, because it's a good way to share the story. To experience it with someone else. Like seeing a movie with someone is sharing a story."

She thought he might be annoyed that she had talked about him to her friends, like he was gossip-material. He was definitely annoyed about something; his hackles had been standing on end for a second. "What?" she said. "Don't you want me to talk about you?"

"No," he said. "But I know you will."

He started unlacing his sneakers, getting ready for bed. He only unlaced the top half of his shoes. She watched with interest as his feet emerged. They were narrow with high arches, sort of beautiful.

"But you just said you want to tell people."

"You don't have to tell them everything."

"I never talk about sex," she said. Unless the sex was terrible, she added silently.

He looked like he was fading fast. After the drive back, the gig, and no sleep last night, he was crashing. She helped him pull off his shirt, then his jeans.

"Aren't you going to brush your teeth?" she asked.

"I don't have a toothbrush on me."

"You can use mine."

But he was already under the quilt, flat out and groaning with contentment.

She went and brushed her teeth, shed her leggings, and came back to bed. He looked asleep, or close to it. She turned out the lights and climbed in next to him. He put an arm around her and she had a moment of hope; maybe he was getting a second wind. But he wasn't. His breathing changed, his body got loose and heavy. She lay still, holding him while he slipped down into sleep.

A few miles away, Angel was wide awake. As far as he was concerned, the night was young. Dan had come home with him after the gig. They sat in the living room drinking beer, Dan sprawled on the couch, Angel cross-legged on the floor. Sukey was asleep in the bedroom. They kept the boom box on low so she wouldn't wake up, although sometimes Angel thought a bomb going off wouldn't wake Sukey.

Angel and Dan talked about the new roadie, how he didn't have much to say for himself but seemed to know what he was doing. They talked about Stringer's new car. Angel thought Stringer had bought it to match his eyes. They talked about the article in the paper. Dan was wondering what Cynthia would think about that. Dan thought Cynthia was beyond-belief wonderful, even though she was most definitely married and had no interest in fooling around with musicians, only in managing them.

"If women are poison," Angel said, Dan's favorite mantra," but Cynthia isn't, she must be a goddess, right? She can't be a normal woman." She didn't look normal; Cynthia was so perfect she looked like an ad for herself.

Dan grunted, refusing the bait.

"You should go after her," Angel said. "That'd cure you. I'll bet she'd like a change from whatshisname."

"Fuck you," Dan said, without heat. Actually, that was the last thing Angel wanted, Dan fooling around with Cynthia. She was a good manager, she was talking recording contracts; Angel didn't want anything to screw that up. But Cynthia had a brain, there was nothing to worry about.

"You oughta lay off Joe," Dan said, as if he wasn't changing the subject.

Angel blew smoke rings and didn't answer. He tried to blow one through the middle of the other.

"All that shit you pull on him onstage. It's unprofessional," Dan said. He was even starting to think like Cynthia.

"If I didn't do it, who would?"

"Who needs to? It fucks up the songs."

"It wakes him up," Angel said. "He was a dead man on that tour until I changed the bass line on him. First time he played that guitar instead of hiding behind it."

Dan squinted at Angel through smoke.

"I was watching out for him," Angel said. "What'd you think?"

"I thought you were paying him back," Dan said. "For fucking Alice," he added. As if Angel didn't know for what.

"I didn't need to pay him back. I had her, he wanted her. I was helping him get through a bad time. Like he always did for me. That's what friends are for, right?"

Dan blew air through his lips, making the pfff-sound of total disbelief.

Angel leaned back into the wall, getting comfortable. "Okay," he said, "I was paying him back. The best revenge is revenge." He grinned at Dan. "But I almost didn't need to, you know? He was so fucking lovesick." He took another drink of beer, warming to his topic. "Who'd of believed it? He goes without a steady woman for years, just enough action so his dick doesn't drop off, and then he falls for somebody like Alice."

"You fell for her," Dan said.

"She fell for me," Angel corrected him.

"Yeah, right."

Angel thought about how to explain what he meant. "Did Joe ever tell you about Donna?"

"Who's Donna?"

"The woman he almost married," Angel said. Dan was stupefied. His jaw dropped. Angel was pleased.

"You're shitting me."

"Nope. She was such a babe. Tall, all this wavy dark hair, and built like a…a…"

"You mean a femme fatale," Dan said.

"Not exactly." Donna wasn't dangerous, any more than a Playboy bunny is dangerous. She was maybe slightly more complex. "She was the kind of woman you go for," Angel said.

Dan's eyes opened wide. "Wow."

"The big deal about her was she could drink anybody under the table. Except Joe, nobody can drink him under the table. Anyway, she showed up at this party. Every guy in the place was hitting on her and she went for Joe." Now he came to think of it,

Joe hadn't given anyone else a chance. While the rest of them were still catching their breath and eyeing her sideways, Joe went over and started talking to her. End of story.

Dan pulled a joint out of his shirt pocket. He wanted to meditate on this. He lit up, sucked down smoke, and passed it to Angel. Angel took a hit, making an ash that was a third as long as the joint, and passed it back. He meditated too.

"So what happened?" Dan asked.

"One night with her, Joe turned monogamous," Angel said. "That was the first thing. Then they were gonna get married. That was the second thing."

Dan toked up and passed the joint to Angel. "What was the third thing?" he asked in a squeaky voice.

Angel thought about the third thing. It had been him. Him and heroin. Donna didn't like it that Joe lived with a junkie. Then Angel had robbed her on payday. Nobody knew that, except him and maybe Donna. It could have been any of the people Angel was hanging out with then. She wouldn't know for sure.

"The third thing was she fell in love with her boss," Angel said. That was also true, but it was the fourth thing. "She married him instead."

Dan made a face. "Oh man," he said.

"The next thing," Angel went on, "was that Joe went back to fucking around with a lot of women. And then none. He couldn't get over her. Just could not."

Dan nodded sagely. Then he shook his head. "I always wondered..."

"Wondered what?" Angel prompted, before Dan could forget the rest of his sentence.

"I never could figure his thing about women. It doesn't make sense."

Angel didn't think anybody's thing about women made sense. And women were just as fucked up about men. When they were into men. Angel thought of the women he knew who were into women. They all seemed completely in the dark about the women they fell in love with. Which was pretty strange, considering they were the same sex. Maybe it didn't have anything to do with sex—maybe it was people. Everyone was a confusion and a mystery to everyone else. Even the people you thought you knew best, the ones you thought you could trust to hell and back—

Dan blew smoke on a sigh. "That poor sucker." He was morose with empathy. "One woman fucked him over, and now he's got another one who's gonna do the same."

"He wanted Alice," Angel pointed out. "Now he's got her."

"I don't hate his guts. I can feel for him. You know she's just using him."

Angel figured that's what everybody was going to think. That Alice took on Joe because she couldn't have Angel. That Joe was a fool. That was revenge, too. But it wasn't a good revenge, it was other people being assholes. About the mother of his child, come to think of it. "Alice doesn't think like that," he said.

Dan took a last toke. "Is that why you sent her the money? Because she doesn't think like that?"

"Yeah," Angel said. "She's broke, she's pregnant, you'd think she'd accept a little help. But she doesn't have good sense. She keeps on believing in elves or something."

"You still have a thing for her?" Dan asked, being way too matter-of-fact.

"Fuck no. She drove me nuts. She wanted to fix me up. I can't stand that shit."

"You should leave him alone about her then. Just forget it. He's gonna blow some day. He's gonna blow sky-high. He almost did tonight."

Angel laughed, remembering Joe's face.

"You want him to blow?"

"I don't care if he does or not. I'm not scared of his fucking ahh-kee-doe."

"I know, I know," Dan said, "you used to fight with knives and broken bottles. I'm not talking about scared. Just lay off him and play the goddamn bass, okay?"

Angel said he'd think about it.

After Dan left Angel picked up the empty beer cans and rinsed them and put them in the deposit bag. He emptied the ashtrays and took out the trash. He did a few dishes. Sukey was into Diet Delite lately. He didn't know why, she was as skinny as a snake. She said it was healthier than the other frozen shit, not so much sodium. At least she wasn't living on candy bars anymore.

He put out his cigarette. Then he went in and stood by the bed, watching Sukey sleep.

She slept peaceful. When she slept she shed everything that had happened to her, everything she'd done. She wasn't like Alice at all. Sukey did as she pleased, and she expected Angel to do the same. That was the beginning and end of her expectations. She didn't want a pact sealed in blood, she didn't want to tear him apart and remake him. But she touched a part of him nobody else had been able to reach. It was like they were related. That sounded so corny, and he would never tell anyone, but that's how he felt about her. Once upon a time, he could have told Joe. Joe would have let him say that without making him feel like a fool. The fucking prick.

Angel climbed into bed and curled up around Sukey. She didn't move a muscle. She was wrapped up in sleep, as far away from him as god.

Mystic River Ink
P.O. Box 441357
Somerville, MA 02144
www.mysticriverink.com